FAKING IT WITH THE FORWARD

WITTMORE U HOCKEY

ANGEL LAWSON

FOREWORD

Readers!

This isn't one of my normal content warning notices. This is pretty much an anti-content warning notice. If you're looking for Royals of Forsyth or Serendee levels of super dark romance you will not find it in this book. If you are looking for reverse harem, it's not here. If you want over the top, mafia style decapitations and cut off appendages? Sorry, this book isn't for you! This isn't a Samgel book, it's an Angel Lawson book and sometimes I get swoony.

Faking It With The Forward does have the following:

- College Hockey M/F Romance
- Fake Dating Trope
- Captain x Team Intern
- Forbidden Romance
- Reformed Playboy
- Slowish-burn to Spicy heat
- Standalone
- Smexy Alpha MC

- Jealous and Possessive H
- Socially Awkward h
- Past Trauma (obviously, this is an Angel Lawson book)
- HEASo for my swoony sports romance lovers… this book is for you! Enjoy!

Angel

1

Twyler

THERE'S nothing more pungent than a locker room full of hockey players after practice. The scent is foul. A mix of new and old sweat, feet, and whatever body spray the guys think they can mask it with.

Trust me, nothing works.

"How was that?" I push my fingers between the tape and his sweaty ankle, barely able to get them in. "I feel like that is as tight as we should go if you want to keep up your mobility."

The size twelve foot shifts. The man it's attached to, a player for the Wittmore U varsity team, nods slowly. "I don't know. It feels a little wobbly."

"Okay, we can wrap it a little tighter next time, but you need to let me know if it's giving you problems."

"Thanks, Twy." Pete slides off the table and yanks my ponytail before offering me his fist. I bump it in return.

"That's what I'm here for." I'm in my second year working with the trainers for the men's hockey team, but it's my first as the official intern. My days are spent taping and wrapping sprains, bandaging broken noses, and checking for concussions. Pete suffered a sprained ankle last season and always feels better with it wrapped tight on the ice.

"Everyone gather around," Coach Bryant steps out from his office into the locker room. He taps his clipboard on a nearby locker to get the attention of the players. The guys have just come in from the rink, filing in the door that leads to the ice, loud and talking trash, tossing pads and their blue and silver jerseys into the laundry bin. "That wasn't too bad," he smirks, then adds, "for a bunch of guys who took the summer off." His tone hardens, the team logo, Bluto the badger, painted behind him on the wall. "Playtime is over. From here on, it's about focus and determination. About hard work and who wants it the most. We have two months until the season starts." His eyes ping from player to player. "Can I expect a hundred percent from each and every one of you?"

As a group, the guys call out their affirmative, some louder than others, but all sincere. Badger hockey is the number one sport at Wittmore U, even football takes second place, which is blasphemy where I'm from. Failure isn't an option for anyone in this room, especially after last year.

"Because if not, I've got a long list of men who didn't make the roster this year, and each and every one of them is eager for a shot."

A voice booms from the back, "We're ready, Coach!"

"Cain," Coach gestures to the back of the room, "step up here."

From my spot near the training room door, I watch a shirtless Reese Cain rise from the bench and push through the other guys to stand next to Coach Bryant. It's not like he's hard to miss. Six-foot-four, broad-shouldered, with dark hair and intense blue-gray eyes. He's got that look that's usually reserved for quarterbacks or underwear models. That kind of genetic superiority that eludes the rest of society. The only visible imperfections are the slant of a formerly broken nose and a thin white scar under his bottom lip.

Neither make a dent in his looks.

I know Reese isn't perfect. There's the fact he knows exactly how good-looking and talented he is. Or how ever since he broke up with his long-term girlfriend, he's used his power to seduce and conquer every female, and possibly a few males, on campus.

Not that I'm keeping track of Reese Cain's life or anything. Everyone knows about his breakup. It was hot gossip for months last year. The rest? Well, it's just part of my job to know the injury histories of our players. I spent the summer going over the roster and their charts, familiarizing myself with each player. Reese Cain, and his broad shoulders, happens to be one of those players.

That's all.

"After three years of stellar performance on the ice, and showing great leadership during last year's tournament, Cain's earned the title of Captain of this years' Badgers."

"Yeah, boi!" A shout from the locker room calls. Jefferson Parks. Cain's best friend. The rest of the room claps and cheers, happy with the announcement. It's not a surprise that he got the position or that his teammates are pleased about it.

"Thanks, guys," he grins with those straight, white teeth. "Last season was rough. We made it to the big time, and didn't get the trophy, but this year, under my leadership, I promise you, we'll get back and take the whole damn thing."

"Hell yeah!" Axel Rakestraw, the team goalie, pumps his fist, and the rest of the guys clap. Our head sports trainer, Coach Green, whistles his support next to me and I catch a dose of the enthusiasm, clapping with the others.

Coach Bryant nods his approval and adds, "Get some rest and I'll see you at morning skate. If you need to stop by Coach Green's office, he and his staff will be available."

Coach Bryant turns and heads into his office while Coach Green, my boss, steps over to talk to one of the players nursing a bruise he got during practice. "Twyler," he calls, "grab me one of those ice packs."

"Yes, sir."

I step toward the training room and hear, "You should let Twy check out your injury, Reid."

I look back when I hear my name. "You have an injury?"

Reid frowns and glances at his buddy. "Nothing you can help with, Twyler."

"Are you sure?" I step closer to Reid. He's a sophomore on the offensive line. "I can take an assessment and—"

"You hear that, Reid?" Jefferson calls. "Twyler wants to *assess* your problem." He smirks in my direction, revealing the dimple in his cheek, and a slow heat rolls up my spine. "Reid has a severe case of blue balls, sweetheart. As far as I know there's only one remedy for—"

"Perkins!" Coach Green barks at me, "What's the status on that ice pack?"

"I'm on it." I take the opportunity and duck into the office, cheeks flaming with embarrassment. I should've seen that one coming. Jefferson always has a way of making me feel self-conscious. They all do.

Taking a deep breath, smoothing down my athletic shorts and Badger hockey T-shirt, I grab the pack out of the freezer and fall into my old habit of just wanting to be invisible. No. No hiding. This is my job, and these guys are all assholes. I knew that when I accepted the position. Clenching the ice pack in my hand I start for the door, but then stop short.

"—how many times do I have to tell you. That girl is off-limits. Not just because you're a bunch of heathens and aren't worth the air she breathes, but because this isn't the time or place. Leave her be. She's not your sweetheart. She's not your girlfriend. She's here for one thing; to do a *job*, and that doesn't include dodging your pathetic attempts at flirting!"

"Aw, come on, Coach. Jeff was just messing around. No one here sees Twy like that."

The humiliation I felt a moment before amplifies by a million when Reese steps in with that little nugget. Of all the guys on the team, he makes me the most nervous. Like palms sweaty, tongue-tied, nervous.

It's not just his looks, although that doesn't help. It's like looking straight at the sun. My real issue is the way he interacts so effortlessly with everyone. There's not a trace of insecurity, and he uses that skill not just to command the team, but to win over everyone around him. People like that make me uneasy. Like how can it be so easy for them, when it's so hard for me?

"Twy's like the little brother we always wanted, right, Sunshine?" Reese adds, noticing me in the doorway and giving me a wink.

Sunshine. Like the way people call a big guy Tiny, Reese started calling me Sunshine.

Because of my not-so-sunny disposition.

A strangled laugh erupts in my chest. "Yeah. No worries here. I'm not into any of you." I wave my hand at the room of shirtless men in front of me. "Like, at all."

The room full of desirable, sexually active, ripped hockey players stare at me like I've grown two heads as if they're trying to figure out how it's possible.

"Good," Coach Green says, stroking his beard. "Glad that's cleared up."

What's been made clear is that in the last ten minutes I've had my hair pulled, my fist bumped, and the captain of the hockey team just declared that I'm not just undateable, I'm reminiscent of a little brother.

And I *agreed*.

Fuck my life.

It's bad enough that for the past two years, the guys on campus have made it brilliantly clear they're not interested in me, but it's worse that Coach Green reinforces this with his little speech anytime one of the guys dares notice that I'm actually female.

But Reese Cain's declaration is the nail in my coffin.

"Now," Coach Green says, walking past me and toward the office, "who besides Reid and his underused balls needs something looked at?"

I walk in the door of my house, tossing my backpack near the door and heading straight to the kitchen. There's a leftover burrito with my name on it, and after a long day of classes and assisting with practice, I'm starving.

The kitchen is small—well everything in the house is minimized. We live in an area called Shotgun, named after the tiny, narrow cluster of houses that were originally part of a community built for the local mill. The mill closed at some point in the seventies, but as Wittmore expanded, it became coveted student housing. A kitchen, living room, two bedrooms, and a shared bath. That's all me and Nadia need.

I can tell she's home. Music pulses from behind her closed bedroom door. That and the kitchen sink is a mess, coffee grounds are all over the counter, and a dirty pot sits on the stove. I grab a plate, toss the burrito in the microwave, and start straightening up. Nadia and I are opposites, proof that the roommate match system through the university has its flaws. She's a business major while I'm studying Kinesiology. She's a social butterfly, while I prefer just hanging out with one person at a time. Her confidence initially made me feel even more insecure. She just understands all the social games I don't. Like social media, or flirting. She's so comfortable in her own skin, it makes me all the more aware of how uncomfortable I am.

I had plans to find a new roommate the following year, but then Ethan happened. She didn't judge me. She had my back, and ever since then I've tried to do the same for her.

Her door opens, music spilling out with her. She's got her phone in her hand, barely stopping to take a selfie, camera angled down to catch the top of her cleavage pushing out of her sports bra. I glance down at my eight-year-old, worn hoodie that I tossed on after practice.

Total opposites.

The microwave beeps and I take out the plate.

"Hey," she says, turning the music down on her phone. "How was the first day of practice?"

"Easy enough. No major injuries." I make my way over to the couch and grab the remote off the coffee table. "They made Reese captain."

"Oh, really," the mention of a hot guy grabs her attention, and she leans against the kitchen door. "Like he needs something to make his ego bigger."

"Right?" I take a bite of burrito and add, "Oh, and apparently, Reid Wilder has a severe case of blue balls."

That really grabs her, and she lifts an eyebrow. "That means he and Darla broke up."

I shrug and turn on the TV, ready to settle into a relaxing night of true crime. "I guess."

She gets quiet, and I look away from the screen to see her scrolling on her phone. Probably looking for proof of the breakup.

"She unfollowed him on Chattysnap."

"There you go." The dating lives of the players is the least of my concerns. It's a revolving door and I learned quickly not to take their interest in anyone seriously. I find an episode of Murders and Mayhem and press play. Leaning back, I sense Nadia watching me and I look up again. She's not just watching me. Her big brown eyes are all droopy and pathetic.

Dammit.

"Nadia, no."

"You know he's in my top five."

"*No,*" I say again, firmly. "You promised."

There's no other way to put it; Nadia is a self-proclaimed jersey chaser. The kind of girl that has made it her mission to hook up with as many varsity level athletes as possible. She's convinced one of these guys is going to be her prince charming, turning her into the wife of a professional athlete.

Little does she know, it's the opposite. I hear the chatter in the locker room, how they feel about the puck bunnies that make it easy on them. Nadia is the type of girl they hook up with —but they don't marry.

Because of our friendship, Nadia has kept her interests to mostly football and basketball players, maybe the occasional fling with someone from the baseball team if she's feeling particularly degrading at the time. She'd, one thousand percent, be into hockey players, but once I started working with the team, I declared them off-limits.

There was no way I could look them in the eye, or sprained wrist, if I knew they were hooking up with my best friend.

"But…" she crosses the room and sits next to me, her bottom lip protruding in a pout.

"You know I love you, but I can't have you sleeping your way through my team."

"Why? It's not like you're sleeping with them."

It's not an insult. It's the truth. "First of all, I can't. I don't want to compromise my position, and even if I wanted to, they think of me as a little brother—firmly reinforced today by Coach Green."

Her eyes widen. "Oh no. What happened?"

"Nothing new." I tell her about the team meeting and the fist bump and how Reese Cain said no one thinks of me as dateable.

"Reese said that?"

I nod, shuddering at the memory. "Then he called me 'Sunshine.'"

Her nose wrinkles.

"Babe," she throws her arm over my shoulder, "that isn't even remotely true. You're hot, in your own athletic shorts-wearing kind of way. You hide behind that tight ponytail and those heavy hoodies. They have no idea what you're packing underneath."

I squirm out from under her affection, tugging at my favorite hoodie that I've had since middle school, and give her the side-eye. "I like to be comfortable."

"I know, but I also know you think it's easier this way—keeping guys from noticing how freaking amazing you are."

"That's not exactly true." It's completely true. My past relationships with men weren't the best and I've learned not to trust my instincts. Dressing down, playing invisible… it is easier.

She gives me a look that says she's calling my bluff. The truth is I'm scared to follow my heart, but Nadia? She goes after exactly what she wants—for better or worse.

"I know what you're doing," I tell her.

She bats her eyes innocently. "Me?"

"You're flattering me, hoping you can butter me up, so I'll say it's okay to date Reid. But I know you. That will be a short fling and you'll move to the next and the next and..." She won't stop until she's bagged them all—until she's bagged their *king*, Reese Cain.

Nadia wants the golden ring.

And I'm the only one standing between her and trying to get it.

"What if I promise to only go after Reid. *One guy.*" She grabs my hand. "He'll only be single for a minute before he's either back with Darla or moved on to someone else."

She's right, and really, is it fair for me to cockblock my best friend?

"Fine," I relent, "but only Reid."

She squeals, throwing her arms around me. "Thank you!" She grabs the remote and turns off the TV.

"Hey! I was watching that!"

"Guess what? The husband did it. He always does!"

"That's not true—"

"Twy, there's no time to waste. I need you to introduce me to Reid *tonight.*"

I still. "What's tonight?"

"Party at the manor."

"A party? At the hockey house? I don't know...can't we just do something more casual? Like on campus?" Panic blooms in my chest. "Like, a good old-fashioned coffee shop meet-cute?"

"No chance. I don't want meet-cute. I want meet-hot, and I can't wear my slutty stuff on campus. I need to make a good impression and fast. Reid won't be single long."

I sigh, already knowing this is a terrible, awful idea. "You know, he may be into you for just you and not your tits and ass."

She cups her ample breasts and squeezes them together in an impressive display of cleavage. "But they're my best features."

The sad part is that Nadia believes that.

Against my better judgment I say, "I'll go, but I need you to promise me something."

"Anything."

"Even if he wants to, you can't sleep with him immediately. You have to give this a real shot. An actual date, not just a hookup." Because that's where it always goes wrong for Nadia. Not trying to be a prude, I've just seen it over and over. "Play hard to get." She glances down at her low-cut tank and raises her eyebrow. "Fine, play *kind of* hard to get. Just... for me?" And for her—because I know Nadia really does want something with one of these guys. A future, and she's not getting it the way she's going about it. "Do that, and I'll introduce you and be your wingwoman for the night."

"Deal."

I reach for the remote, certain I can get in a few episodes while she gets ready, but she holds it out of my reach, and pulls me off the couch, instead.

"What's happening right now?"

She looks me up and down, her eyes filled with excitement. "You're showering, changing and doing...something with your hair."

"But—"

"Twyler, I know one thing for certain; my wingwoman doesn't wear hoodies to parties."

2

Reese

"Fuck, it's crowded in here."

Jefferson holds the two cups of beer, one, for him and the other I assume for whatever girl he's planning on hooking up with tonight, over his head, trying to keep from spilling them on the floor. It works because he's six-five and just to get through the room people have to give him space.

"Yeah, I think Reid made a video and put it on blast." I eye the crowd. Every frat and sorority showed up, as well as the rest of the varsity athletes. The bigger the better is how I see it. More options for the end of the night.

"Ginna's looking for you."

"I saw her," I say, lifting my own bottle of beer to my lips. As captain, and the guy responsible for my teammates getting to early skate on time, I get one drink and I'm trying to make it last. "She looks good."

More than good. Ginna's got this straight blonde hair, big eyes, and pouty lips. Everything she wears is for show, leaving little to the imagination. That's what I like about her. She's a no-nonsense puck bunny. No games. No mystique. No strings. She's here for a good time and happy to provide it.

"If you can't drink," Jeff says, "you may as well get your dick wet, don't you think?"

My best friend is the one that commiserated with me when I broke up with Shanna. He's the one that told me I was making the right decision to throw our four year relationship out the window for my goals. He's also the one that encouraged me to stop having a pity party and to get over my ex by sowing some oats. That was five months ago. It's not an exaggeration to say I've planted an entire crop at this point.

Holding up my bottle, I clink it to his red cup. "Go have fun. Just don't make me drag your ass out of bed in the morning, okay?"

"Got it," he says, leaving me to go push through the crowd toward the backyard where a volleyball game is in progress.

The Manor is the biggest house in Shotgun—formerly the foreperson of the mill's home. Two stories, a big front porch and backyard. It's been claimed as the hockey house for years now, passed down from one teammate to the next. I moved in sophomore year—and now that I'm a senior, this will be my last. Jeff, Reid, and Axel all live here, too.

Everything is riding on this season for me. The team, the tournament, and my future.

"There you are," Ginna says, appearing out of the mass of people. Her arm snakes around my waist. This girl gets it. She knows what I need and how much I have to give, which isn't much between hockey and school. Especially not with how much is on the line. "Thought maybe you took off."

"Nah, just keeping tabs on everyone." I grin down at her. Okay, fine. I grin down at her tits. "Making sure no one does anything stupid."

"That's right, I heard the news. Congratulations on being named captain." Her reaction is genuine. My position is beneficial to both of us. She gets to fuck the leader of the team and I, well, I get to fuck her and anyone else I want. No obligation. My favorite kind of relationship. "Want to take a break from duty and go upstairs?"

The good thing about drinking less is my dick is always ready to go. "I think I can spare a few minutes before the guys get in too much trouble."

She nudges me toward the stairs, but I hear my name called over the music. Jeff's head pops above the rest. "Cap!" He waves me over. I'm about to tell him to talk to me after Ginna sucks me off, but he's got a serious expression on his face.

"Give me a second." I drop a kiss to her mouth, and she doesn't miss the opportunity to swipe her tongue against mine.

"Don't be long."

I push through the crowd, an easy feat when you're taller than most people in the room and outweigh them by fifty pounds. Outside I see a small circle of people and there's a body on the ground under the volleyball net.

The red hair is a giveaway. Reid.

I'm not the first to get to him, a hot girl with curly long dark hair is already next to him. Her hair shields her face, and I don't recognize her small frame. She's wearing jeans and a black shirt revealing a wide strip of skin on her lower back. She leans over Reid, touching his forehead.

"Move," I command, pushing everyone aside. I crowd next to the girl, my shoulder knocking into her, but I don't give a shit.

Reid is my responsibility. He's on his back, his shirt long gone, but he's awake, thank God—although I spot the glassy look in his eye. "I've got this under control." I push the girl's hands away.

"Do you? Because nothing about this seems under control," she bites back. "Reid, how many fingers am I holding up?"

I know that voice. I do a double take.

Reid, even in his dazed state, says it first, "Twyler?"

"Yeah." She wiggles her fingers in front of his face. "How many fingers, Wilder?"

"Holy shit," his eyes dart to me then back to her, "you don't look like..." he swallows, "...you."

She sighs. "Well, it's me."

"But you never come to our parties." Again, he looks to me like he needs help figuring this out, but I'm with him. Twyler, *this Twyler,* is a surprise.

"Dude." She snaps in his face. "How many fingers?"

He squints. "Four."

She exhales. "Good. Anything else hurt?" She's still going through concussion protocol, tracking his eyes, feeling the back of his head for swelling. While she does all of this, I'm stunned speechless, trying to reconcile the girl next to me.

The very attractive, very much not like a younger brother, girl.

Reid sits up on his elbows. "I don't have a concussion, Twy, I'm just drunk."

"Of course, you are." She looks over her shoulder, eyes narrowing at me. "A little help?"

I snap out of it, moving into action, helping Wilder off the ground. "Nothing to see," I announce. "Everyone give him some air."

The crowd thins once they realize nothing dramatic is going on. When he's steady on his feet, I let go, and turn to her.

"Sorry about that. I didn't recognize you." Now that she's

standing, I give her a full once over. She isn't dressed overtly sexy. Just that tight midriff-revealing shirt, and a pair of high-waisted jeans. For Christ's sake, she's still wearing sneakers, but there's the hair, and her eyes... That's the thing about the intern; she's got these big, blue, innocent eyes and pouty lips, but it's all lost in a permanent resting bitch face. But damn, who knew Twyler had a tight body under those hoodies? For a hot second, a bad idea forms in my mind before Coach Green's lecture comes roaring back. Besides, she's made it perfectly clear she's not into guys.

I can respect that *and* check out her tits.

"Thanks for being so quick to get to him," I add. "He turns into a real dumbass when he drinks."

"No worries." Her eyes never make contact with mine, instead hovering somewhere around my neck. "Just doing my job."

"He's right, though. You never come to our parties."

"Well," her fingers push at her hair, flipping it over her shoulder and then back again, "I've never been invited."

"That's not true," Reid says. "You're one of the guys, open invite."

A girl steps forward, one I hadn't noticed in the mayhem, although I'm not sure how. She's got the look of a girl ready to party—the kind just about every guy on the team is happy to see–except she's scowling down at Reid. "She's not one of the guys, you idiot." She points at Twyler's chest. "Do guys have tits like this?" Then spins her around and slaps her butt. "Or an amazing ass?"

"Nadia! Oh my god." Twy covers her face, like she's hoping she'll just vanish. From under her hands she mutters, "Ignore her. Please."

Of course, all it does is make me look at her, watching the

red streak up her neck, and my gaze goes lower, and I check out her tits. Yeah, they're not bad.

My eyes dart up and meet hers. She's scowling.

"Did you seriously just check me out?" she asks.

"It's her fault, Sunshine." I point to the girl. "She brought it up." Whoever "she" is.

"I know you're God's gift to hockey and the women on campus, but I'm still the same girl I was this afternoon." Her arms cross over her chest, which isn't helping the way she thinks it is. "Let's go back to that please."

Ah, the little brother line. For the life of me, I can't figure out why I'd ever say that.

"Reid, if you're okay," Twyler sighs, shifting away from me, "will you go get my friend Nadia a drink? Please."

Reid's been staring at Nadia ever since she made herself known. He grins happily. "Sure, come on, there's a whole bar in the kitchen."

We're left alone. Ginna is waiting, but it feels rude to step away. She did come to Reid's rescue. But even though I'm used to Twyler being around the locker room or taping ankles or handing out ice packs, she never talks much. If anything, like now, she mostly seems annoyed by us.

"You, uh, want a drink or something?"

"No, I'm going to head home. All Nadia wanted was an introduction." She looks through the window to the kitchen where Reid and her friend are mixing drinks. "Mission accomplished."

"Ah, so that's why you came. To play wingman to your girl." I look at her friend, trying to place her. "Or uh, wingwoman?"

"That's exactly why."

"Why haven't I seen her before?"

She looks at me straight on for the first time all night. "Because I forbid her to hook up with any hockey players."

I laugh. "Seriously? Why?" I give her a slow smile. "Trying to keep us to yourself, Sunshine?"

"Don't call me that. And God, no." She blanches. "Nadia's a... well, to put it bluntly, a jersey chaser. High level."

"Yeah, I got that vibe." And there *is* a vibe. It's in the clothes, the comfort level around athletes, the confidence.

The extreme opposite of the girl in front of me.

"I just didn't want her to, you know…" She makes a face. "Do her thing where I work."

"Gotcha." Makes sense. Things can get messy, and I don't know much about Twyler, but it's obvious she's dedicated to her internship and working with the team. "So, why tonight?"

"Reid's blue balls," she admits, pushing a lock of that long hair behind her ear. "She realized he's single and she's always had a crush on him. I told her she gets one chance—one guy—and no one-night stands."

I take another glance toward the house. Reid isn't wasting his time cozying up to her friend. "You think she'll hold up to the deal?"

"The only certain thing about Nadia other than her desire to be a trophy wife, is her loyalty. She won't screw me over."

I nod, hoping she's right. Being on the cusp of something big changes people. "I get that. Loyal friends are important."

"Well, I guess I'll see you at practice." She gives me a tight smile. "I'd appreciate it if you don't let this go too far." She gestures to the party. Jeff is on the patio playing quarters. Axel, as usual, is shirtless and has two girls sitting on his lap by the firepit. The other guys are hanging out with a group from Zeta Sig, which usually means trouble, but what the hell. What's the point of all this hard work if you don't get to have some fun? "Hangovers make for mistakes and mistakes lead to injuries."

"I'll take care of it," I reply, but she's already walking off, headed toward the back gate. "Hey, you need a walk home? I can send a rookie."

She rolls her eyes. "Nah, I live in the teal house. It's just down the block."

That close? I'd never noticed. "Well, thanks again."

"Any time."

Up on the porch, Ginna is still waiting on me, her pink nails tapping on her phone. I walk over and pick up my beer from the porch rail.

"Who is that?" she asks, wrapping her arms around my waist. Her body presses into mine and I remember what we were planning before we were interrupted.

"Team trainer." I glance at Twyler, watching her back as she crosses the yard. A tug of guilt gnaws at me. My mother would kick my ass if she found out I let a girl walk home alone from a party in the dark. "Shit," I grimace. "Gin, do me a favor, head upstairs? I need to do something real quick."

Her hand travels below the belt, grazing over my cock. Blood rushes downward. "Don't keep me waiting too long, Captain."

I smile down at her. "I won't."

Once I'm out of the gate, I can see Twyler half a block away. I jog after her, calling out, "Hey, hold up."

She doesn't turn and I grab her by the shoulder, but she jerks away, like my touch burns. "What are you doing, Cain?"

"Walking you home."

She turns and eyes me. "I know you've got the Captain America thing going on with the team—they think you're a superhero--but I can walk myself home. You may have just realized that I'm a girl, but I'm still an undateable girl, so I should be fine."

I frown. "The guys were just messing around—no one thinks that—"

"Trust me, Cap," she says, something dark and different flickering in her eye, "I learned a long time ago that the scary shit out there isn't hiding in the dark. It's right in front of you." The moment the words are out of her mouth, the intensity in her eyes vanishes and her expression shutters again. "Forget it. I'm fine. My house is right down there."

I open my mouth to argue, but she turns on her heel. After a beat, I do the same, heading back to the Manor. This girl isn't my problem. She's not even my friend. I have no obligation to anyone but myself and my team. What I do have, is a half-naked girl waiting for me up in my room, and that's exactly where I plan to spend the rest of my night.

3

Twyler

THE ONLY PERSON I know that is awake at this time of day is my mother. So when my phone rings on my walk to campus at six-thirty in the morning, I know it's her without even looking. She claims she likes to get an early start on the day, but I know she just has a hard time sleeping now.

"Hey, mom," I say, crossing the street. I take a sip of my ice coffee hoping the caffeine will jolt my brain awake.

"Walking to practice?"

"Yep." Every Tuesday and Thursday, the rink is open for the guys that want to come in for some extra work. Since I'm the intern, Coach Green decided I'm the one that gets to supervise. "What's up?"

"Just wanted to check in since I know you'll be busy all day." She pauses and I wait for whatever's coming next. It doesn't take long. "I was using the Find your Family app to see if your sister made it back last night and saw that you left the house."

And there it is. My mother is obsessed with my social life. Or lack thereof. Other moms worry about their kids partying too much. Mine worries about us not partying, or being social, enough.

"Nadia wanted to meet one of the players on the team, so I took her to a party."

"Oh!" In my mind I can imagine how big her eyes are, while she's also trying to feign disinterest. "That sounds fun."

"It was okay." I spot the arena in the distance. "I didn't stay long."

"Oh."

Yep, there's the disappointment.

"I had to get up early," I remind her. "And it was pretty lame. Just a bunch of stupid hockey players acting like idiots."

"But are they cute idiot hockey players?"

"Mom..."

"I know, I'll stop." But she doesn't. "I just know it's been hard for you, but you can't meet someone if you don't put yourself out there."

"I'm out here right now." Literally. But I know what she means and the thought of it just makes me anxious. "I'm working on it. I promise."

"I'm not trying to pressure you, Twy. I just know that you struggle with this. Going to that party was a good first step."

I grunt, not willing to admit that it had been sort of nice to get out and do something other than watch TV. It wasn't my first party, Nadia manages to drag me out on occasion, but I'm just more comfortable in a small group.

"Okay," I say, walking up to the door of the rink, "I'm here and need to go."

"Okay, sweetheart, have fun!"

"Wrangling a group of hungover players isn't really fun, Mom."

"Stop, you know you love it."

Refusing to agree, I say a quick goodbye and hang up, tucking my phone into my pocket.

I don't mind that Coach Green doesn't come in until later. There's something peaceful about the training center early in the morning. The smell isn't so bad since the cleaning crew comes in overnight and douses the place with something lemony-smelling that manages to cut into the funk that permeates the locker room.

I like having a chance to work independently. I tape ankles and wrists, document any concerns in the player's file, and then head out to the rink to prep for practice. Part of that is managing the water station. Each player has a bottle with their name and number on it, just like every other piece of equipment. The guys are particular about their things. A mixture of preference and superstition. Thank God that's not my job. There's a separate equipment intern, Jonathan, who handles that.

Thirty minutes later the guys start rolling in, bleary and half awake.

These extra practices aren't mandatory, and the coach isn't here, but the majority of the team exits the locker room and hits the ice. The guys are in better shape than I expected. I guess Reese managed to keep the party under control after all. Even Reid looks steady on his feet as he skates over to grab a water bottle.

"How are you feeling today?" I ask, taking another sip of coffee. I know it's counterintuitive to have a cold drink inside the rink, especially when I'm bundled up in sweats and a jacket, but ice coffee is my lifeblood.

"Good. Told you, I was just drunk."

"Well, maybe next time you don't get so wasted you can't stay upright."

"Maybe. But where's the fun in that?" He squirts a stream of water into his mouth. "You should come to more of our parties." His forehead screws up and he stares at me for a minute before saying, "And wear your hair down more. It looked good like that."

Ignoring the hair comment, I retort, "Why? Because I hand-delivered a hot girl to you?" Nadia was home and in bed by midnight—a record for her. It's a good sign she stuck to our deal.

He grins. "Nadia *is* hot, so thank you for that, but also because it's pretty awesome to have a trained medical professional on hand."

"Ah, I see." I bring hot girls *and* provide medical attention. "Unfortunately, I don't think my job description includes keggers, Wilder."

"Just saying...open invitation," his eyebrows waggle, "for you *and* your friends."

He hands me his bottle and skates off.

"Morning, Sunshine."

At the sound of Reese's voice, a weird sensation rolls down my spine. Our interaction the night before was tense and awkward *before* I blew off his nice gesture to walk me home and made the comment about not being afraid of the dark. Why did I say that? Even though he's cocky as hell, it's obvious he cares about his teammates, and by extension, that includes me.

"Ignore him," he adds. "He knows you saved his ass last night. He just doesn't know how to say thank you."

I glance out at the ice. "I'm not worried about Reid."

Guys like Reid don't rattle me like Reese does. Reid's a goofball–serious about hockey and having a good time. He's too caught up in his own energy to focus on me, and I like that.

I wait for Reese to skate off, but he was the last one to come out of the locker room, and from the looks of it, he's still not quite ready. He leans his stick against the wall and tugs at his gloves. Finally, I ask, "Do you need something? Water?"

"Just wanted to make sure you made it back okay."

"Ah, and they say chivalry is dead." I start rearranging the water bottles just to give my hands something to do. "I made it home in one piece, just like I said." And changed into comfortable clothing and binged a documentary on serial killers.

My phone buzzes in my pocket and out of habit I check.

Ruby: I heard you went to a party last night.

I roll my eyes. My mom tells my sister *everything*.

"Problem?" he asks, eyebrows arched.

"No." I shove the phone away. "It's just my sister, being nosy as hell."

He nods. "She's older?"

"Yeah. She graduated last year from State and apparently has nothing better to do than to text me at 7 a.m. about my social life."

"She sounds intense."

"You have no idea," I mutter, focusing on the guys on the ice. The guys swarm around the area in front of the net, taking shots on Axel.

"Well," he says, "you were right about your friend. She didn't sleep with Reid." Against my better judgment, I look over and see his helmet is askew on his head, not yet secured under his chin. His very sharp, chiseled chin. "Not for lack of trying on his part though."

"Yeah, she was home pretty early."

Reese snorts.

I narrow my eyes. "What?"

"Hooking up doesn't only happen after midnight, you know that, right?"

The accusation of being naïve makes my cheeks burn. "Nadia has a pattern," I tell him. "And coming home before midnight doesn't fit it."

A player skates up and asks. "Twy, got a towel?"

"Yeah." I toss it over and he wipes the sweat dripping off his face. Reese watches me—waiting apparently for me to continue. Fine. "Normally, she vanishes all night, turns off the location app on her phone, and drags in looking like hell the next day."

A strange expression crosses his face, and I can't help but ask, "What's that look for?"

"Just trying to figure out if I have a pattern," he asks, at the moment Jefferson skates up.

"Probably a trail of used condoms and morning-after pill packets," Jefferson jokes. "Come on, Cap, the guys are ready."

Although I wrinkle my nose at the thought, my pulse quickens at the idea of his casual hookups. I've heard the rumors about Reese's exploits. The talk in the locker room and I saw the girl waiting for him on the porch last night. It's just so easy for him and Reese doesn't even have the sense to look guilty at Jefferson's comment, a small smirk lifting the corner of his mouth. "If anything, that's *you*," he says to his best friend, securing his helmet. "And stop being gross in front of Twy. She's not into it."

"Sorry, Twy," Jefferson says, pushing off with his skate. Without another word, Reese grabs his stick and follows.

I stare at his name stretched across his shoulders: CAIN, the number fifteen underneath. He's a powerhouse, commanding both the ice and his team, which is probably why he makes me nervous. I don't like feeling out of control, but every exchange with him sets me on edge, like he's two steps ahead and I'm, predictably, falling behind.

I don't like it. No, I don't like the way he makes me feel.

But unfortunately for me, it's Reese Cain's world, and like everyone else, I'm just living in it.

EVER SINCE THE PARTY, he's everywhere.

Reese Cain.

It's like the phenomenon when you're shopping for a new car and then suddenly all you see is that brand of car on the road. Everywhere I go his massive frame looms. Between classes, always surrounded by a group of teammates or puck bunnies hanging onto his every word. Or he's on the quad, sprawled out trying to catch a few of the remaining rays of sunshine before winter takes hold. Twice, I see him over in Shotgun. Both times I was walking out of my house as he was on the way to campus. I ducked back inside, peering out the window, and not leaving until he passed.

Why am I avoiding him? Fuck if I know.

There's something about him that is a sharp reminder of how I'm perceived—uninteresting and unattractive. The opposite of people like him and Nadia. And the people who do take notice? They aren't good for me anyway. That lesson has been learned.

I can't avoid Reese at practice, but I've managed to ease myself to the background, helping Coach Green when I'm needed and luckily, he's not one of the ones that needs trainer assistance at the moment. It's outside the training facility that seems to trip me up.

"Twyler?"

My name is called by the barista, and I step forward to get my iced latte. I grab the cup and turn, crashing into a brick wall. No, not a brick wall. Reese Cain.

His hands stabilize my upper body, fingers tight around my

biceps. It's not enough to keep my drink from sloshing onto my shirt.

"Seriously?" I mutter. If I didn't know better, I'd accuse him of stalking me. The problem here is that I *do* know better. I'm just cursed.

"Shit, sorry," he says, reaching behind me for a wad of napkins. "Here."

I take them, wiping the droplets of coffee off my hoodie.

"I didn't see you," he says, taking the trash and tossing it into the nearby bin.

Of course he didn't.

"George!" the barista shouts.

"That's me." He steps over to the counter and grabs his drink. To my surprise he returns to stand next to me. On the side of his cup the name "George" is written in block letters.

I raise an eyebrow. "Having to go incognito?"

He shrugs those big shoulders. "It's just easier."

"Ah, the life of a celebrity." He doesn't respond to my jab, which is probably an indicator of how true it is for him, and takes a sip of his drink, wincing when it's too hot.

"Damn." His tongue flicks out, and my belly does a flip-flop.

"That's why I stick to ice. No burned tongues." I look at his cup. "So, who's George?"

"My family dog. Chocolate lab."

I should say something here. My mom and Ruby would tell me this is my moment to practice. I could mention my cat, Bertha, back home, or something silly about pets, but no words come. Outside of the locker room I can't seem to complete a full thought, so I hold up my cup and say, "Alright. Later then."

"Wait," he says, voice raised.

"Yeah?" I turn to face him. His eyes dart behind me toward the door.

"Just..." his hand lands on my hip and he yanks me forward, "...don't freak, Sunshine."

"What are you talking—"

My question is cut off when he invades my space and pulls me flush against his hard body, dropping his mouth to mine. There's zero time to react, and even if there was, I probably wouldn't. I'm in shock. Complete shock when I feel Reese's soft, warm lips press into mine.

What the fuck is happening?

But even that part of my brain shuts off as he deepens the kiss, tongue licking at the seam of my lips in gentle, hypnotic strokes. I part for him, taking him inside, aware that every inch of my skin is aflame, and my heart threatens to rupture through my ribcage.

The weight of his other hand settles on my lower back, fingers curled into my shirt. I'm still clutching my drink between us, one hand clinging to his forearm. Just when I wonder if I've truly, completely, lost my mind, he slowly withdrawals, pressing his forehead to mine.

"What the hell?" I whisper, already squirming away.

His hold on me is tight, the implication clear. He's not letting me go. Not yet.

"I'm sorry," he says quietly, and I wonder if he can hear how hard and fast my heart is beating. Am I having a heart attack? Is that what happens when you kiss a guy like Reese Cain? Your body overheats and implodes?

He asked me not to freak, but here I am, one second from a full-on freak out.

Again, I repeat, "What. The. Hell."

He glances over his shoulder toward the crowded line and looks... well, seriously flustered. He eases his grip, but doesn't release me. His eyes meet mine, filled with regret. "That was... I apologize. I know you're not into me—guys."

"Who was that for? I'm not dumb. Was this some kind of game?" I scan the room. "One of the guys on the team? A bet? Did Jefferson bet you to do that?"

I'll stuff his cup with Icy-Hot.

He touches his lips with his index and forefinger and shakes his head. "No. My ex."

I look around his massive body and see her. Shanna Wentworth. Everyone knows about her, or at least *of* her. She and Reese were high school sweethearts. Destined for the NHL and a perfect marriage. He gave her a promise ring for high school graduation that she wore in a profile of him in a *Sports Illustrated* issue about the rising stars of college hockey. That is, until last year when they broke up and Reese went full manwhore.

"So you kissed me to what? Make her jealous?" I'm still reeling as I take in her stick-straight hair with perfect makeup and lacquered nails shaped like talons. Her clothes are expensive, already looking like a socialite hockey wife. Me? Well, I'm in my ratty coffee-stained hoodie paired with track pants and running shoes. I look like... well, Reese's twelve-year-old younger brother. "Me? You think I'm making someone jealous?"

His eyes narrow. "You don't see yourself very clearly, do you?"

"What–"

"Oh, shit. She's coming. Play along." His eyes dart over my head and he raises his hand in a small wave.

"I will not."

"Please?" Is that desperation? Can someone like Reese sound desperate? I've seen him slam a two-hundred-and-forty-pound man into the wall while skating twenty miles an hour. Or once play with blood gushing out of his nose, and he still managed to score the winning goal. This man is fearless.

Or so I thought.

"Why should I?" Because there's no way this ends up with me not looking like a fool.

His jaw tenses and I think he's about to give it up, when he says, "I'll get Reid to ask Nadia out on a date. For real."

The bargain comes in a rush, and I don't have time to agree before he tucks a lock of hair behind my ear and traces his fingers along my jaw. A rush of goosebumps spreads down my arms, and he lasers the full effect of his charm on me in one mega-dose.

"Fine," I hear myself say over the rush of blood thrumming in my veins. As if I have a choice.

"Hey!" Shanna's voice carries over the music and noise of the coffee shop. "I thought that was you."

Yes, because there are so many six-foot-four, drop-dead handsome, ex-boyfriend hockey players roaming around campus. This bitch.

"Shan," he says, the picture of ease, sliding his arm over my shoulder. "Didn't see you come in."

I guess everyone is lying today.

"Obviously not." Her eyes dart to me—to us—and I see the question in them. Trust me, Shan, I have questions too. She thrusts out her hand. "Hi, I'm Shanna."

"Oh," I step forward to take her hand, or try to, but Reese's muscular arm keeps me locked in at his side. I offer a tight smile instead. "I'm Twyler."

"Twyler... that's an interesting name."

It's a crazy name. Some family lore about the summer my grandmother, Twyla, lived in Tyler, Texas and met my grandfather and subsequently fell in love.

Her gaze shifts over and up to the face of the man next to me. "How are you?"

"I'm great," he says a little too casually. "The season's looking good. Coach named me captain..."

"I heard." She gives him a grin. "So proud of you." Again, she looks to me, or at me, my ponytail and hoodie. "And you two..."

"Twy's the intern for the sports trainers," is all he says by way of explanation.

"Ah, the sports trainers. Right." There's a glint in her eye. Something... troublesome. "Well, you make a cute couple. Hope everything goes great with the season. Good luck, Reese, you deserve it."

"Thanks," he says, followed by a beat of silence between the three of us. "So, we should go. Twy has class."

"Well, it was good seeing you." She smiles at me. "And meeting you."

"Same," I say, allowing Reese to lead us out the door. Once we're outside and clear of the coffee shop entrance, I waste no time disentangling myself.

"I'm sorry," he says again, running his hands through his hair. "I just panicked."

"You panicked by assaulting my mouth!" Am I yelling? I can't tell over the blood pounding in my ears.

He tilts his head and his lips quirk. "That seems extreme."

"Whatever, Cain. Explain yourself."

He stiffens and shrugs. "She gets under my skin."

"So you decided to shove your tongue down my throat to make her 'jealous.'" The finger quotes are my emphasis, because Jesus, that's the most absurd plan ever. "If you want her back just go get her."

"Getting her back is the last thing I want." His expression turns hard. "I broke up with her."

I stop short. No one knows what happened between Shanna and Reese. Their breakup was quiet and without drama. Even being privy to locker room chatter, this is the first I've heard that he's the one that initiated it.

"Why the hell would you do that?" I ask, although the image of an endless line of puck bunnies seems like a good enough reason.

"It's complicated," he says easily, but his hand is tugging at his hair again. "I just don't want to give her any openings."

I don't ask what that means, and I also don't miss the way he's looking at me. Weird. He's looking at me weird.

"Again, I'm sorry. I appreciate the cover even if it did gross you out."

Gross me out? That's nowhere near what that kiss made me feel. My heart still feels like it may rip through my chest.

"Well, you did promise me something in return." I smile, ready to collect on my bribe. I grab the ties on his hoodie and yank. "You owe me one date between Nadia and Reid."

He looks down at me, an odd expression flitting across his face. It's gone in a blink, and he nods, confirming. "I'll make it happen before the end of the week."

4

Reese

Sweat drips off my chin, and my arms feel like they're made of gelatin, but it doesn't stop me from saying, "Add ten more to each side."

Reid's standing over me, his red headphones hanging around his neck. "Are you sure, Cap?" he asks, eyeing the weight on the bar.

Jefferson's nickname has spread through the group and now everyone is calling me Captain or Cap, only occasionally tagging on the "America."

I don't deserve the title. Especially not this week. Not after the debacle in the coffee shop.

Fuck. I acted like a fucking pussy.

"I'm sure," I say, wanting to feel the burn.

Seeing Shanna on campus messed with my head. I'd

managed to avoid her since arriving back at school. She no longer hangs out with my circle of friends, instead immersing herself in her sorority and some of the frats on campus. Seeing her in the coffee shop had been a jolt. I probably would've kissed anyone standing next to me.

But it wasn't anyone. It was Twyler.

She'd been shocked, her standard bitchy expression replaced by utter surprise. That, her big blue eyes, and… Jesus, her mouth. I hadn't expected a kiss like that. Or to still be thinking about it a day later.

I definitely didn't expect to get a semi every time I think about it.

It's not the only thing I can't forget. There's also the date I agreed to make between her roommate and Reid. Meddling in my teammates' love lives isn't something I want to do, but a deal's a deal.

"How's that?" Reid asks, hands on either side of the bar, ready to spot me.

I push the weight up and over the bar, feeling the burn instantly in my biceps. It's a good sensation. Something real and true. Not like what happened between me and Shanna.

We'd met through a group of friends and up to that point, girls had never been on my radar. I'd been completely consumed by hockey since I was a little kid. Not that there was any other option with my dad. As a former professional player and then my coach, he put skates on me as soon as I could walk. The NHL was our goal. In middle school he moved me to a school for kids that specialized in sports or specific talents. I went half day and the teachers cooperated with sending me work when I was on the road for games and tournaments. There was no time for girls either, but Shanna was determined and undeterred by my chaotic schedule.

She went out of her way to get to my games. Met me after

practice or was happy to just do homework together. It felt like I'd met this person that understood how important my future was and she was willing to do what it took to be with me.

She was positioning herself for a specific role, hockey wife, and I was ready for it.

Until I realized the position was more important to her than I was.

Behind my head, Reid's phone is blowing up in his pocket, the vibration going off every few seconds.

"Avoiding someone?" I ask, when he ignores it.

"Darla." He grimaces. "She's been calling all week."

Shit. I thought that was over. Guess that makes two of us dealing with lingering relationship drama. "Is that a bad or good thing?"

"I dunno." He watches the bar as it rises and falls. "Bad, I think. Easy, obviously, but I think we're done."

I understand. Things with Shanna felt easy too. Comfortable. Until it wasn't.

"Maybe it's time to move on." I huff out, pushing the bar up again.

He grunts, not committing one way or the other.

"What about that chick, Nadia?"

"Nah," he says. "I don't think she's interested."

"Why do you say that?"

He shrugs. "I followed her socials and slid into her DMs, but nothing came of it."

I push through the last two, arms wobbling from the pressure. Reid spots me, but never touches the bar, not until he helps lift it over the rack. "Jesus," I breathe, sitting up and wiping the sweat off my face with the hem of my shirt. "Brutal."

"Beast mode, man." He gives me his fist and even though I can barely lift my arms, I save face and bump it.

"She could be playing hard to get." Or abiding by the rules

her best friend set up, I want to say, but can't. "Maybe," I say, trying to find the right tone, "you should ask her out."

His eyebrow raises. "Ask her out," he repeats.

"You know…" the word feels weird on my tongue, but I push it out anyway, "…on a date."

"You want me to ask a jersey chaser on a date."

"It's one way to let Darla know it's over."

"I don't know, man." He grabs his water bottle and takes a drink. We're quiet for a minute, nothing but the sound of the other guys moving around the gym. I'm going to have to tell Twyler this isn't happening. These guys don't date. They fuck around, more serious about the game than settling down. Which is how it should be. Committing to a woman is a distraction, like Darla blowing up Reid's phone all day. I'm about to tell him to forget it, and I'll just have to make it up to Twyler another way, when he wipes his forehead and says, "You know what? I'll do it. She's hot. I had fun with her the other night. One date won't be the end of the world, and you're right. Maybe it'll send a message."

We part, him heading to the free weights and me to the treadmill. Once I'm finished, the gym is pretty cleared out, and I see a notification on my phone from Shanna.

It's the third time she's contacted me since the coffee shop. One was a text telling me she was glad to see me. The next was a throwback photo on her Chattysnap where she tagged me, and now a video of a badger winning a fight against a leopard with the note: *This is how I see you on the ice!*

Running my fingers through my hair, I can't help but see the irony in the fact I'm giving all this advice and telling my teammates how to handle their shit, when it's pretty fucking clear I have my own ex that needs to get a message.

I shower and change, grabbing my bag to head out. Passing the training room, I stick my head in. Twyler's bent over, organizing the supply closet. Damn, Nadia's right, she does have a pretty amazing ass.

My dick twitches.

She turns, and I straighten, dragging my eyes, mind, and cock out of the gutter.

"Hey," I say, leaning against the door.

"Oh, hey." I watch as her skin turns pink, something that happens every time she looks at me.

"Just wanted to report that I think the date's a done deal. Reid should reach out to Nadia tonight."

Her eyes light up. Which is saying a lot, they are the most expressive part of her face. "Really? That's great."

"Sure, told you I'd take care of it."

"Well, thank you. Even if it doesn't work out, I just want her to give it more than a one-night stand, you know?"

"More than a jersey chaser."

She nods and closes the cabinet doors. I'm still standing there when she grabs her jacket and zips it up.

"Are we good?" I ask, stepping into the room. "I know that was out of line the other day. I really am sorry. I know you think that *I* think I'm god's gift, but under normal situations I wouldn't just kiss someone without asking. Especially someone that has made it clear they're not into me." I give her a small grin. "I'm all for consent."

Her eyes linger somewhere between my mouth and chest. "We're fine."

"Promise?"

"Mmhm." She slings her backpack over both arms.

She doesn't sound sure, but I let it drop. We walk out together, and then turn, taking the same path back to Shotgun. "For the record," I announce. "I am not walking you home. Just headed the same direction."

She cuts me a glare. "I know."

We continue in silence. Normally I have no problem talking to people. Girls. New faces. Adults. But Twyler is tough to crack and dare I say it, immune to my charm. My phone buzzes and I ignore it, afraid to even look.

"I've been thinking about something," she blurts as we cross the street, leaving campus and walking into our neighborhood.

"Oh, yeah?"

"You said that you know I don't like guys..."

"Right. I mean, whoever you're into, or not into, it's not my business."

She stops walking and takes a deep breath. Closing her eyes, she says, "That's the thing, I do. I do like guys. Men."

Huh. I take in her sporty vibe. It's not screaming, *I want to kiss girls*, but it's also not encouraging anything else. Asexual, maybe? I haven't thought too much about it. Then I think back to that outfit at the party and how my body responded to her and... well, fuck.

"What are you saying?" I ask, trying to gauge where this conversation is going.

"I'm saying that there's this assumption I'm not into men, but I am." Her chin juts out. "I've had a boyfriend before."

A boyfriend. Noted.

"Okay."

"I'm just more comfortable like this," she tugs at the workout pants, "and it works for the job. It's not some kind of sexual identifier."

"Of course not." As someone who spends their days in workout clothes or practice uniforms, I get it.

"I just..." God her face is so red and her hands twist around the straps of her backpack. "...I want to make that clear."

"So, what you're saying is that you're into guys, but you're just really awkward."

"What?" Her jaw drops. "I never said that."

"Okay, I inferred it." But I hear what she's saying. We've been making a lot of assumptions and jokes—treating her like a kid, or one of the guys, when so far, she's proven that she's a smart, capable woman. "But that explains the kiss. Because that wasn't the kiss of a woman who isn't attracted to men."

Or me, but I'm afraid she'll punch me if I say that out loud.

Her cheeks go red again and that's when it clicks that her normal bitchy expression is a shield to hide her vulnerability. The phone in my hand buzzes. Shanna. I press the device against my forehead and mutter, "Not again."

"Something wrong?" Twyler asks.

"Apparently, kissing you didn't do anything to deter Shanna. If anything, it seems to have fueled her interest again." The phone buzzes again. *"Shit."*

"I told you no one would believe it."

I laugh. "That's where you're wrong, because this?" I hold up the phone. "*This* is insecurity. And you made her insecure."

"Unlikely."

"You hide behind that bitchy scowl and that ancient hoodie." I rake my eyes down her body. "I told you before, you don't see yourself clearly, Sunshine."

She scowls. *"Don't* call me that."

Fuck, she's cute riled up, but any follow up is cut by the buzz of my phone.

"Is that her again?" she asks, peering at the screen.

"Yep."

Studying me for a minute, Twyler holds out her hand. "Give me your phone."

"What? Why?"

She makes a grabby gesture with her fingers, and I relent. I think she's going to look at the messages, but she doesn't, instead saying, "Give it."

She opens my Chattysnap app and turns on the camera. She

shocks me by grabbing a fist full of my shirt and dragging me down. "Get closer," she says, then arranges us for a selfie, faces pressed close together. She smells good, like something fresh and clean. Without a second glance at her hair or the angle, she presses send and shoots it out to the universe. "There."

I raise my eyebrows. "You posted that?"

"If she's texting you, she's watching your social media." She shrugs like this is the most obvious thing ever. "Now she knows why you're not answering. You're with me."

I blink, trying to figure out what's happening. "How do you know that?"

Twyler presses the phone back in my hand and laughs. "I live with Nadia, the queen of making men *and* women jealous on social media."

"Interesting."

She starts to walk forward, but I grab her by the arm, dragging her back. "Wha—"

"One more." I position us this time, pulling her close. She doesn't smile, but rolls her eyes at the camera, and that's when I turn my head, kissing her on the temple as I snap the picture.

"Reese!" she shouts, pushing me off.

"You started it," I call as she storms off toward her house. I smile and wave when she reaches the front porch. She flips me off, then turns, slamming the door behind her.

Twyler Perkins may like guys, but I'm definitely not one of them.

5

Twyler

Regret.

That's how I feel about taking that stupid selfie.

So many freaking regrets.

I don't even know why I did it. It was completely out of character for me to do something like that. With someone like Reese. Like, what in the world compelled me to put my face on Reese's social media and blast it to the world?

Okay, maybe not the world, but I checked when I got home, and he has over a hundred thousand followers. No, a lot of *fans*.

But even as I wallow in a bag of chips and my regrets, deep down I *know* why I did it.

Shanna Wentworth.

Being shy is the norm for me. I'm used to being overshadowed by big personalities like Nadia, or the cocky, ego-driven guys on the team. But hearing that Shanna started texting Reese more after seeing us together?

Well, that's just a bitch move.

That dismissiveness lit something inside of me, and for once I just couldn't sit by and take it any longer. So, I acted. Rashly, and according to the little tracker next to the photo of Reese kissing my cheek, twenty-two thousand people heart it.

I'm not even venturing into the comment section.

I've got my hand shoved in the bottom of the chip bag when the door swings open, banging into the wall. "Tell. Me. Everything," Nadia says with a wide, beaming grin.

"I'm assuming you saw the photo."

"*Everyone* saw the photo, Twy. What the fuck?" She flops next to me on the couch and takes the bag from me. "Reese Cain? Why is he kissing you and posting it online?"

I open my mouth to tell her—everything. About the *other* kiss in the coffee shop–the one I felt in my bones. How just being around him flusters me and makes me feel a little unhinged. The obnoxious follow up texts from Shanna and how irritated he seemed. But most of all, how I wanted to prove to her I wasn't just an inconsequential ant to be stepped on.

In the end, I keep all of that to myself, and say, "We were just messing around."

"Messing around," she says slowly, "with Reese Cain."

I snatch the bag back from her. "There's nothing going on, if that's what you're thinking."

"There's *something* going on." She pulls out her phone and opens the Chattysnap app. "Do you know how many girls have made it onto Reese's feed? Three." She holds it up for me to see. "His mom. Shanna. And now you. Ever."

"Which should tell you how little his account means. You know guys don't pay attention to all that."

She laughs. "Please. They pay attention. More than they'd ever admit."

"This isn't a big deal." I crush the empty bag in my hand and stand up, crossing the small space to toss it in the trash bin.

"Twy..." Nadia starts, but I shoot her a look. Not that it stops her. "What's really going on? Do you like him?"

"God, no," I blurt—a little too quickly. "You know he's not my type."

In the past I went for emo guys in skinny jeans and shaggy hair. The complete and total opposite of a guy like Reese. Lately? I haven't gone for anyone.

She rolls her eyes. "Reese is everyone's type."

I'm not ready to admit to myself that Reese gives me feelings—albeit crazy, neurotic, frustrated feelings—much less Nadia. She wouldn't understand. She crushes on everyone. There's an endless list of guys on campus that she's always got her eye on. Ever since I broke up with Ethan, I've kept that part of myself closed off. There's just something about Reese that makes me want to consider it again. Not with him exactly, but maybe someone.

"It's okay if you do. I mean, he's very good looking, and have you seen him without a shirt?" She shoves the phone at me again, a photo of Reese, Jefferson, and Axel, all shirtless, hanging out at the lake. All of their bodies are insane.

"I work with the team. I've seen them all shirtless." And Reese is cut like marble, all hard-packed muscle, complete with a climbable ladder on his abdomen, and a deep-set V that plunges below.

"Ethan totally mindfucked you, Twy, but he doesn't get to own your future."

My chest constricts at Ethan's name and that same panicky feeling lingers. "I know."

"It's okay to dip your toes back in the dating pool, even if he seems out of reach."

"Reese Cain isn't some kiddie wading pool. He's a freaking ocean caught in the middle of a hurricane." I know it's impossible, but I can still feel his lips on my cheek, the scratch of his scruff, and the flutter of butterflies racing in my stomach. "But we are friendly, and I've been trying to put myself out there more."

"I'm proud of you." She grins and sets her feet on the coffee table. "Just watch, that picture of you and Reese is about to change your life."

∽

Later, as I get out of the shower, I catch sight of the tattoo on my upper thigh in the bathroom mirror. The design is a crown, shaded dark with whimsical flowers and swirling lines surrounding it. I run my thumb down the ink and feel the scars hidden underneath.

An eternal reminder of the effect Ethan, my first real boyfriend, left on me.

We met the first week of school on the lawn outside the freshman dorms. Nadia had already found herself some baseball players to hang out with, and I refused to join. I spent all of high school surrounded by the jocks I worked with in our sports training program. College was going to be different and I was determined to find my own crowd.

Ethan was the opposite of a jock. He wore all black, including jeans, even though it was still summer. He had a lanky build, with a narrow face and sharp cheekbones, floppy hair hanging in front of his eyes. A sliver ring pierced his eyebrow, and I was drawn like a moth to a flame. The jocks never paid me much attention, but Ethan... he looked me right in the eye and asked if I wanted to hang out with him and his friends.

From the start it felt electric with him, and at that time in my life I just wanted to *feel* something, to *be* something to someone. But in hindsight, I understand that Ethan was smarter than me, calculated. He saw me coming, set his sights on me like a hunter with prey, and from there it was a slow descent into an inferno of pain. Mental and physical, and it's taken me a long time, and more than a little therapy, to move on with my life.

Or at least try to.

Ruby and Nadia both think I'm stuck. Lodged in a place where I feel safe. But what's wrong with feeling safe?

You know who doesn't make me feel safe? Reese Cain. Not because he's dangerous, but because he's the first person to push me out of my comfort zone in a long time.

The first person to make me want to feel something more.

Looking away from my reflection, I tug on a clean T-shirt and shorts. My hair is wet, hanging loose, and I think about Reid suggesting I wear it down. Another reminder of how I allowed Ethan to change who I am and how I present myself.

Grabbing a hair tie, I pick up my phone and head into my room, opening Chattysnap to Reese's account. The picture of us has even more likes now and hundreds of shares. Reese looks devastatingly handsome, of course. His lips are pressed against the side of my face, amplifying the angle of his scruff-covered jaw. His body dwarfs mine, and you can't see anything but my face. My eyes are huge. I know it's from the surprise, but in the moment, I just look happy.

No one knows the nerves that were crashing inside of me.

I stare at the hair tie. So small but, so meaningful.

I toss it on the bedside table, run my fingers through my hair and loosen the waves.

Nadia's right. It's time to leave the past behind and embrace the future.

6

Reese

AFTER A FULL DAY of classes and practice, I'm fucking beat.

Axel is the only one that parties regularly, his body able to take a beating on the ice even with whatever toxins he decides to ingest. Some of mine is just habit. Those years of training with my dad were more than just workouts and practices. It was creating an entire mindset around success.

"What's going on with you and the trainer?" Jeff asks, after deke'ing my player on the screen. We ate dinner in the athletic dining hall and came back to play a few rounds of video games before I needed to study.

"You saw the pic?"

"Everyone saw it, dude." He winces as I slam his guy into the boards. "Or was that the point?"

Jeff knows me and I shouldn't be surprised he's suspicious of the photo of me and Twyler. "Shanna's been sniffing around again."

"Shit? For real?"

All night I expected another text or some kind of response from Shanna. Hell, I wouldn't be surprised if she showed up at the Manor door. But that never comes and I'm relieved when it doesn't happen. I have zero interest in dating Shanna again, but the simple fact she's waiting around for the right opportunity to weasel her way back in? That's enough to make me consider something extreme.

"What does that have to do with Twyler?"

"We were walking back to Shotgun when one of the texts came in. It was just a way to maybe shut Shanna down."

In my peripheral I see him nod. "She was okay with that?"

I laugh. "It was her idea." I manage to score, the light flashing behind the goal. I toss the controller on the coffee table. "Okay, I've got a paper to write."

An hour later, I have half a paper written for my communications class, but there's a restlessness gnawing at me. That's what Shanna does to me. She worms her way into my brain, distracting me from my goals. I mean, that's the real reason why we broke up. She wanted me to go pro this year, leaving my college degree behind. But I decided a long time ago that I wanted to graduate. A professional career has to wait until I get that diploma in my hand.

I refuse to make the same mistake my father did.

She doesn't give a shit about that or what I want. Which is why she's trying to reinsert herself in my life. She doesn't want me. She wants the lifestyle.

I can't let her fuck with me again, especially not in the preseason. Every practice, every workout is important. I know she hasn't changed her mind about what she wants me to do, and I sure as fuck know I haven't either. One thing stopped her in her tracks, for now at least: the photo with Twyler.

Tossing my laptop aside, I grab my phone and open the official team chat. Scrolling down until I find the right number, I type a message and press send.

OneFive: It worked.

The message is instantly read, but there's a long pause before the small bubbles of a new message appear.

InternTwy: What worked?

OneFive: Shanna stopped texting me.

InternTwy: Oh, well good, I guess.

OneFive: But now my roommates are asking what's up with us.

InternTwy: Tell them the truth. That you assaulted me. Again.

OneFive: I could just tell them the actual truth, that you were being a supportive friend and were happy to help me with my ex-girlfriend worries.

InternTwy: "Friend" feels like a stretch here.

OneFive: Ouch... although there's something else we can do.

InternTwy: What do you want, Cain?

Her impatience amuses me, and I can't help but wonder what she's doing right now. And, what she's wearing. I smirk. I already know the answer. That ratty worn-out hoodie and shorts.

Shit, did my dick just twitch at the thought of peeling that hoodie off her body?

OneFive: I was thinking maybe we could tell them what we told her, that you're my girlfriend.

InternTwy: ....

Lying in bed, I stare at the line of bubbles as they fluctuate, waiting for her response to come through. Except they vanish.

Shit. I scared her off. Twenty-minutes later, when I know for certain she's not going to reply, I video call her.

"Hey," I sit up when her face appears on screen, "Don't hang up."

"I should," she says warily, which is fair after what I proposed.

Her hair is back in a ponytail, but it's messy, hair loose and curled around her face. At the bottom of the screen, I spot the top of that royal blue hoodie. Called that at least.

"Just hear me out, okay?"

"You have three minutes before my microwave popcorn is ready and the next episode of 'I Survived a Cult' starts."

That answers the question about what she's doing.

"You actually watch that garbage?"

The camera swings to the microwave where the timer is counting down: 2:43. "You're wasting time."

"Okay." I take a deep breath, feeling a little dumb now that I'm facing her. "I'd like you to consider being my girlfriend." She opens her mouth to argue and I continue, "Not a real girlfriend, but just... we can pretend for a while. Just until the season gets going. Shanna needs to understand this is over."

"Thanks for the offer, Cain, but I'm a hard pass."

"What?" Honestly, I'm reeling a little bit. "There are a dozen–no, two dozen–girls on campus that would be thrilled to get this offer. You didn't even consider it!"

"Reese, even if I wanted to help you out, which I don't, you made it perfectly clear today that I am super awkward around guys and I don't see how that will help you." Her eyes narrow. "I know you're not this desperate."

"Hey, you're the one that sent out that photo. People are asking questions. Shanna thinks we're dating. The only way she's going to buy it is if we play along for a while."

In the background I hear a buzzer going off. Shit, I'm running out of time.

"Seriously, Twyler. I need to get her off my back. She's toxic and bad for my mental health." I take a deep breath and confess something I've never told anyone, not even my parents. "When we were dating, she fucked with my head. There were some ultimatums, and she didn't like my answer." On screen Twyler watches me closely. "I just want the team to have a kick-ass season. I want to help them win it all and make up for screwing up last year."

"You didn't single-handedly lose that game, Reese."

"Maybe not, but I was distracted and dealing with personal drama and wasn't giving it my full attention. I vow not to do that again."

"And you think getting into some fake dating scheme will provide *less* drama to your life?"

I laugh, but take one last shot. "Honestly, it could help you, too."

I hear the microwave open and slam shut. She opens the bag and a gust of steam blows into her face. "Exactly how does this help me?"

"You said it yourself. People think you're not into guys, but you are. There's a misconception going around that you're undateable. One that I may have inadvertently encouraged." I give her an apologetic look. "Being seen with me will fix that."

"No one would believe it."

"Shanna did."

And to be honest, when my lips met hers, I forgot all preconceived ideas that I had about her, too. That kiss, well, she may be awkward and inexperienced, but it sure as fuck didn't feel like it.

She pauses, shoving her hand into the bag of popcorn. She's thinking about it, I can tell. All I need to do is nudge her over the line. "Look, we both need something. I need to look like I've moved on. You need to look—*in your words*—dateable. It's win-win." I rest a hand behind my head and lean back on the headboard. My camera lands on my bare chest and I see her eyes dart down. Yeah, maybe this girl isn't immune to me after all. "At the very least maybe you can gain a little confidence and become a little less awkward around guys."

"Dammit." Her hand comes to her forehead.

"Drop your popcorn?" I ask.

"No." She sighs. "Fine. I'll do it."

"Don't act like you're being so put out." I smile. "You're getting to date the unbelievably hot captain of the hockey team, you know."

"Don't push me, Cain."

"I'd stop," I laugh, feeling another surge of relief, "but it's just so much fun."

7

Twyler

I'm five minutes from class when my sister's name lights up my phone. I'd ignore it, but that won't discourage her. She'll just call back.

"Hey—" I start, but she cuts me off.

"I can't believe you didn't tell me."

"Tell you what?" I ask, keeping my voice low. I've already had more than my share of attention today as I walked across campus. "What are you talking about?"

"I saw the picture of you and Reese Cain floating around."

I stop abruptly, apparently right in front of another student who mutters, "Watch it," as he dodges me.

"Sorry!" I move to a bench outside the Arts and Sciences building. "Where did you see this?"

"I follow the College Mail page. It was on their daily wrap up."

"Oh no." My skin gets hot. I obviously knew people on campus would see it, or maybe some of Reese's hockey fans, but a major college gossip site? This blew up more than I thought. "It was nothing," I say, using the same excuse I gave Nadia. "We were just messing around. *Joking* around."

"Please," she dismisses me. "You, of all people, don't mess around with hot, superstar hockey players."

"Sure I do!" Although we both know it's a lie. "I have a sense of humor. I have friends."

What I really have, if Reese was serious last night, is a hot, superstar hockey player *fake* boyfriend.

That part I keep to myself. Ruby would never understand. And worse— "Just don't say anything to Mom, okay? She'll get the wrong idea."

"Oh, I won't. She'd probably drive down there to see it herself." She laughs, but we both know it's not a stretch. "I'm just kidding anyway. Reese Cain is wayyy out of your league. Obviously, it's nothing serious."

Am I offended? Yes. Do I say anything? No. Why? Because I never do. I let that little jab pass and take the opportunity to move on.

"How are you?" I ask, changing the subject to Ruby's favorite subject: herself. "How's the job?"

My sister is two years older than me and graduated from State in the spring with a degree in education. It's her first year teaching fourth grade.

"It's good. The kids are fine, although their parents are a pain in the ass."

I laugh. "I bet."

Ruby's love of bossing people around seems to make her a pretty good teacher. The kids love her, and she has a lot of enthusiasm, but I can see her struggling with demanding parents.

"I'm glad things are going well, but," I say, standing up, "I need to get into class. Seriously though—don't tell Mom about the picture."

"I won't," she promises, but we'll see. Secrets are never kept long between those two. We all get along, but I was always closer to my dad.

I walk into my History of Rock Music class and find Nadia saving me a seat. Although we're in different majors, we both needed a humanities class this semester and lucked into a spot in the popular class.

My dad loved music. Rock, country, blues, annoying stuff with horns that my mom always called "marching band music" but is really just something called Ska. He tried his hardest to influence me and Ruby with his eclectic taste in music and to be fair, I resisted it for a long time. But now that he's gone, taking this class seemed like the perfect homage.

"Hey," I say, taking off my backpack and sitting next to her near the middle of the room. The class is held in an auditorium with stadium seating. Professor Kent often shows videos of the musicians we're studying on the screen behind the podium.

"Hey, you'll never believe what happened," she says, eyes wide when she looks up from her phone. "Oh my God, your hair looks amazing."

I wore it down and have regretted it every step across campus. It feels hot and heavy on my neck and now Nadia's attention makes me feel more self-conscious. I swallow some of that back and manage, "Thank you. Now, tell me what happened and please don't let it be about the photo of me and Reese going viral." I take out my laptop. "Because I heard."

"Nope. That's old news." She grins in a way that tells me it's not old news, but she's moving on. "Reid and I have been texting a little, and last night he asked if I wanted to go out tonight."

"Oh," I feign surprise. "Like a real date?"

"A hang out maybe?"

"But just with him?" I push, resting my elbow on the little desk and facing her. She nods. "Where are you going?"

"I suggested the Badger Den."

The Badger Den is a bar—more specifically—a hockey bar. "Hmm. Does that really count as a date if you go to a bar with all his friends?"

"I don't know." She shrugs. "I'm the one that suggested it."

I'm not exactly surprised. Nadia doesn't know how to date any more than I do. She just hooks up and I just... well, do nothing.

Professor Kent steps up to the podium and the class quiets, which allows me to distract myself from the guilt I'm feeling over not telling her that I orchestrated the whole thing. It's not like me to meddle, but I just want her to be safe and happy.

As Professor Kent starts a new video about the evolution of rock music from southern spirituals, I have no idea how I'm going to explain to her what's going on with me and Reese. I'd been pretty adamant that the intimacy in the photograph wasn't real, yet now that's exactly what Reese wants me to pretend is happening. Do I tell Nadia it's fake? What are the rules around this? The more I think about it, the more anxious I get and the more this seems like a terrible idea.

There was no morning skate today, so I haven't seen or heard from Reese yet. I'm not convinced he wasn't drunk or something when he made the proposition. It's completely possible he's changed his mind since last night.

Except, when we walk out of the class an hour later, I spot Reese's massive frame leaning against the wall across from the hall. His gray eyes are pinned on me, and his lips are curved in a sexy smirk.

Have mercy.

I have a strong suspicion he hasn't changed his mind.

"Hey," I say, nudging Nadia toward the main entrance. "I'm,

uh, going to stop in the bathroom, but I know you've got a hike to get to your next class. You don't need to wait."

Normally we walk across campus together before splitting off. She has a class in the business school, and I have to set up for afternoon practice at the rink.

"Are you sure?" she asks, hitching her bag over her shoulder.

"Totally."

She smiles gratefully. "Okay, cool. I can tell Professor Walker is kind of done with me dragging my ass in late every week."

"Go!" I push her playfully, telling her I'll see her at home later. Once she's out of sight, I linger in front of the women's room door for a minute longer before taking a deep breath and turning to face him. I know he's still there. I can *sense* him. Reese has that kind of presence. Big and commanding. When I finally get the courage to make eye contact, I know one thing for sure: Ruby's right. This guy is completely out of my league.

My palms start to sweat as he pushes off the wall and crosses the hallway.

"How did you find me?" I ask, well aware of everyone watching him approach me. How many have seen that photo?

"I asked around." His tongue darts out, wetting his bottom lip. The action has me mesmerized, propelling the memory of our kiss to the forefront of my mind, and all those feelings rush back to me. Which is why I'm not prepared for the kiss he plants on my cheek, or the way he takes the backpack off my shoulder in one seamless move.

"You don't have to do that." Meaning both the kiss and the backpack.

"Sure I do," he slings my bag over his broad shoulder, on top of the one he's already carrying, "*girlfriend*."

I take a deep breath and exhale. "So you're serious about this."

"Dead serious."

The back of his hand brushes against mine and he tries to hold it. I shift nervously, stuffing my hands in the front pocket of my hoodie. He adjusts by laying his arm over my shoulder. Oh god.

"This is weird," I say quietly, as he holds the door for us to walk outside. Two girls stare up at him with dumb grins on their faces.

"It's not weird," he says, trying to assure me. But it doesn't work. Every eye on campus follows us as we walk across the quad. I'd like to say they're just looking at Reese, but I feel their eyes shift from him, down his muscular arm, to me. That's when their expression turns from awe to incredulous gaping.

"People are watching."

He chuckles darkly. "Welcome to my world."

"Jesus," this time it's a group of guys swooning over Reese as we walk by, "no wonder your ego is so fucking big."

"It's not just my ego that's big, Twy." He raises his eyebrows suggestively.

I stop and crane my neck to look up at him. "Did you seriously just say that?"

This time his laughter is more genuine, and the action lights up his face. "Just trying to break the tension." He tilts his head. "Did it work?"

"No."

In fact, it made it worse. Now I'm thinking about how big he is—*everywhere*—and another thought comes to mind. Does he expect us to experience that firsthand? Like how far does being Reese Cain's fake girlfriend go? What are the expectations?

Oh, God. I can't breathe.

"I can't do this," I blurt, ducking out from under his arm. "Sorry, I just—"

I don't finish the sentence, bolting across campus toward the training center. There's a short cut by the agricultural building, and I take it, hoping Reese doesn't see me. He hasn't caught up to me by the time I enter the building, and thankfully the locker room is quiet. Coach Green is in a private therapy session with one of the players down the hall. I exhale, feeling settled for the first time all day.

This... this makes sense to me. The smelly locker room. The laundry running down the hall with the guy's clean uniforms. The lingering scent of antiseptic and bleach. I first joined the sports training team at my high school on a whim. I was new to the school and a girl I'd become friendly with suggested it. Before that it'd never been on my radar, but there's something about working with the team that came naturally. Probably because here I'm behind the scenes, not on the field–or ice–as the case may be.

Grabbing the clipboard with the list of jobs Coach Green leaves out for me every day, I skim the list.

First up: Organize supply closet.

Perfect.

I'm in the middle of sorting the bandages by size when the door opens behind me. Looking over my shoulder I see Reese as he enters. His cheeks are pink and he's breathing heavy.

He tosses my backpack at my feet.

I frown. "What's wrong with you?"

"After you ran off, I jogged to three different places on campus before I realized you'd probably come here." Sweat soaks through the collar of his gray T-shirt. "I'm going to need to put a fucking tracker on you."

I still can't tell when he's joking or not, and that's half the problem.

"Thank you for bringing back my bag." I push it aside with my foot. "But, I'm serious. I can't do this. I'm not the right girl for this job. In fact, I'm not just unqualified, I'm completely *under*qualified."

He glances into the hallway and shuts the door behind him. "I think you're overestimating what it takes to be my fake girlfriend."

"I think you're overestimating my ability to pretend to be a functional person, much less a girlfriend." I inhale, feeling my cheeks turning red before I even speak. "I told you I had a boyfriend before. He wasn't a great guy, and it took me a long time to accept that how he treated me wasn't my fault. But it also took me a long time to really establish boundaries with myself and the people I surround myself with. I feel like getting into this situation isn't sticking to the rules I've set up for myself."

"So that's why you put up that shield."

"What?"

"You have this tough exterior—almost like armor. I've seen it fall a few times," he reaches out and brushes a lock of my bangs aside, "and it's like you become a different person."

Hearing Reese say this is both uncomfortable and exhilarating. It's why he makes me nervous. He *sees* me.

"I really think we can both benefit from this, Twyler. You need to build up your confidence and learn to handle social pressures. I can help you do that."

I start to roll my eyes at his egotism, and he shakes his head.

"I'm used to being the center of attention." His massive arms cross over his chest. "People looking and talking about me is just part of the position–I'm not just a hockey player, I'm a product. But because of that, I can help you elevate your status so that you can get what you want."

"I'm not interested in being a social climber."

"I know, but you do want to change your image, right? A boyfriend, maybe."

That's exactly what I'm looking for. There's no doubt I could use his help–any help–but I'm struggling to understand why he really needs me.

"Is Shanna really a problem for you?"

"You don't know how determined she can be." The lines around his eyes tense. "She thought I would cave to her demands, and when I didn't, she had to reassess."

"Why not another girl? There are plenty around."

"Shanna won't back off over a basic puck bunny, but you're a real girl, with a real understanding of what my obligations are to the team. I also don't have to worry about you catching feelings." He winks. "You've made it pretty clear that you're not into jocks."

Butterflies race through me and that should be warning enough to back out of this now. But against my better judgment, I say, "*If* you're really serious about this, I think we need to establish some parameters."

His eyes light up, knowing he's got me, but he asks, "What are you thinking?'

"No other women," I say.

He nods. "Or guys for you."

I laugh. "Thanks for the vote of confidence, but my two-year dry spell predicts that won't be a problem."

"Maybe, but once the male population on campus sees you with me, you're going to be swatting them away like flies."

"So vain," I mutter, rolling my eyes. "This can't affect my internship. I worked too hard to get here and really need Coach Green's reference. That means we keep this professional during practices and games."

"That's fine. I don't need the distraction either."

"And no more kissing without notice and consent," I shift uneasily, feeling like this is where it's going to get tricky. "In general, I'm not really into PDA."

He rubs his jaw, but I don't miss the way his eyes drop to my mouth. "Define PDA."

"Kissing, hand-holding, groping, sitting on each other in public—"

"Sunshine, come on—"

"Pet names," I add. "No pet names. Especially that one."

He's been calling me Sunshine since last year–no doubt because of my lack of sunny disposition. He thinks it's cute. I think it's annoying as fuck.

"Twyler," he says, over exaggerating my name, "you're going to need to compromise on this a little if we're going to make it believable. Not just for Shanna, but everyone else."

"Should I bring over a box of condoms and Plan B for you to spread around?" I ask. "Will that make it believable?"

He winces and shakes his head. "Fuck. I deserve that."

I shrug. "I work in a locker room. I've heard worse."

"Hey," he takes a step toward me, close enough I catch his scent; detergent and sweat–mixed with something intoxicatingly manly. "We'll take this super slow. Nothing you're uncomfortable with."

"Okay."

He closes the distance and takes my small hand in his massive one. Gently, he splays my fingers and links his with mine. "How about this? Yes or no?"

Warmth spreads up my arm–and I look past his broad chest to his gorgeous face. I swallow thickly. "Yes."

With his other hand he runs his fingers down my jaw. A shiver runs through my body, pebbling my skin—my nipples. God, he's good at this, I think, until he drops his hand to my neck and my spine straightens, and I squirm away.

"I don't like that."

"No?" he frowns, eyes narrowing in concern. He's probably reconsidering, realizing that I may break, but I won't. I never do. But I've spent a long time learning about setting boundaries and if we're really going through with this charade, Reese is right. I need to use it as a learning experience.

I take our linked fingers and place his hand on my hip,

letting it rest there. His other hand moves back to my hair, pushing it behind my ear, then trailing down my jaw.

"I like your hair like this." His fingers splay behind my head. "It's kind of wild and uncontrollable. A little bit like you."

His neck tilts and I know what to expect now. Or I think I do. His lips brush against mine, soft and sweet, a small kiss, before he pulls back, tongue darting out like he's tasting me on his mouth.

"We'll keep it simple for now."

Easier said than done, I think, feeling the intense heat from his gaze. Reese Cain doesn't have an off switch. That may feel easy to him, but my entire body reacts in a way that is decidedly not simple. My lips burn from that barely-there kiss, and I swallow back the desire to make things complicated.

"Do you have any rules or expectations?" I ask, stepping back to put a little distance between us. His hand remains on my hip, fingers applying the slightest pressure to hold me in place.

Possessive.

"You're off the hook for coming to games," his lip quirks, "but we'll need to go to a few parties together. Hang out with the guys or your friends."

"Okay, I can do that."

I think.

"Then there's the athletic department alumni fundraiser. The guys usually bring dates."

"That feels like a work/dating conflict, don't you think?"

His gray eyes hold mine, like he's considering it, but ultimately he says, "How about we play that one by ear?"

Preseason games start this weekend, and then the fundraiser kicks off the season at the end of the month. Do I really think Reese will still want to keep this up?

"But first," he says, "come to the Badger Den with me tonight. Everyone will be there."

"That's not the selling point you think it is."

He laughs, squeezing my hip. "The earlier we rip this Band-Aid off the better."

He's right. Dammit. "Reid and Nadia are going to be there tonight."

"Good. We'll come out to the team and your friend all at once."

The thought is terrifying, but I know this needs to happen. Something in my life has to change. "I'll meet you there."

"Not a chance." He shakes his head. "I'll pick you up at eight."

Reese doesn't give me an opportunity to push back. He presses a fast kiss to my forehead and exits the closet, leaving me, my pounding heart and burning lips, to process the fact that I officially just agreed to be Reese Cain's girlfriend.

8

Reese

The door swings open before I have a chance to knock. That's not what surprises me. It's Twyler herself.

Fuck, she's cute.

"Hey." Her fingers tug her jeans. The nervous action draws my eyes to her waist and the strip of pale skin exposed by her cropped sweatshirt. My cock twitches in appreciation. Why did I agree to abstain from hooking up during this?

Shifting, I blink, taking in the curve of her hips. Then she's gone, stepping back inside, saying, "I'm almost ready."

She doesn't invite me in, but she also doesn't slam the door in my face, so after a beat, I step inside the narrow house and shut the door behind me. The Shotgun homes, other than the Manor, are uniform. Long and skinny, just enough room for a couple of people. A couple of normal-sized people. With my height, I feel like a giant, like if I stretched my arms out, I could probably touch both walls.

"No rush," I say, looking around. There are two doors—both

open. I glance in one and see it decorated in bright oranges and pinks—it also looks like a tornado recently passed through. The one right next to it is a bit darker. Gray, black, and a little light pink. Not spotless, but tidy. Twyler's trademark blue hoodie hangs over the back of her desk chair.

"It's just you and Nadia that live here?" I ask, giving the open bathroom door some space.

"Yeah, we've been roommates since freshman year."

"I've lived with Jefferson since then, too."

She walks out of the bathroom, hair down, and curled in long waves. Her eyes are smoky and dark, making the blue three shades brighter. Three silver hoops hang in both ears and a chain loops twice around the base of her neck—a small medallion resting against her throat. I think back to how she reacted to me touching her neck earlier today, the panic and discomfort in her eye.

If I didn't know better, I'd think she was scared.

Twyler said something about a shitty ex doing a number on her, and seeing her like this, I have to believe it, because there's no way guys on campus wouldn't have noticed her if she'd wanted it.

She's more than cute. She's bordering on hot.

"I just need my coat and we can go."

She passes me, stepping into her room, and I wait in front of a massive bulletin board hanging on the wall between the two bedroom doors. It's filled with photos, including a furry black cat that seems to be the star of the board. Otherwise, it's mostly Twyler and Nadia. There are other mementos, like silly handwritten notes and a dozen ticket stubs held up by push pins. I thumb through them, noticing they're all from the same band; The New Kings.

There's one photo of Twyler and two other women out in front of the arena. All dressed in Badger yellow and black. One woman is older, and one about the same age as Twyler, all with identical blue eyes.

She steps out of her room, and I point to it. "Is this the sister?"

"Yep."

"And your mom?" I guess.

Honestly, the woman in the photo looks pretty young, but Twyler replies, "That's us. The Perkins girls."

No mention of a dad.

"You all look a lot alike."

She snorts. "Don't tell Ruby that."

"Why?" I study the women. The genes are strong. Ruby's face is a little narrower and her hair a shade lighter, but the eyes and nose are the same. Twyler's got a rounder face, thick, dark lashes, and pretty, soft, pink lips.

"Because she thinks she's better than me. Better looking. Better in school. Better daughter. Okay," she says, finally stopping to look at me. Her eyes start at my head and slowly move down before pinging back up. "Ready to get this over with?"

I laugh.

"What?"

"I've never been out with a girl so ready for our date to be over with." I open the door, while she puts on her coat. "Well, unless it was just to get to the stuff at the end of the date."

Her gaze dropping back to the ground, she says, "You say stuff like that just to make me blush, don't you?"

"Yep." I can't deny that it's impossible not to mess with her when she gets so flustered, but I know if I'm going to get her to go through with the rest of the night, I need to ease off. "You okay with walking? I can call a ride if you'd rather."

"Walking's good," she says, and we head down the sidewalk toward the main road that cuts through campus and leads to The Strip, the hub of Wittmore's nightlife.

"If we're going to pull this off," I say, falling in step, "we should probably learn a little about each other."

"What do you want to know?" she asks, tucking her hair behind her ear.

"Where are you from?"

"Tennessee."

That comes as a surprise, although I'd noted the hint of a southern twang in her accent. "Really? How did you end up here?"

"I was ready for something new, I guess. My aunt and uncle live a couple of miles from campus, and we would visit in the summers. I always thought the campus was pretty and I could see myself here. When I saw they had Kinesiology as a major, it seemed like a perfect fit."

"So how did you get into sports training, anyway?"

She tells me about the program at her high school and how her coach was more like a mentor. He got her interested in pursuing it as a degree. "It's hard to explain, but I like being part of the game experience, you know, feeling the energy, but sitting with the crowd always felt a little boring and overwhelming. I'd rather be busy, and this way I get to do both."

"That makes sense." I press the crosswalk button. The row of bars and restaurants start a block down and the glow of lights travels to us. "But why hockey?"

She laughs. "Oh, that was kind of a fluke. I wanted to be assigned to the basketball team, but when I turned in my internship application my advisor pushed me to take the open position for the hockey team. Truthfully, I think they were looking to diversify the staff—since you guys have a whole bro-culture going on. I guess they figured I may be the only female that could handle working with a bunch of alpha-male jocks."

"They weren't wrong." We cross the street and I shift to the side nearest the road. Up ahead groups of students are stepping into the various establishments. The neon sign for the Badger Den shines in the dark. "The guys like you. I know a couple would rather have you do their wraps than Green."

"Why? Because they don't want to look at his mustache?"

"I'd like to say no, but... maybe?" Coach Green has a signature, thick bushy-mustache, that is his pride and joy. I laugh. "Fuck, that thing is a beast, right?"

"Yes! It's like an animal glued to his upper lip," she agrees. "I don't know how his wife stands it. I'd make my husband shave it off or he couldn't come in the house."

"Oh, so that's how it is with you? Your way or the highway?"

She shrugs, but doesn't hide her smile. "I'm just saying, a little scruff is okay, sexy even, but a weasel on your face is a hard no."

By the time we approach the door she's loosened up a little. "Hey." I tug on her jacket, slowing her down. I can tell through the window it's already packed. I like this. Talking to Twyler. Learning about her. Once we get inside it'll be loud and crowded. "You didn't ask me any questions."

"Oh." Her eyebrow lifts. "I guess I don't need to."

"Really?" Is she that disinterested? "Why?"

"Because, Cain," she pauses, her hand wrapped about the bar door, "there's nothing you can tell me that I don't already know."

˜

"Breathe, Sunshine."

Her neck cranes and those blue eyes meet mine. "Don't call me—"

I can't help but grin because messing with her is the only way to get her out of her head. She scowls when she realizes it. "You good?"

"Not in the least."

"Well, it's happening." We're just inside the door and any loosening up she'd done on the walk to the bar vanished when we stepped across the threshold. I slide my hand into hers, adhering to our preestablished rules. Also, I don't put it past her to bolt again and I'm not jogging all over town again to find her. She's fast for someone so short. "But I promise to stick by your side all night."

The Badger Bar is a Wittmore hockey landmark. It's also a dive. Framed photos of past teams line the walls, along with signed pictures of the guys that went on to go pro. There's an entire section for past Frozen Four winners and matted newspaper articles. It's basically a shrine to local hockey and even as a kid, when my dad brought me here for the first time after watching a game, I knew I wanted to be on the wall.

On game nights, fans pack the place to watch the game on one of a dozen screens. On other nights, like this one, when we don't have late practice, the team congregates looking to blow off a little steam. It's not just hockey players though, there are plenty of girls that hang around, which means guys from all over campus will be here. I spot a group from Zeta Sig hogging the dartboard.

"Do you see them?" she asks, fingers tightening against mine. Her hand is so small and frankly, a little sweaty. She's the complete opposite of Shanna, or really any of the girls I hang out with. They love athletes because they love competition. Going up against one another to see who can attain the attention of a jock. Twyler doesn't seem to care–at all. She's nervous and I like it—better than hiding behind that tough exterior. Nervous I can work with.

"Cap!" Reid's voice carries from the back corner. His hand shoots up and waves us over. Keeping a tight grip on her hand, I lead her through the crowd to the booth. Teammates, girls, fans, they all say hello as I pass. If anyone notices me dragging Twyler behind me, they don't mention it. That doesn't mean they don't see her though. I hear the guys' excitement when they spot her, calling out her name.

"Hey!" Axel looks past me and grins down at her. "This makes twice in one week."

"Axel," she says, voice quiet over the noise and music. She looks him up and down. "I see you found a shirt to wear tonight."

Pete laughs behind his hand. "She called you out, man."

Axel's lips quirk and he reaches for the hem of his shirt, exposing the waist of his low-slung jeans. "I can lose it if you want."

"Shirt on," I say, giving him a hard look. "Remember what Mike said last time."

Axel sighs and drops the fabric. "Maybe next time, TG."

"TG?" Twyler asks.

"Trainer Girl," he replies with a wink. Axel gives everyone a nickname. I'm never sure if it's because he doesn't actually know their real names or if he just likes handing them out. Regardless, once he's given someone a name, it's a done deal.

"Who's Mike?" Twyler asks as I lead her past the pool tables where a puck bunny I hooked up with last week plays a game with one of the rookies. She grins and I give her a friendly but disinterested nod. "And what did he say last time?"

"Mike is the owner of the bar. A former defenseman from back in the nineties. Due to Axel's need to strip down everywhere we go, he had to enforce a strict no clothes-no service policy."

We approach the booth and there's no missing the way Nadia's jaw drops when she sees us. To her credit, she recovers quickly. "You didn't tell me you were coming..." She says, eyes pinging between us, "...*with* Reese."

"Last minute plans," Twyler says, sliding across from Nadia.

Reid gives her the once over and says, "Like the hair."

"Why does everyone get so weird when I wear my hair down?" she asks, tugging at one long curl.

Nadia grins. "Because it takes you from cute to smokin' hot, babe."

"She's right," Reid says, adding a wink. "Smokin'."

Twyler rolls her eyes, and she may think Reid's messing with her, but I know better. I see the spark of interest in his eye, like he's seeing her for the first time too. These guys have spent two seasons around Twyler in her ratty hoodie and pulled-back hair. But unwrap those layers, revealing the woman underneath, and they see what I've started to notice too.

And I don't fucking like it.

"Come on," he says, drawing me out of my irritation. "Let's go hit the bar."

"So what's up with you and the trainer?" Reid asks after we've fought the crowd and ordered from the bartender.

"I decided to take my own advice." I shrug. "It's time for something new."

He leans his elbow against the bar and snorts. "Well, she's definitely something new for you."

There's no denying that Twyler is the opposite of any girl I've been seen with before. From Shanna to the puck bunnies, I've always had a type. Twyler goes against it—which is exactly the point.

"I'm focusing on the season," I tell him. "And that includes cooling it with the puck bunnies for a while. Also, Twyler's fun to hang around. It's nothing serious."

He lets it drop as the bartender pushes the pitcher of beer across the bar top and Reid grabs it as I pick up two new glasses. Or at least I think he does. He turns to me, his red hair glinting in the neon lights behind the bar, and says, "She's a cool chick,

Cap, and I really like the way she deep tissue massages my hamstrings." His expression is dead serious. "Don't fuck this up."

I can't tell him that there's no way for me to fuck this up when the whole thing is fake and Twyler Perkins has zero interest in me anyway.

9

Twyler

"Just let it go," I say to Nadia after she asked me a dozen questions about me and Reese showing up together. *Are we on a date? How did he ask me? What were his exact words? Does that mean the picture he posted was real?* "We're just... feeling things out."

My friend blinks at me and says, "Girls don't just feel things out with guys like Reese Cain. They fuck him or they marry him. There is no in between."

"Who says I can't be one of those?"

We both know it's a stretch, but I get the sense there's something else lingering under Nadia's disbelief. Jealousy. In her world, there's no other option for a woman who wants to be with an athlete. Jersey chaser or wife. If I fall into something in the middle, her whole life plan falls apart.

Our stare off is interrupted when two guys approach the table. Two cute, non-hockey playing guys.

"Well, hello," Nadia says, instantly intrigued.

"You're new," the tall one says, grinning down. His shirt has the symbol of the rowing team stamped over his heart. "I'm Knox." He sits next to Nadia and his ridiculously good-looking friend stares at me. "That's Miller."

"We're, uh..." I look over their shoulder searching for Reese. He promised to stick by me all night.

"Nadia," my friend says, eyeing the rower. Not her team of choice but I know her, and any varsity athlete will do.

"And what about you, beautiful?" Miller says, reaching out to touch my hair. "What's your name?"

"Not interested," a voice says. We all look up and to see Reese and Reid back from the bar. "You're in my seat, Hansen."

"Cain. I didn't know you were sitting here." His lip quirks in a way that says he definitely knew it. "How's the season looking?"

From the expression on Reese's face, it's looking like he's one heartbeat away from ripping this Miller guy's head off at the neck. Knox seems to get the picture faster than his friend because he stands up and says, "Nice to meet you." He nods at Reid. "Later, dude."

Reid nods and slides into the seat Knox vacated. Nadia smiles at him.

Miller takes his time getting up. I don't know who this kid is, but he has balls, that's for sure. He winks at me and says, "See you around," before rising and merging with the crowd. The last thing I see is him palming the ass of a blonde before getting swallowed up.

Reese glares at his backside and sits next to me.

"I'm sorry," he says quietly. "I should've known that if I left you alone for two seconds the vultures would descend."

"It's okay." I'm rattled although I'm not sure why. "Who was that?"

"Miller Hansen–frat boy degenerate." He sets the two glasses he was carrying on the table. "I know you're supposed to be learning how to relate to guys, but *absolutely not* with that one."

I'm not going to disagree. Reese is out of my league. Miller seems like the Devil looking for a new plaything. Shifting, Reese's massive thigh presses against mine. A flutter tickles in my lower belly, followed by a slow-spreading warmth. Am I so desperate that I'm falling for a jock-manwhore like Reese? No. It's just biology and going way too long without a boyfriend. But ugh, how can one guy smell this good?

"I apologize for the beer," he says a little louder, sliding a glass in front of me. "Reid ordered before I could get a word in."

"What? PBR is a classic."

"It's watered-down piss." Reese shakes his head. "At some point last year Reid decided he wanted to go old school with beer. Only brands made before the nineteen fifties."

"Hey, this beer was made in the eighteen hundreds." He starts pouring the pitcher into glasses. "If it was good enough for our forefathers, it's good enough for me."

"You know these people didn't have indoor plumbing, right?" Reese says, clearly diving into an old argument. "Progress isn't a bad thing."

"I like it," Nadia says, smiling over at Reid. "Beer is beer."

"It's really not," Reese mutters, but lifts his glass and takes a sip. He grimaces and gives me an apologetic look. "Seriously, you don't have to drink it. I'll get you something else."

"It's fine," I say, taking my own sip. I'm not really into beer one way or the other. It all kind of tastes like piss to me. I prefer my alcohol flavored with syrup and sugar. "Mmmmm, so good."

"See?" Reid says, feeling vindicated. "Twyler's got good taste." His eyes dart to Reese. "Mostly."

Beer issue settled, the table sinks into conversation, the guys talking about the first preseason game coming up. "Anderson's off the injury list," Reese says. "Which means that Hartford will be a lot more dangerous this year."

"Maybe." Reid doesn't look bothered by this news. "But they lost three seniors, including Boozer to Wisconsin."

"Fair point," Reese says. "I just wish we were playing at home and not away."

"Oh, that reminds me," I look across the table to Nadia, "we'll be on the bus when tickets go on sale. Are you still good for buying them?"

"Yep. The online sale starts at nine."

"You can't oversleep," I tell her.

"I won't. I promise. I have the whole morning cleared." Nadia lifts her glass and takes a drink. "I already set my alarm."

"Tickets for what?" Reid asks.

"The New Kings," Nadia replies before I get a chance to. "It's Twyler's favorite band."

"New Kings?" Reid says. "I haven't listened to them since high school."

"You mean since they had a song in that superhero movie, and they played it on the radio all the time." Fairweather fans. They're the worst.

"How many times have you seen them?" Reese asks.

"Eight."

"Eight *tours*," Nadia supplies. "That's not including multiple shows at each stop. She's hardcore."

The New Kings were indie for a long time, but exploded a few years ago. It's great that they've had such huge success, being on that soundtrack set them up, but for the majority of the fanbase, we're not in it for their fame. Two best friends front the band, and their lyrics are about life and struggling with depression. The good and bad stuff. It's all real, and I'm not surprised a party boy like Reid isn't into it more than superficially. Their music has helped me through a few rocky times—including the one with Ethan.

"So, you're a fangirl," Reese says, looking at me like he's trying to unlock some code.

"Is that a surprise?"

"Maybe," he says, "but as someone who had a shrine to Wayne Gretzky in my bedroom, I don't think I can judge."

"They're coming to the city next month," I explain, running my thumb over the condensation on my glass. "I haven't seen them at the arena before and I just want good seats."

"Twy," Nadia says, reaching across the table and grabbing my hand. "I've got this. Wake up, get in the queue, sit there bored out of my mind for two hours, snag awesome tickets."

"Thank you." The tension in my shoulders eases, and I brush against Reese. God, he smells so good. Some kind of intoxicating mixture I can't put my finger on. I just know it makes me want to lean in and huff him. "I just haven't missed a tour yet. I'd ask Ruby, but she's working the reading bowl that day for her school district."

"Ruby doesn't need to do it. I'm doing it."

Reese nudges my knee with his, sending another round of butterflies hurling through my stomach, and says, "I'm sure Nadia can click a few buttons, aren't you?"

Reluctantly, I agree. Nadia isn't the most reliable person. She's terrible at communicating and answering texts. I'd feel better if Ruby was getting the tickets, but I'm just going to have to trust that Nadia won't screw this up.

I nurse my beer while Nadia and Reid empty the pitcher. Next to me, Reese sticks to his one drink limit, a self-imposed rule he put on himself for the season. His dedication is impressive and as someone busting my ass to help the team, I appreciate it.

Another thing? He sticks by me all night, even when a steady stream of teammates stop by to ask him to play a game of pool or various girls linger to flirt, just like he promised.

"Hey," I say when Reid gets up for a refill. "Can I get out? I need to use the restroom."

"Sure." He slides out of the booth, then takes my hand to help me scoot out. He bends down and asks, "Want a chaperone?"

"I think I can handle it." I lock eyes with Nadia. "Y'all stay here so we don't lose the table."

Shockingly, there's no line for the bathroom, although two girls, clones of one another with stick-straight hair and tops with plunging necklines, stand at the mirror applying makeup. One I recognize from stopping by the table to talk to Reese and Reid. The girl from the party. Ginna, I think.

When I come out of the stall, they're still there.

"Hey," one says, as I squeeze between them to wash my hands. "You're the girl from Reese's Chattysnap, right?"

"I guess."

I pump the soap and lather up.

"And you came here with him tonight?"

"To meet up with some friends." Why I add this, I don't know. Maybe it's the way they're both looking at me. Like I stole their pet.

I turn off the faucet and grab a paper towel.

"Well, if he takes you home, let me give you a little tip." She faces me. With all the makeup and the boobs and the confidence, I feel like I'm talking to some older, wiser woman, when rationally I know we're the same age. She leans forward, her perfume wafting, thick and oily. "He loves it when you bite the head a little bit. Just a little nibble."

"Okay," I say, heat rising to my cheeks. "Good to know. Thanks."

I don't miss the sound of their laughter as I rush out. Because although I told Reese earlier I know everything about him, I realize it's not true. I definitely didn't know *that*.

Just outside the door I slam straight into a brick wall.

A wall with tattooed hands.

"What you running from, TG?" Axel Rakestraw's hands are wrapped around my upper arms, holding me upright. He peers behind me just as the bathroom door opens and Ginna and the other girl walk out. "Ah, vipers."

"Come on, let's get a drink."

I follow him, only because I don't want another run-in with those girls.

"Two shots of…" he looks from the bartender to me, "…what's your poison? Tequila? Jack? Fireball?"

"Something sweet?" I ask.

"Jäger," he orders, leaning on the bar.

He's a little shorter than Reese, but he's got the wingspan of an Olympic swimmer. All the better for blocking the goal. His white-blonde hair sticks out like a devilish halo, and dark tattoos peek out from the neck of his shirt.

"You gotta ignore girls like that," he says, nodding over to where Ginna now has her body plastered up against Pete. "You intimidate the fuck out of them."

"That's ridiculous." Across the room, Pete stares at her tits like a deer in headlights. Fuck, now I'm staring at her tits. "No one intimidates a girl like that."

The bartender pours the two shots and pushes them over. Axel hands me one and lifts his.

"Girls like you do, the kind that wears comfortable clothes, looks hot while doing it, and spends her time pursuing a career, not trying to fuck the entire hockey team."

I tip back the shot, allowing the burn in my throat to avoid acknowledging any of the nonsense Axel is spewing. He's a huge player and spends every night with one of the girls he's talking about.

"Speaking of… did you get any of Linkletter's presentation on ligaments last week?"

Axel is in my anatomy class. He spends the majority of each class with either his headphones on listening to music or sleeping.

Before I can answer, a strong arm wraps around my shoulders, tugging me into a hard chest. I'm engulfed in the best, sexiest scent known to man. Reese Cain.

"There you are, Sunshine."

I look up into Reese's face. His, if I'm not reading it wrong, annoyed face. "Yep. Here I am."

Axel's gaze drops to Reese's arm and the way his fingers tighten around my bicep. He smiles. "Hey, Cap."

"What are you guys talking about?" Reese asks, looking between us.

 "TG and I both have Linkletter for our anatomy class." Axel grins. "We were just comparing notes."

Is it me, or does Reese pull me a little closer to his side. "I didn't realize you had class together. That's cool."

"To be fair," I say, "we're both in class, but only one of us is awake for the majority of it."

"You know how it is. Late nights. Early practice." He shrugs like every player in the room does the same. "Plus, Linkletter bores the fuck out of me."

"It's a little like listening to paint dry," I admit. Unlike Axel Rakestraw, I need to pass the class and get my degree. He's already been drafted.

Axel and I share a knowing look and we both laugh, but he adds, "Maybe we could meet up and go over some of the notes before the midterm—"

"We should go," Reese blurts, sliding his hand from my shoulder down to my waist. His fingers brush over the bare skin above my waistband. I stiffen at the contact, fighting off the shiver that threatens to run down my spine, but I don't move away.

Then he takes it a step further and presses a warm kiss to my temple.

"Now?" I ask, my voice a squeak.

"Yep. All this talk about anatomy is giving me ideas." He winks and licks his bottom lip, forcing my eyes to zero in on his mouth. Fuck. Reese overload.

With his arm firmly around my waist, he nudges me toward the door. "Later, man."

"See ya, Cap." He grins and claps me on the shoulder. "You too, TG. We'll talk about class later."

"Bye," I call out as Reese continues toward the door, barely acknowledging his teammates as he passes. "Wait." I stop. "Should I tell Nadia we're leaving?"

"You can text her. Let her and Reid finish their date," he says, pushing me outside. The cool night air feels good against my overheated skin. He doesn't stop moving until we've passed the pizza parlor next door and are close to the crosswalk.

I wiggle out from under his grasp. "Okay, what the hell was that?"

"What?" he asks. If he's playing dumb, he's super good at it, because his expression is a mix of innocence and confusion.

"What's with the rushed exit? I was talking to Axel... doing what you said I should do. Socialize a little. Gain some confidence."

"I did say that, but..." he weighs his words, finally adding, "... not with Axel."

"Why not? He's popular and social. We have a class in common and something to talk about. He—"

"He's out of your league." He cuts me off like he can't bear for me to continue.

It hits like a slap to the face. Eyes stinging, I say, "Oh. Right. Okay."

Reese grimaces. "Fuck. No. Wait, that's not—"

"No. I hear you," I assure him before spinning on my heel. I check the crosswalk, it's flashing, warning that the time to cross the street is ending. I dash forward at the last minute, hoping to put some distance between us.

Behind me, I hear Reese calling my name, but then the flow of cars blocks us. I brush a hot tear off my face. Fuck. Why am I crying? What Reese said is nothing but the truth.

"Twyler, hold up." I hear his feet hit the pavement behind me. His stupid long legs allowing him to catch up faster than I hoped. "I didn't mean it that way."

"Sure you did." I refuse to let him see me cry. "Axel Rakestraw is definitely out of my league. Just like you are. Everyone thinks so. Nadia. Ruby..."

He grabs me by the shoulder, forcing me to stop. We're a block away from Shotgun, the streets over here are quiet. At least there aren't witnesses to my humiliation.

"I didn't say that because I think you're not good enough for him." He takes in my face, frowning at the tears I can't hide. "If anything, you're *too* good for him. Axel is a—"

"A fuckboy."

His eyebrows raise.

"I know Axel's reputation, Reese. God, it's like you think I live in a cave like some naïve innocent. I know he's slutty as hell. Just like the majority of the team." I eye him. "Just like you."

If that hurts him, and it probably doesn't because these guys wear their promiscuity like a fucking badge of honor, he doesn't show it. "Listen, this isn't about reputation or fuckboys or anything else. This is about the fact that as far as anyone is concerned, you and I are together right now. We have to establish ourselves and unless I marked my territory a little bit in there, he was going to think you were fair game."

I brush aside a tear. "Why would he care?"

"Sunshine, I know Axel. I know what he looks like when he's interested—and he was interested in you."

My jaw drops. "Don't be stupid."

"I'm being serious."

I take a shaky breath and feel his hand on my hip. It's strong and firm, and I know it's mostly to anchor me to him so I can't run off again.

"We just had our first official fake date." His other hand reaches out and his warm thumb wipes a tear off my cheek. "There were some hiccups, but we survived. For better or worse, you definitely got the attention of the guys on the team."

"I think Nadia bought it, even if she's not sure she understands it."

"Oh," he says with a smirk, "Nadia bought it enough that she felt the need to threaten me with slight bodily harm if I fuck this up."

"Oh my god," I choke out a laugh, "she didn't."

"She did." He laughs, gray eyes bright. Warmth spreads through my limbs when he squeezes my hip. "It'll get easier from here."

"You think?" I ask.

"Yep."

Sliding his hand into mine, he threads our fingers together and we walk, hand in hand, to my house. On the front porch, I stand on the top step, and he's two below, making our faces level. I tense when his hand reaches out, thinking he's about to touch my neck, but he only pushes my hair over my shoulder. "If we were really dating this is when I'd kiss you goodnight."

I roll my eyes. "You want me to believe you drop girls off on their doorstep with nothing but a kiss?"

"I said *dating*. Which is different from my normal–"

"Hookups," I supply.

"Yeah, I guess."

His hands cup my face and his eyes dart to my mouth, and I think for a second, he may kiss me. And for a second, despite our laid out parameters, I think I *want* him to kiss me. Instead, he tilts my head forward and presses a kiss on my forehead, before stepping back. "Night, Sunshine."

I don't exhale until I'm inside, door locked behind me, and say to myself, "Don't call me Sunshine."

10

Reese

Rolling over, I wake up with a wince at the sharp throbbing between my legs. I want to say it's just biology—morning wood—but it's been like this since I left the bar with Twyler the night before.

Rubbing one off in the shower did nothing to abate it.

It's not like it's a challenge to get me hard. I get a semi every time I see a hot girl on campus. Sometimes even if they're not hot. But being close to Twyler all night? Fuck, we passed semi after she licked that shitty beer off her lips and moved onto full-on boner. I haven't been able to get her off of my mind since–or if I'm being honest–longer than that.

I flop on my back and let my cock breathe, tenting under the sheet.

Sunshine really doesn't get how cute she is, even with Axel panting on her like a dog. After months of being surrounded by chicks wearing little to nothing, there's something refreshing about her more modest outfits. That little strip of skin between her shirt and jeans? Wondering how big her tits actually are? Fucking tantalizing.

Axel noticed it for sure.

The instant I realized she was talking to him; something came over me. I muscled my way through the crowd at the bar, not giving a shit who I bumped into on the way. She had that bitchy-amused look on her face as he bent down to speak in her ear, a cocky grin tugging at his mouth.

Nope.

Fuck no.

That's all I thought as I slung my arm around her shoulder and marked my territory without crossing any of her boundaries. A fucking kiss on the forehead and I'm over here humping the mattress like an animal.

Fumbling under my shorts, I release my cock and give it a long stroke. I hadn't thought this part through when I made the arrangement. No hook-ups with other girls and no hooking up with the one I'm pretending to date. My dick is going to get real familiar with my right hand. It'll be like high school all over again.

I shut my eyes and go through the playbook. Puck bunnies, porn, the underwear models that have supplied my spank bank for years. My brain latches onto one familiar scenario, and I pump my dick to the image of Scarlett Johansen dressed like the Black Widow on her knees, her big eyes looking up at me as she begs for my cock. Her lips make a perfect circle—the perfect place to bury myself. Except when I look down again, her fair hair turns dark, the length long and hanging over her shoulders. Then those eyes, dammit. Ice blue.

Yep, my fantasy just slipped right back into what I was trying to avoid.

Twyler Perkins.

I'm too far gone to pull the plug on this so, I lean into the fantasy, guiding my hand up and down my cock with long strokes. Watching the tip as it slides across that puffy bottom lip. My balls pinch and my breath grows heavy—

Bang bang!

"Yo, Cap!" Jefferson calls.

"Yeah?" I muster, shuddering through a tight breath.

"Breakfast in ten."

"Got it. Be right out."

The image of Twyler vanishes, replaced by Nadia's accusatory glare. She'd given me more than a warning last night.

"Twyler's not like most girls." There was an underlying tone—hostility if I had to guess.

"Obviously you want to say something to me." I lifted my chin. *"I'm all ears."*

"Twyler is special."

"Okay."

"She's been through a lot with some super shitty men in her life and the good men...well," she swallowed, *"she can't rely on that either. She doesn't need games, Reese. She needs kindness and stability and someone willing to help her work through her vulnerabilities and if you're not here to be that for her, stop whatever the fuck this is before she gets hurt."*

There was a fierceness in Nadia's eyes that made my balls shrink up a little. Twyler told me that the one thing about Nadia that she could count on was her loyalty. After last night, I don't doubt it.

"Look," I said, holding her eye. *"You're right. She's different and in a good way—a great way. I like her. She's funny and quirky and..."* A fucking great kisser. *"She surprises me, and it's been a long time since I've been around a woman that does that."*

Across the bar Twyler had emerged from the back hallway, and I'd quickly looked back across the table. *"I'm not going to hurt her, but if I do, you have free rein to kick my ass."*

Nadia thrust her hand across the table. *"Deal."*

We'd shaken on it. And here I am, hours later, with my dick in my hand, exploiting her friend in my depraved masturbatory fantasies.

For the *second* time.

Jesus, I think, dropping my dick and feeling my balls deflate. I'm a fucking asshole.

~

I don't see her again until I'm in the gym that afternoon, getting in a pre-practice workout.

She's back in her trainer uniform—although the gym is hot, and she's ditched the hoodie for a Wittmore Hockey T-shirt and a pair of shorts.

The workout room isn't crowded. Practice doesn't start for another thirty minutes, but I felt the need to work off a little energy. The other guys in the room must feel the same way, either that, or they're here for a prearranged meeting with Coach Green or Twyler.

Lifting a set of free weights, I discreetly watch her work with Hartman on the mat as he stretches out his calves. "That's right," she says, kneeling in front of him. A flash of my fantasy comes barreling back. "Spend a little time doing each of these exercises before and after practice and I think it'll reduce the tightness."

Hartman's eyes are glued just below her chin, directly at her tits.

Hell no.

I rack the weights with a loud clank, and cut across the room.

Coach Green steps out of the office and looks up from his clipboard. "You need something?"

I blink, knowing I need to say something. "Oh, yeah, I'm

feeling a little tight after that last practice. I thought maybe a stretch could help?"

"Perkins," he says without looking up, "when you finish with Hartman, Cain needs some attention."

Her gaze shifts over, but she keeps her expression neutral. "Sure. We're almost finished."

I grab some water and wait, feeling stupid. Feeling territorial. We'd made a firm agreement not to let this interfere with her work, yet here I am, interfering.

"Thanks, TG," Hartman says, obviously catching on to Axel's nickname. He grins at me. "Hey, Cap, having a problem?"

"Nothing a little stretch can't fix." He looks over at Twyler again and irrational annoyance licks up my spine. "Why don't you get a head start on the ice," I tell him, arms crossed over my chest. "Work on wrist shots before everyone gets out there."

He nods, looking a little guilty. Wrist shots are a weak spot for Hartman, and I just called him out on it.

"Good idea."

He exits, hustling to the locker room. I face Twyler and she grabs a file out of the slot on the wall and opens it. I see my name on the tab. Reese Cain.

"What's going on?" she asks, a hundred percent professional.

"Um, my uh," I think back to what Reid said about Twyler being great at massaging his hamstrings. "My hamstrings. They've been really tight lately."

She frowns. "You've been stretching?"

"Yep."

"Okay, well," she jots something down in the file and then points to the mat. "Why don't you get on the floor and I'll take a look."

"Sure." I drop to the floor, hands flat on the mat behind me. She stands before me. My eyes wander to her thighs. Is that a birthmark?

"Give me your foot," she says, returning the folder to the slot. "I'm going to apply some pressure. You let me know if it hurts or feels uncomfortable."

Twyler offers her hands. I drop back to my elbows and put my shoe-covered foot into her cupped palms. She adjusts, leaving one hand to brace my foot at the heel and the other moves to my calf. She gently massages the back of my leg, then leans forward, stretching the muscles. Damn, maybe my hamstrings *are* tight.

I groan. "That feels good."

"Lie back a little more." I do, and she bends, leaning over me, and I get a straight shot of what Hartman was ogling before. Her shirt gapes, giving me a full view down the neck. She's wearing a black athletic bra that pushes up her tits, and it's not sexy, or is it? Shit. I don't know anymore. And neither does my cock.

"Yeah." With a wince, I rise up, bending at the waist in an attempt to cover my semi. "I think we're good. Thanks."

"Are you sure?"

"Yep." I glance over my shoulder. "I can do that against the wall, and it looks like Schwartz is waiting." I jerk my chin at the first string offender. "You go ahead, man."

Adjusting myself, I'm halfway to the locker room when Reid catches up to me. "Everything okay, Cap?" he asks with a knowing smirk.

"Shut up," I grunt, heading for the locker room, ready to get on the ice.

Something's gotta cool me off.

If I don't get a handle on myself it's going to be a long fucking month.

11

Twyler

Reese's concerns about Hartford are unfounded. Even their best player, Anderson, isn't a match for the extra hours and hard work the Badgers have been putting in since the practice started.

"Four-zero!" Jefferson shouts as the last of us climb on the bus. By last of us I mean Coach Green, Jonathan, the equipment manager, and me. The guys are chatty, full of energy from the win, and it's contagious. I wasn't lying when I said I wanted to work with the basketball team, but something about Badger hockey has gotten in my blood.

I glance back at Reese, sitting near the back of the bus next to Reid, our eyes meeting. No, someone's gotten under my skin.

"It's so much better when they win," Jonathan says from the seat next to mine. We tend to pair up on the bus, taking the second row of seats behind the coaches. "Don't'cha think?"

"Way better," I agree, searching for my phone in my bag.

We've both been on the bus after bad losses. The guys can be angry. Or sad. Sometimes there's a fight, or worse: tears.

The Frozen Four loss last year was a lot of both.

The driver closes the door, and the lights flicker off on the bus. We've been on the road since nine this morning, but I had to be at the arena before that to pack up and get everything ready. Then we had a two hour drive to Hartford U and the guys got fed lunch before the early afternoon game. After that, while the guys warmed up, Coach Green and I prepped everyone who needed ankles, wrists, and muscles wrapped. Double checking for any pre-game injuries while getting everything prepped for the actual game and quick fixes between periods. Post-game we had to check over anyone with injuries, hand out ice packs, and wait for the guys to shower and change. It's been a long day, and the staff is exhausted. The guys? Well, the win seems to have given them another surge of adrenaline.

Me? I'm tired, but what I really want to know is if Nadia got my tickets.

I finally find my phone at the bottom. Opening the screen, I see messages from my sister and mom, but I bypass those, looking to see if Nadia texted about the tickets.

"Hey, man, swap seats with me?"

I look up to see Reese standing in the aisle.

"Oh, uh..." Jonathan fumbles in the seat next to me. He looks at me, as if asking for permission. I nod and he jolts up. "Sure. Yeah, I'll go to the back."

Reese drops into the seat, taking up twice the space Jonathan did. His hand whips out and he tugs the tie out of my hair, releasing it in long waves.

"Hey!" I snatch the tie back and stuff it in my pocket.

He grins and looks at Jonathan walking down the aisle. "I think I make him nervous."

"Oh, you definitely make him nervous," I reply, distracted. I open my social media accounts looking for a message from Nadia there. Nothing.

"You've got to be kidding me," I mutter, going back to my texts.

"What's up?" Reese asks, turning toward me. "No, what's wrong?"

"Today was the day Nadia was supposed to get my New Kings tickets. She never texted."

"Okay," he says slowly. "I'm sure it's fine. She probably just forgot to text after she got them."

Panic thrums in my veins. "She was still asleep when I left, but I texted her around 8:30 and she replied that everything was a go."

"Then why are you worried?"

"She's always doing stuff like this. Forgetting things or getting distracted. She knows how important this concert is to me."

I send her a text: *Did you get the tix?*

"See?" I say after there's no reply. "She flaked. I knew it. I knew this would happen."

Going back to the phone, I pull up Chattysnap and search New Kings. A series of posts shows up. All about how quickly the show sold out. "See?" I hold up the phone so he can see the screen. "They sold out! Just like I knew they would."

"Sunshine," Reese says, his big hand capturing mine, "You've got to chill. She could be in the shower. At the gym. Fucking Brent Reynolds."

"The quarterback?"

He shrugs, but I see the small smile on his mouth. "You never know."

I take a deep breath and look down to where our hands are clasped. Then crane my neck to see if Coach Green, who is seated across from us, has noticed. His head is back against the seat, eyes closed, headphones in. Exhaling, I detangle our fingers and shift closer to the window.

"You know the rules," I say quietly.

"I do." He nods, plucking the phone from my fingers and tucking it into his jacket pocket. "But I still wanted to check up with my girl after a big win."

I smile, not because he called me his girl, although... "You had a kick ass game. Two goals!"

He grins eagerly. "You saw them?"

I wince. "The first one, but I missed the penalty—you know, when Kirby came out with a bloody nose."

It'd been a gusher.

"Right."

"But I'm sure I can catch it on a replay."

"How about I give you a play-by-play?"

Before I can argue, he launches into it, drawing in the guys behind us with his overexaggerated and animated retelling. Soon half the bus is leaning over us, and I listen as they recreate the entire game; every slapshot, every crash into the boards, every penalty and goal. Halfway through, when Reese leans back in his seat and winks at me, I suspect he's just trying to distract me from harassing Nadia. *Successfully* distract me.

He's right though, she could be doing anything, and she knew how important it is to me. I'm sure everything's fine.

Coach Bryant finally yells at the guys to get their asses in their seats and the bus quiets down. Reese doesn't leave, but he closes his eyes and keeps to his side of the seat. Resting my head against the window, I drift off to the rocky vibration of the bus barreling down the highway. I don't wake until the brakes hiss and the vehicle jerks to a stop.

"Wake up, Sunshine."

My face is plastered against something hard—and it's not the window. Jolting up, I blink at the realization that I was asleep on

Reese's shoulder. I sit up, putting distance between us. That's when I see it. "Oh my god."

"What?" he asks, stretching his arms over his head.

I grab his jacket sleeve, heat licking at my cheeks. "I drooled on you."

He peers at the spot and laughs. "You must've been comfortable."

That's the thing. I *was* comfortable. I completely passed out, and totally forgot about— "Give me my phone."

"Perkins!" Coach Green calls from the stairwell. "Wake up and help me unload the supplies."

Reese steps into the aisle, and I grab my bag before climbing down the small staircase to the parking lot outside the arena. There's a crowd waiting. Family, girlfriends, puck bunnies, and general fans. He pushes his hand in his pocket and pulls out my phone. "Here you go."

"Thank you," I say, checking the notifications. Nothing from Nadia. "And thanks for being a big cushion."

"You're welcome." He presses the phone in my hand. "Listen, we're having some people over tonight. Feel free to drop by or I can come pick you up? People will be expecting us to be seen together anyway."

"A party?"

"A gathering," he clarifies.

"We'll see if I can stay up that long." I cover my mouth and fight a yawn.

With his bag over his shoulder, Jefferson walks up and claps his friend on the back. "Ready?"

"You want me to hang around? Wait for you to finish?"

"Nah, you never know how long it'll take." Coach Green likes for everything to be organized when we get back so we're set to go for the next practice. "But thank you."

He shrugs, like it's no big. Isn't offering something like that what a boyfriend would do?

Jeff looks at me. "Coming over tonight, TG?"

"Maybe."

"Alright, see you then," he replies as though I said yes. Hate to break it to them, but I'm going home, confirming my tickets, and going to bed. The last thing I want to do is hang out with a bunch of drunk hockey players. The two of them walk off and I head over to where Coach Green is dragging our kits out from under the bus.

It takes us an hour to unload and unpack before I'm dismissed. I call Nadia on the way home, but she doesn't answer. I pull up the ticket sales page as I walk, confirming that the concert is sold out already. I don't see the person sitting on the bench outside the student center who rises when I approach.

"Twyler?"

My head jerks up when I hear my name, dread inching down my spine. "Hey," I say, hands getting sweaty. "Ethan. Hey."

He gives me a smug grin, the piercing in his eyebrow glinting in the light like an evil wink. God, I hate that stupid piercing.

"It's been... awhile." I've managed to avoid him for months and when I did have the bad luck of running into him, I'd ducked and hid. It's immature, but necessary. Unfortunately, tonight I've been so distracted by the ticket situation I've stumbled right into him. I look around. It's quiet, but the student center has all kinds of activities going on. Movies, performances, special events. "What are you doing here?"

"Waiting on a friend." He steps closer. "I've been thinking about you. How are you?"

Shifting back, I say, "Good. Great, really. Busy with my internship."

His gaze shifts to my team outfit—the uniform we wear for

the games. The yellow badger sits above my heart. "You're still doing that."

"Yep." Ethan didn't like me working with the hockey team—or anything that took time away from him. "It's going great. They just won their first game of the preseason."

"Mmhmm." His expression reminds me of how much he hates sports and the long rants he and his friends would go on about how jocks are nothing but pawns of corporate machines that profit off condoned violence. As if he has the right to judge violent acts. "I saw that picture of you and the hockey guy. What's that about?"

"Reese?" I ask, surprised he saw it. He loathes social media. Or so he says. He's a hypocritical shit. I know that now. "Yeah, we're friends."

"Sure, *friends*." He says the word with exaggeration, but there's no time for me to process it. His eyes skim over me. "Is that what's up with the hair? Does your 'friend' like it down better?"

I force myself not to touch it—not to show how insecure he makes me feel. How he knows my insecurities and uses them against me. Choking back the bile threatening to rise in my throat, I grind out, "You know, I don't have to answer that. We're not together anymore. We're not even friends. It's none of your business one way or the other."

"You're right." His fingers twist the silver rings on his left hand. My stomach drops seeing them. "Your decisions are your own, no matter how basic they are."

Hell. No.

"If anyone is basic, it's you," I say, allowing the anger to roll through me, which is so much fucking better than sadness and tears. That's how I used to feel around him. Desperate to please. "With your stupid piercings and lame tattoos and..."

He smirks and fuck. Fuck. *Fuck!* This. *This* is what he wants.

To show that he can still get under my skin. To make me lose my temper so I'll feel like shit and give him the upper hand.

The student center door opens, and a girl walks out. I recognize her purple hair and green eyes under the thick layer of mascara. Joan. She'd been part of the larger group that we'd hung out with. I shouldn't be surprised they're together.

I use her arrival as an excuse to walk off, leaving him and his condescending asshole ways behind me. Although, I can't help but wonder if he hurts her the way he hurt me?

The anger barely dissipates on the walk home, but I'm happy to see that the lights are on and that the door is unlocked—meaning Nadia is home.

I toss my bag on the floor and kick off my shoes, shouting, "You'll never fucking believe who I just ran into."

Nadia walks out in a Wittmore sweatshirt and barely visible shorts under the hem. Her expression... it tells me everything. She doesn't even have to say it. I already know.

"You didn't get my tickets."

"I'm so sorry, Twy. The craziest thing happened last night. I got a match on my hookup app at like 3 AM." Her eyes light up. "It was Brent Reynolds."

"The quarterback?"

Why does this feel like déjà vu?

"Yeah, he slid into my DMs and he asked me to meet up and I went."

"I texted you this morning."

"I was still there." She tugs at the ribbed wrist of her sleeves. "I was planning on leaving but then we, we..." She shrugs. "You know."

"You were fucking Brent Reynolds instead of getting my tickets."

"You know how long I've been waiting to hook up with him!"

I shake my head, my head and heart a swirl of angry

emotion. First Ethan. Now this. Two gut punches in a row. And how the hell did Reese name drop Brent tonight? Did he already know?

"What about Reid?" I ask.

"What about him?"

"I thought he was the guy you'd been waiting on."

"We went out. He's a nice guy, fun to hang with, but there were no sparks." Her chin lifts. "In fact, since there were no sparks, I intentionally didn't sleep with him—for you."

"Oh, well, thanks for thinking of me before you boned one of my hockey players."

"Twy, we'll figure something out. Find tickets on a resell page or—" she starts.

"No." I edge back to the door, looking for my shoes. "You fucked me over, Nadia. I asked for one thing, and you couldn't keep your legs shut for one morning to make it happen."

Her jaw drops and red rims her eyes. "Are you slut-shaming me?"

I laugh. "No. I'm reality-shaming you. You're a shitty friend who is more into chasing jerseys than anything else. Those guys are always your priority. *Always.*" I take a deep breath. "And the worst part is you're *never* going to be theirs."

"Screw you, Twyler," she says. "I knew you were always judging me, it's about fucking time you said it out loud."

She spins and runs to her bedroom, slamming the door behind her. I finish putting my shoes on and open the front door. Nadia isn't the only one I'm angry with tonight.

If I'm burning bridges, I may as well do all of them.

12

Reese

As much as I'd hoped the post-game gathering at the Manor wouldn't be too big, my teammates had other ideas. First, Pete showed up with a keg. Then Axel invited every puck bunny in his contact list and half the rowing team, which meant Zeta Sig also showed up and they're notorious for taking everything up another level. Reid plugged in his playlist and by eleven, we have a full-scale, bass-thumping rager going on.

"We have to stop letting Axel invite people to these things," I say to Jeff as I stub out a lit cigarette someone left on the porch. "He has zero discretion."

He shrugs, eyeing a new group of girls coming up the path. "I know you hate the frat boys, but they always bring a nice selection of sorority girls with them."

"Sure, if they don't burn the house down first." Eyeing that little Zeta prick Miller Hansen take a drag from a joint and shotgun it into his girls' open mouth. "Or get us busted for possession."

"Dude," he says, "you've got to chill out. When did you get so uptight?" Probably when I decided to get into this relationship with Twyler which includes no sex. "Where's your girl? Is she coming?"

"Not sure. She had some stuff to do."

"Hopefully she gets here soon so she can help you relax." He winks and heads back into the party.

"Congratulations, Captain. Two goals, very impressive." Ginna steps onto the porch and presses a cup in my hand. I sniff it and then take a sip. Jack and Coke.

"Thanks," I say, sitting in one of the rocking chairs. "It was definitely what we needed to kick off the season."

She comes closer, perching on the arm of the rocker, her short skirt riding up and showing a wide swath of her upper thigh. "You alone tonight?" she asks, hand landing on my shoulder.

"Alone? Yes." I take another sip of my drink and cut my eyes to her. "Available? No."

She frowns. "So you're really dating this girl? The meek little trainer I saw you with at the bar?"

I don't like the description, but I don't owe Ginna any explanations. "Twyler and I are together, yeah."

"Then why isn't she here?" Her hand runs down my arm, fingers squeezing my bicep. "Because part of the perk of having a big win is having a hot girl ride your dick."

She's not wrong, and that's exactly what the majority of my teammates will be doing before the night is over, but it's none of Ginna's fucking business. I'd hoped Twyler would come, but it was obvious she was both tired and eager to get home to find out if Nadia got her concert tickets. I open my mouth to tell Ginna to cool it when I see a familiar head of dark hair step off the sidewalk and stride purposefully toward the house. I stand, ignoring the way Ginna's hand tugs me back, walking down the steps to meet Twyler.

"Hey," I say, unable to contain my smile. "You came."

"And you're a dick," she snaps, stopping me in my tracks. I get a better look at her face. Her eyes are ice cold and filled with rage, but more than that, I see the red rim underneath and the pink in her nose.

"You're crying." My stomach clenches. *Shit*. "Why are you crying?"

"Because you suck. You and Nadia and Ethan. You all fucking suck."

Ethan? The ex? What the hell?

On the porch I hear a snort and look to see Ginna and a few other puck bunnies watching us. I shoot them a dirty look and realize I need to take this somewhere quieter.

"Hold on," I say, resting a hand on her lower back and leading Twyler around the front of the house. There's a side door that leads to a small, enclosed porch that we never use. I open the door and usher her inside the dimly lit space. Once we're alone, I say, "It's completely possible that I'm a dick, but do you think you could give me a few more details?"

"Nadia didn't get my tickets because she was fucking Brent Reynolds." Her arms are folded over her stomach. "Sound familiar?"

It does sound familiar. I'd made that joke earlier in the day, but it'd been just that. A joke. "That's... fucking uncanny. I didn't know. I swear. I was just fooling around because I know Nadia has a history of jersey chasing and what bigger jersey is there to chase than the quarterback of the football team?" I give her a cocky grin. "Well, other than mine."

She glares at me, but I see the quiver in her lip. She wants to laugh. At me maybe, but that's better than the murderous look she was giving me when she got here.

"Hey," I say, stepping closer and resting my hand on her shoulder. I resist the urge to pull her closer, but I do hold her eye. "I promise that was a bizarre coincidence. I didn't know anything."

"I believe you." She sighs and then shocks the hell out of me by leaning into me and pressing her cheek against my chest. Slowly, I wrap my arms around her shoulders, drawing her into a hug. I rub her back and the feel of her body sinking into mine is unreal.

"It sucks that Nadia flaked—and for Reynolds too. What a douchebag."

She laughs, the vibration bouncing off my chest.

"He *is* a douche, right?" she asks, wiping her nose. "Ugh, that's twice today I've left fluids on your body. First my drool. Now my tears and snot." She frowns. "I'm sorry I barged into your party and accused you of being a dick. It's been a shitty day."

"I'm just glad you came." I brush her hair behind her ear, finding it impossible to keep my hands off of her. "Do you want to go join the party? Have a drink?"

She looks down at her outfit—the same one she wore all day for training the team. "In this? No way. I look terrible."

"Sunshine, you have a way of making a T-shirt and joggers look pretty sexy."

She rolls her eyes. "Stop."

"It's true." I shrug, even though I know she doesn't believe me. "But if you'd rather go, that's fine too. Do you want me to walk you home?"

She tenses. "I don't want to see Nadia yet." She looks up at me, expression guilty. "But you go back inside and hang out. You deserve it after the win today. Go have fun. I can just…" She looks around at the small room. There's nothing in the room but a small metal table and chairs, some dead potted plants and a worn-out loveseat we pushed out here the day we moved in. "I can stay here."

"We can both hang out here," I tell her, taking her hand and leading her over to the small couch. I take up more than half the space, but it's an excuse to sit close to her. "So stuff is bad between you and Nadia?"

"Yeah, we had a big fight and we both probably said a few things that crossed a line."

She doesn't say more, so I let it drop. Getting between chicks when they're fighting is a no-win situation.

"I'm sorry about the tickets. I'm not sure why it's so important to you, but I know it is."

I don't know if it's the dimly lit room, the only real light coming from outside, or the fact we're truly alone for a minute, but I feel a shift in Twyler. She looks down at our intertwined hands and says, "I first got into the New Kings in high school. They were pretty indie back then. Kind of obscure, but everything about them just resonated with me." She keeps her eyes down. "I struggled with some depression—and making friends. I was lonely and things got kind of dark. William and Trey, the guys in the band, their lyrics hit on a lot of those things, and it helped me find my way out."

I don't like the idea of teenage Twyler being alone and depressed any more than I like the idea of her being hurt now.

"My dad took me to my first New Kings concert. I didn't have anyone else to go with. He got the tickets, drove us down to this shitty little club in a terrible neighborhood. He always supported my need to be part of that community."

"That's cool that he gets you like that."

She looks up at me, and there's something written on her

face that makes my gut drop. "Got me," she says. "He died three years ago."

"Fuck, babe." There's zero hesitation as I wrap my arms around her, and I expect her to fight it—to fight me—but for once she doesn't, just allowing me to pull her small frame against my chest. "I had no idea. I'm so sorry."

"It sucks." Her voice is small, not like the ball-busting, quirky girl I've gotten to know. "He was always there for me, even when shit got dark." Exhaling, she adds, "When they announced this tour, I figured it would be impossible to go with the team's schedule, but then they added a location locally, and it happens to be on Dad's birthday." She takes a deep breath and lays her hand flat on my stomach. "It seemed like fate that it was all aligning, but..."

But Nadia.

Now *I'm* pissed.

She leans into me for a moment longer and I feel her breathing even out and her limbs relax. Fuck, this girl feels right in my arms, and the way her hand rests on my stomach makes my pulse quicken. Unfortunately, it also sends an alert to my dick, sending a false signal for it to wake up. Twyler's confiding in me as a friend—leaning on me for comfort—not as a gateway to a hookup.

"Hey," I say, running my hand down her hair. "I know you don't want to party, but how about we go make an appearance. Let Nadia and everyone else know we're on good terms and then I'll walk you back home."

She shifts, turning her gaze to mine. "Sure. We can do that."

We disentangle and I help her off the couch, using it as an opportunity to keep my hands on her a minute longer. I have more questions, like why she was ranting about her ex, but I know Twyler well enough to realize the amount of personal information she shared tonight was huge.

"Wait," I say. Lifting my sweatshirt over my head, I place it over hers, dropping it over her uniform. It engulfs her, hanging down below her thighs. "That's better."

Following her through the door that leads back into the house, I keep my eyes on her, the way she looks in my shirt—how seeing her wearing it makes me feel.

Terrified.

I like it.

More than I should.

~

"You're disturbingly good at this."

Reid shakes his head in disbelief as he takes another shot after Twlyer lands her tenth quarter in a row, directly in the red party cup across the table.

"It's a gift." She grins, and the action lights up her face. Other than a little smear of mascara under her eyes, there's no evidence of her earlier upset.

At first, she didn't want to play, but the guys egged her on, pushing at her buttons until she relented. Me? I just sat back and watched my girl go on a winning streak.

"Rematch?" she asks Reid, holding up her lucky quarter.

"Nope. I'm out," he says, eyeing a puck bunny across the room. Guess whatever happened between him and Nadia was mutual.

"Anyone?" Twyler asks, looking around the room.

It's getting late, and the adrenaline the guys came into the party with has started to fade. They're either drunk or horny—or both—and ready to settle down.

Reaching out, I grab Twyler by the waist, dragging her in my lap. "Looks like you're the reigning champion, Sunshine," I tell her, pressing a kiss to her cheek. It's been hard to keep my hands off her tonight. She turns to face me, and her eyes are clear enough to tell me that the beer she drank over the last two hours hasn't given her more than a slight buzz. She shifts again, dragging her ass over my dick in the process. The innocent look in her eye tells me she has no fucking clue what she's doing to me. It's sweet.

And frustratingly hot.

I desperately want to taste her again. Full mouth, lots of tongue.

But we made an agreement and I'm not seeing a loophole here.

"You spending the night, Twy?" Jefferson asks, grabbing two bottles of water out of the cooler on the porch. I shoot him a dirty look and he winks back. I know what he's doing. He knows Twyler hasn't spent the night yet and he's trying to get me laid.

"Nah," I say, resting a hand on her thigh. "I'm going to walk her back soon."

"You know," she says, brushing her fingers over my knuckles, "maybe I should just stay."

"If you want." I don't know who she's saying it for. Jefferson, to continue the ruse, or herself, because she doesn't want to go home. If I had to guess, this is about Nadia. "I'm happy for you to stay."

"Aww, have fun, you two," Jeff says, gesturing for the girl waiting for him by the doorway to follow him up the stairs. "See you two in the morning."

Slowly everyone takes off. Some for home, some for couches or beds inside. It's not unusual to wake up to five guys sprawled out in the living room after a party. I nudge Twyler. "You sure you want to spend the night here?"

"Is that okay?"

"Of course it's okay." I ease her off my painfully throbbing dick and rise off the chair. "I just don't want to make you uncomfortable."

Leading her up the stairs, I take her to my room. It's tidy-ish, although I didn't expect to have a girl up here tonight. The bed is made, a habit from childhood, and most of my clothes, clean and dirty, are in separate baskets. My desk is a mess, but that's how I keep it, relying on some kind of internal organization system.

"So this is where the magic happens," she says, walking over to my dresser. She lifts the MVP award I got last season, despite the shit show at the Frozen Four. I kick off my shoes and when I look up again, she's studying a poster hanging on the wall. She juts her thumb at it. "You go to bed every night looking at your face?"

"I mean, you could bring me a photo of you—preferably in a bikini—and I'd happily go to sleep looking at you every night."

It's not a bad idea.

She rolls her eyes. "You're ridiculous."

"The team PR department gave me that after I was named captain. I left it rolled up in the tube it came in. Jefferson and Axel thought it would be hilarious to hang it up." I shrug. "I just didn't move it."

While Twyler snoops around my room, I grab a pillow off the bed and an extra blanket from the closet. I toss both on the chair in the corner of the room. She turns and says, "What are you doing?"

"Sleeping in the chair. You can take the bed."

"What? No." She shakes her head. "You take the bed; I'll sleep on the chair."

We stare at one another for a long beat, a standoff brewing between us. I break it off first, dropping my hands to the hem of my shirt and pulling it over my head.

"Did you just use your chest as a way to distract me and get your way?"

She blinks, managing to both look away and stare at my chest at the same time. She looks like she may have a stroke just from seeing my upper body.

"Did it work?" I ask, because yeah, I'm vain. I work my ass off to keep in top shape. But there's a little vindication that after making it clear she wasn't into jocks, Twyler likes my body.

"No."

Liar.

If this is how she reacts to my upper body... "Unless you want to see my junk, maybe turn around," I say in warning.

"Oh, right." She spins, facing the wall, and I drop my pants and grab a pair of shorts from the top dresser drawer.

Pulling them on, I say, "You're in the clear."

She's slow to turn, peering at me with those big eyes. I head to the bathroom and smear toothpaste on my toothbrush. I point to a drawer. "If you want, there's an extra toothbrush in there. T-shirts are in the top drawer of the dresser." My eyes drag over the sweatshirt she's been wearing like a dress all night and our eyes meet in the mirror. "Or you can keep that on."

She watches me go through my routine and as I'm walking out and dropping onto the chair. It's not uncomfortable, just a little small for my frame. There are no arms to hold me in, but I can manage. One of the skills learned from years of travel hockey is how to sleep anywhere.

"Do you do this a lot?" she asks, still standing by the bed. "Have to offer girls toothbrushes and clothes?"

I snort and drag the blanket up to my waist. "Their mouths are usually too occupied, Sunshine, to worry about a toothbrush."

Her nose wrinkles and her cheeks move past pink to flaming

red. Her glare is intense. "You're doing it again. Trying to embarrass me."

I lean back and arrange my pillow. "Wrong. Most girls that come up here with me have their clothes off before we cross the threshold. None stay long enough to stay the night. I'm not trying to be a dick. It's just the truth."

She watches me closely for a minute, then enters the bathroom, shutting the door behind her. I hear the water run, and the sound of her brushing her teeth. I don't know if Twyler is a virgin or not. She obviously has had a boyfriend, and despite her arguments otherwise, she's a pretty fantastic kisser. But kissing and fucking are pretty far apart.

I'm still thinking about it when she emerges from the bathroom, still wearing my sweatshirt. Then there's the bundle in her hands—another look down her legs and it's clear what she's holding. Her joggers. Fuck me.

I drag my eyes away from the lure of her pussy, but not before I see the flash of ink on her upper thigh. A tattoo?

Hell, I want to see it.

Just the sight of her climbing into bed wearing my shirt and no pants, does something to my insides. My cock? It raises a flag, like it wants to stake a claim. *Mine.*

But from my chair across the room, I know this girl isn't mine to claim. Not in any real sense. I understand better what Nadia meant by her being vulnerable and not having men to count on. That fucking sucks about her dad, and I wish I'd been there when it happened to support her.

What I can do, is not fuck this up, and support her now.

I reach for the switch on the lamp on my desk. "Night, Sunshine," I say, turning off the light.

Across the room, I hear her sigh at the nickname and after a beat, she replies, "Goodnight, Reese."

13

Twyler

I can't sleep.

Not in Reese's bed that smells so good. Not knowing he's shirtless and asleep in the chair across the room. Not after feeling his erection jamming into my ass when he pulled me into his lap downstairs, and definitely not after seeing his perfect torso. Christ on a cracker, I wanted to touch him.

Nope. My whole body is too warm. I already stripped off Reese's heavy sweatshirt trying to cool off but nothing—

"Son of a—"

The curse hits my ears before the crash does, the loud bang and clatter cutting through the dark of night. It sends a jolt to my heart, and thrusts me upward, sheet clasped between my hands. Then I hear a groan.

"Reese?" I whisper.

"Down here, Sunshine." I grapple for my phone on the bedside table and turn on the flashlight, shining it toward the chair. Except there is no chair, or at least it's on its side. Reese is crumpled on the floor in all his bare-chested glory, rubbing his head.

"Oh my god, are you okay?" Fuck. Does he have a concussion? Or a broken bone? What if he's injured? A million injuries run though my head as I scramble off the end of the bed down to him on the floor. One of them being, how the hell will I explain this to Coach Green?

"I'm fin—"

A tap sounds at the door. "You two okay in there?" Reid's muffled voice calls out. "I heard... something. It could've been sex, or it could've been a serial killer breaking in. I just wanted to check."

"We're okay, Reid," Reese says, stifling a laugh. "Thanks for checking on us."

"Sure, um... Twy?" His voice sounds like it's right next to the door. "You okay?"

"All good," I call, my voice scratchy with sleep.

"Alright, I'll leave you guys alone."

Neither of us speak, listening to the sound of his feet padding down the hall and the click of his door. When I look back at Reese he's sitting inches away, sprawled out on the floor. I kneel before him, resting my light on the floor. "That was sweet," I say, reaching for his arm to feel for any breaks or swelling. "You know there's still that ongoing case in North Dakota where four college students were slaughtered in their house one night."

His lips curve. "No, I didn't know that."

"Then there's Ted Bundy and the sorority house murders."

"Mmhmm." He mumbles, watching me as I assess for injuries.

I apply light pressure to his wrist. "Any pain here?"

"No."

"Did you hit your head?" I hold the light up to his face to

check his pupils. He winces from the light and pushes my hand away.

"No."

"Swelling? Contusions?" I move closer, pressing my fingers to his chest, his very muscular, defined chest. He grunts another no, and as I get lower, checking his kidneys, his hand snaps out and cinches around my wrist.

"I'm good, Sunshine. Nothing's broken, but you gotta stop touching me like that."

He shifts, as though he's uncomfortable, and I start to question it, when my eyes land below the waist of his shorts. *Oh.*

My eyes lift, meeting his for a beat, right before his drop down to my chest and the black boy shorts covering my lower half.

"Where's my sweatshirt?" His Adam's apple bobs when he swallows.

"I got hot and took it off. It's in the bed somewhere." His eyes are glued to my top, which isn't exactly sexy. "Do you want—"

"Get back in the bed, Twyler," he says, voice gruff and filled with warning.

I grab the phone and sit on the edge of the bed, and push back on my heels, scooting back to the middle.

He stands, groaning, and holding his back. "Did you—"

"It's not the fall. It's the chair. Just slept weird." He bends to shift the chair upright.

There's no way I can inflict that on him again. Not if it's causing him pain and if the chair itself won't support him. "How about," I say, feeling my cheeks heat, "we share the bed and stay on our own sides."

He straightens and I see the length of him, the full glory of all six-foot-four of Reese Cain, shirtless and in nothing but shorts, the front tented with an obvious erection. It was one thing to feel it pressed against my ass, but a whole other to see the thick bulge straining at his shorts. The first one I blew off like it was just biology, I was sitting on him for god's sake, but now that I see the heat flickering in the back of his eyes, I know better.

Reese Cain is horny.

"You sure?" he asks, not so subtly adjusting himself.

"Yes," I slide back to one side of the bed, pressing against the pillow. I turn off the flashlight, preferring the darkness right now. "It's your bed, you shouldn't be uncomfortable."

My eyes acclimate to the dim light coming from the window as he grabs his pillow and blanket, tossing them next to me before climbing in. He winces again at the pain in his back.

"Roll over." I nudge his shoulder.

"Huh?"

"Let me check your back. Roll over." He shifts, the bed sinking under his massive weight. "On your stomach."

He lies flat, giving me an impressive view of his muscular back and, well, amazing ass. Taking a deep breath I ask, "Where does it hurt?"

His hand reaches behind him, and he gestures to his lower right side. "About here."

I run my fingers over the spot he's talking about. "I'm just going to get in a better position." I straddle his body and sit on the back of his rock-hard thighs. The thin material of my shorts is barely a barrier.

He groans, fingers twisting in the sheets.

"Am I too heavy?"

"Light as a feather, Sunshine."

He bends his elbows and rests his cheek on his hands. The position makes his biceps flex and that flutter of want is back. I want to blame it on being in the presence of perfection, the expanse of muscles running down his back, but I can't. He's ripped. It's like muscles on muscles, each section of his back carved and buffed out of stone. There are other guys on the team with bodies just as fit—but none of them make me feel like my ovaries may explode.

I press the heel of my hand down and he moans in response, "Fuck, that feels good."

"So it's right there." I feel around, poking and prodding. His body twitches when I find it.

"Yep, that's the spot." He exhales. "Fuck, your hands are like magic."

Using my thumbs, I make tiny circles in the area, attempting to work out any strain. Slowly, the length of muscles along his back untense. After a few minutes, he turns his head and says, "The other night you said you know everything about me, what does that mean?"

"It means I read up on all my players. It's my job to be familiar with your medical files, articles about your career, status reports. If it's been documented, I've read it."

"Medical files I get, but why do you need all of that other stuff?"

"Because your history tells a story. Like, how you broke your femur in the fourth grade, not on the ice, but on the monkey bars during recess at school. I know that it healed clean and hasn't caused you any problems since."

"Okay," he says thoughtfully. "But why stats?"

"Because if you're a center forward and the number one scorer in the region, then the wear and tear on your shoulders and wrists are going to be higher than a simple defender who takes and gives a lot of hits. That tells me what muscles and ligaments need to stay strong and healthy for you to achieve maximum results."

He makes a little face, like he's impressed. "What else?"

"I know that you're lactose intolerant which is why you drink your coffee black and you try to eat gluten free, but that's not an allergy, you just want to stay as lean as possible."

He lifts his head and a small grin curves his mouth. "Twyler Perkins, are you stalking me?"

I pinch his neck, applying pressure where I know he'll feel it. He seizes and presses his face in the mattress, suppressing a howl.

But I'm on a roll and keep going. "I know you've only had the one girlfriend, Shanna, who you dated all through high school and college, but suddenly broke it off last year—although now I know that you were the one that broke up with her. I don't think you really said why."

"We had different ideas on my career," he says, eyes fluttering shut.

"I know New York wanted to draft you last year and you said no, which means you'll become a free agent after the season is over. It was considered a risky move when you had a sure thing locked up."

His breathing evens out, but I can tell he's not asleep, just fully relaxed. Quietly, I add, "I know you call me Sunshine because it bugs me, and you try to shock me by saying outrageous, dirty things."

"That's only partially true," he answers without opening his eyes. "I say outrageous, dirty things because I'm a hockey player and that's just kind of how we are. It's a bonus that you look so fucking cute when you blush."

I'm pretty sure he says *that* to make me blush. I move away from the area I was massaging and spread my hands across his back. His skin is hot to the touch, and I just want to explore him, feel the power and strength under my fingertips.

This man and his body are the complete opposite of what it was like to be with Ethan.

"Do you want to know why I turned down the deal with New

York?" he asks suddenly.

"Sure, if you want to tell me."

He rolls over, but keeps his hand on my hip, not allowing me to shift off. I'm now straddling his lap, looking down at his gorgeous face. There's no mistaking the hard length of his erection pressing against my core. He doesn't look a bit apologetic about it either.

"My father took a similar deal when he was in college. Junior year he got drafted by Boston. He started in the minor league and after a year made it to the NHL." The angles in his face are so sharp in this light, making his cheekbones seem even more dramatic. "He married my mom, and she got pregnant with me, and he promptly had a career-ending injury."

I actually know all of this. I've read his father's history as a player and coach—Reese's coach.

"The fact he never got a degree fucked him, Twy. He didn't have the opportunity to go back because he was a husband and dad. He had to work and the only thing he knew was hockey. The best he could do was coaching at the junior level, barely able to support us the way he wanted to. It caused a lot of strain in the family." His thumb rubs against my hip. "I love hockey. Like, I fucking love it. But I want something secure to fall back on just in case."

"That's understandable. I think you're smart to get your degree. Career-ending injuries happen all the time."

He laughs darkly. "Shanna didn't think it was smart. She wanted me to take the deal, get the signing bonus, and marry her. All she wanted was to start building a life as a professional athlete's wife."

"And that's why you broke up?"

He nods. "She gave me an ultimatum. Her or college. I think she really thought I was going to cave and was shocked when I didn't. That's why she's been coming around again."

And why he needs me to pretend to be his girlfriend.

Except the way we are sitting right now, the way he feels underneath me, and how he looks at me. None of this feels fake. Not the conversation. Not the way my body is reacting. Not the way his fingers brush against my skin.

I reach out and press a hand to his chest. The thrum of his heart feels like wings. "Your heart's beating so fast."

"It does that when I've got a hot girl straddling me in my bed wearing nothing but booty shorts and a bra."

"Reese..."

He sits up, bringing his face to mine. I've still got my hand pressed against his warm chest and his fingers fan over my cheeks and then graze under my chin. "I call you Sunshine because when you occasionally venture to smile, it lights up the whole damn room." His mouth is inches from mine. "You're not easy, Twyler. You're tough and can wrangle a locker room of asshole hockey players, which is fucking impressive. You wear a shield over your heart, but the few times you've let me see inside, I'm overwhelmed by who you are."

"You're crazy," I tell him, unsure of how to accept what he's saying. From the start, the one thing about Reese that has made me nervous was the fact I felt like he saw me when no one else did.

"Maybe." His fingers curl under my jaw and he lifts my chin. "Can I kiss you?"

I should say no. I should get out of this bed and go home because this isn't what we agreed to. He's got a hundred other girls that would happily be in his bed, and a sophisticated ex that wants him back. But I don't say no. I nod my approval and he tilts his head, licking his bottom lip. I think my heart is going to burst through my ribcage.

Like the last time, he starts slow, setting a tentative pace, like he's afraid I'll run. Fair. It wouldn't be the first time I took off on him. But his mouth parts, and mine follows suit, and when his tongue slides against mine, every nerve in my body stands on end. Reese Cain is a fantastic kisser. Calm and confident on the outside, dominating underneath. The same way he is on the ice. The reason he was named captain. He's a leader—a partner. He knows what he wants, and how to get it.

His big hands flatten against the bare skin on my lower back, and I loop my arms around his neck, threading my fingers through the fringe of hair. I pull him closer, wanting to feel his body against mine. The heat between my legs builds, and I grind against him, biting down on his bottom lip with my teeth.

He growls, flipping us over, pressing my back against the mattress. He hovers over me, breathing hard, no longer kissing me, no longer touching me at all. His eyes are wild with lust. His fingers graze my jaw, dropping to my neck. I flinch instinctively, and he jerks his hand back.

"We..." he says through a shuddering breath. "We should stop, before I do something I'll regret."

I withdraw my hand. "Okay. Right. Too far. We made an agreement," I move to shift away from him, back to my side of the bed, "and this goes way outside the boundaries we set."

His hand clamps down on my hip, keeping me still.

"Don't." His fingers graze down my cheek and his gray eyes hold mine. "Don't you fucking think this is because I don't want you. I've wanted you since the first time we kissed. But this isn't what you agreed to, and we need to reassess when you're not sprawled in front of me half-naked."

His confession stuns me, which is why I don't argue as he presses his lips to my forehead and then rolls onto his back, next to me. The room is quiet, other than the two of us trying to catch our breaths.

I move to curl on my side, but in the dark, his hand catches mine. That's how we both finally fall asleep, linked.

14

Reese

"I'm making eggs," Jeff says as I walk into the kitchen the next morning. "You guys want some?"

His eyes dart behind me, looking for Twyler. Take a look, bud, she's not here. She wasn't in my bed when I woke up and her side of the mattress was cold.

There's only one possibility. I scared her off.

Reid looks up from his bowl of cereal, a line slashing his forehead. "Cap, where's Twy?"

"She left." I head straight for the coffee, thankful someone already started it.

"Please tell me you didn't kill her last night."

Okay, so apparently if you're Reid, there's another possibility. I'm a murderer.

"What the fuck are you talking about?" I grab a cup and fill it to the brim. Black. No milk. Just like Twyler said.

"I just heard all that noise from your room last night, and they didn't sound like your standard sex moves so—"

"Wait," Jeff says, taking his plate and sitting at the bar. "I'm curious what the difference is between murder sounds and sex sounds. Describe please."

"Jesus Christ," I mutter, knowing there's no way to stop them when they get started on early morning bullshit.

"You all have them," Reid says, as though keeping track of his roommates' sex sounds is completely normal. "Axel likes it rough and definitely chooses screamers, so overturned furniture and that kind of sound coming from his room wouldn't be a surprise." His eyes shift to Jeff. "You love a good wall fuck, bro. Half the time I think you may come through our shared wall. I've stopped hanging anything up because it falls and scares the shit out of me."

"Are you sure it's not a ghost?" I ask, getting in a jab.

He rolls his eyes, like *that's* ridiculous. "Reese is usually pretty quiet, other than that squeak in his mattress and a little headboard banging." He shrugs, but then points his spoon at me. "Oh, can't forget the sound of whoever he's fucking chanting his name like he's just lit the lamp."

"Oh, Reese!" Axel moans in a high-pitched voice from the couch across the room. Fuck. I didn't even see him. "Don't stop! Your tongue is ammmaazing."

They all crack up, Reid dropping his head on the counter, in full body shakes.

"Hi-fucking-larious." I lean back against the counter. "I can't help that when I go down on a chick she wants to worship me like I'm a higher power. It's a gift." I take another sip of coffee, feeling my brain slowly wake up. "And stop listening to everyone fuck. It's creepy."

"Seriously, dude," Jeff says, barely concealing a grin, "the walls are thin, but get some headphones like the rest of us."

Reid shrugs, making it clear he will not be getting headphones because he's a perv.

"Regardless," I say, feeling the need to clear this up, even if it's with a lie, "I didn't kill her. She just had to leave early. No big."

Although it *feels* big. I've asked plenty of girls to leave after we had sex. I've never had one take off before I wanted her to.

"Probably didn't want to do the walk of shame out of the Manor in broad daylight," Axel says, stretching out on the couch. He adjusts himself, cupping his hand over the crotch of his black boxer briefs. Otherwise he's got nothing on, his ink on full display. "TG's not the kind of girl that wears a fuck like a badge of honor."

Huh. He may be on to something.

Because last night had been amazing. Not the first part where she showed up crying and accusing me of knowing about Nadia's quarterback hookup. Or even when I went to bed with a raging boner, restless, and unable to sleep, which is why I flipped out of the fucking chair. But the part after that, where she straddled my ass and ran her hands all over my body? Hell yeah. I can still feel her hot little pussy pressed up against the back of my thighs. But worse? How wet she was when I flipped over, and my cock drilled in between her legs.

Two strokes. That's all it would've taken.

Which is why I had to put a stop to it before I embarrassed myself and traumatized her for life.

Lost in my thoughts, I exit the kitchen, leaving them to their inane discussion. It's Sunday, which means we only have one practice—at two.

OneFive: Morning, Sunshine. Imagine my surprise when I woke up and found my bed empty.

I give her a minute to respond. She could be asleep. Or in the shower. Or reconsidering all her life choices from the last twenty-four hours.

Ding!

InternTwy: Sorry. I woke up early and couldn't get back to sleep. I figured I'd get home to deal with this Nadia situation.

OneFive: How did that go?

InternTwy: She wasn't here.

OneFive: Sorry about that. I'm sure you two can work this out.

InternTwy: Maybe.

I step in my room, looking at the broken chair and messy bed. For two people not having sex, it sure looks like we destroyed the room last night. I straighten the covers out of habit, looking for my sweatshirt in the process, but it's nowhere to be found.

OneFive: So... are we good? Everything cool after last night? Because I may need you to check in with Reid and assure him that I didn't commit murder last night.

InternTwy: Will do :)

It's not until after my shower and I'm tying my sneakers to leave for practice that I check my phone again. The last message hangs like an undropped bomb. A smiley emoticon is good, right? But she definitely didn't answer my question.

So are we? Good?

With an enigma like Twyler Perkins, hell if I know.

I'M ALMOST to the arena when my phone rings. I open it without looking, hoping it's Twyler.

"Reese! Great game yesterday, son." My dad. I try to hide my frustrated disappointment. "Two goals *and* an assist."

"Thanks. I think we played well." I enter the arena, but stop just inside the lobby outside the locker room to continue the call.

"You did, and if you keep it up, I can see you getting to the Frozen Four."

My dad knows hockey. He knows better than anyone what it takes to get to a championship and then to win one. And he sure as hell knows the hard work that goes into getting to the NHL. He's not a bullshitter so a compliment from him means a lot.

"I know the breakup with Shanna last spring was hard, but if the result is better focus and a championship season, then it'll be worth it. Taking the option to go as a free agent means you have to be better than the rest."

My father thinks the reason that Shanna and I broke up after losing the Frozen Four last spring was because I wanted to focus solely on hockey. He's unaware of the ultimatum she gave me, and some of that is because I was afraid if he found out, he may agree with her. He wasn't completely on board with my decision to not enter the draft, but ultimately, he respected it.

Being a free agent is risky, but it comes with a lot of power.

"Securing that trophy will have the big guys knocking on your door," he adds. "Including New York."

"I hope so."

"And taking a break from dating this year is smart. Women, no matter how much we love 'em, are a distraction."

There's an unspoken addendum here: they also steal your dreams. I know my father regrets being tied down so early in life. Same with having a kid and responsibilities. Even after his injury he could have taken more risks in coaching if he hadn't had a family to drag along.

We talk a bit more, shifting the conversation from my team to his. He's coached the Hurricanes for fifteen years and he's got a good eye for cultivating youth athletes. "You should see this kid," he says, talking about a fourteen-year-old named Johnny. "Fast as lightning and has good stick handling skills."

"Sounds like you found a winner," I say, happy to hear his team is shaping up.

Axel and Reid walk in the door, bringing in a burst of sunlight.

"Okay, Dad, I probably should go. Practice is about to start."

We say our goodbyes, and I follow the others into the locker room.

From the minute we hit the ice Coach works us during practice in a way that you'd think we lost by four instead of won. "Now isn't the time to get content. That was one game. We have three preseason games left and then an entire season. I don't want you just to win. I want you flawless." He slams his fist on his clipboard. "Let's get on the ice and set the tone that gets us to the playoffs!"

While Coach busts our balls on the ice, I'm aware of Twyler behind the bench the whole time. She's busy, splitting her time between basic tasks like handing out water or ice packs and assessing any injuries from the first game. Pete's still paranoid about his ankle and Kirby's nose is a fucking disaster. His whole face is purplish-green, and Coach Green makes him sit out, adhering to concussion protocol.

I try my best not to focus on her.

Try *and* fail.

If she's aware of me, it's impossible to tell. Not once does she look up from her work to find me on the ice. That doesn't stop me from obsessing over how her dark hair is pulled up and she's got on her ratty old hoodie and joggers. Now that I know what she looks like half-naked—smooth skin, nice sized tits, a pussy that cradles perfectly between my thighs—I want to peel off the rest of the layers and explore what's underneath.

"Cain!" A puck skitters a foot away, snapping me out of my daydream. "Get your head out of your ass and start the play!"

By the time Coach has us skating lines, I'm dripping with

sweat and my entire body aches. I rest my hand on my back as we skate off the ice and head down the tunnel.

"Is your back still bothering you?" she asks, finally acknowledging me when I lumber past. I don't miss the wrinkle of ill-placed guilt in her eye. "Do you need me to check on it?"

"Maybe later, Sunshine," I say quietly, giving her a wink that elicits that pretty shade of pink I'm starting to imagine running down every inch of her body. She doesn't bother responding, but I see the small curve on her lips as she turns away.

Yeah, later is when I'm going to kiss the hell out of that mouth again.

Except 'later' is cockblocked, or maybe mouthblocked?, by Coach Bryant. He has us hit the showers and then orders us into the media room, the film from the prior game already queued up. There's a collective groan, no one wanting to spend their Sunday afternoon replaying mistakes. Coach Bryant is on fire, going on and on, like he's channeling a preacher in the front of a packed church. We're held captive, going through replays of the video, until Kirby's stomach churns so loud the whole room hears it.

"Alright," Coach says, annoyed that we require things like food and have homework to do, "we'll call it a day. See everyone here tomorrow afternoon. On time. No excuses."

"Dinner?" Jeff asks, hitching his bag over his shoulder. "Dining hall is still open."

"Uh..." I'm distracted by the text I'm attempting to compose for Twyler. "Give me a minute."

He peers over the screen. "Still trying to figure out why you woke up in an empty bed?"

"Shut up."

But yeah.

He just laughs and shakes his head, grabbing Reid and heading out of the arena.

The locker room empties out and I sit on the bench, wavering over the message. How desperate is too desperate? Is thirsty hot or a turn off? Never in my life have I spent this much time on a simple text. What's wrong with me?

I settle on, *"Can we meet up?"* and have my thumb over the send button when a loud, slow-moving crash sounds from down the hall.

Stashing my phone, I run down the hall. A low curse comes from behind the storage closet door.

Jerking open the door, I find Twyler crumpled on the floor, surrounded by hundreds of tiny square packets of antiseptic wipes.

She looks so pissed off and annoyed that I know better than to laugh, although it's really fucking hard not to. Thrusting out my hand, I ask, "Need some help, Sunshine?"

15

Twyler

I stare at Reese's big, manly hands and try not to remember how incredible they felt against my bare skin.

How needy and hungry they were, even after he pulled back and put some much needed distance between us. He'd held onto me like he didn't want to let go.

So obviously, in typical Twyler Perkins fashion, I snuck out under the cover of dark. I'd barely made it to the sidewalk before I texted Ruby: *"I just spent the night in Reese Cain's bed,"* because someone had to know even if she wouldn't get it until she woke up.

Even though I'm still angry with her, I would've caved and told Nadia too, but she wasn't at the house when I got there. Her bed empty and bag gone. Guess I wasn't the only one running away.

"Afraid I'm going to bite?" he asks, running his tongue over his bottom lip. "Because if I'm remembering correctly, you were the one gnawing on my lip last night."

Oh, he's remembering correctly.

I'd pretty much mauled him after he flipped me onto his lap. *He* was the one that stopped. Not me.

Giving him my hand, because there's no way I can stand up in this mess on my own, I let Reese help me off the floor. He lifts me easily, but my foot slips on the packets. I don't fall because he's got his hands on me, holding me steady. We're chest to chest in the tiny space and he's clean from the shower and smells intoxicating.

"Are you okay?" he asks, pushing a loose strand of hair behind my ear.

"I'm fine," I say looking past his muscular arms at the mess I made. "According to Coach Green, the closet is an abomination and needs to be rearranged *immediately*. I heard Bryant going off on you, too." Which is really unfair after the amazing game they had the day before. "I have no idea what got the coaching staff riled up today, but they're taking no prisoners."

"Preseason makes everyone nervous. Especially when the team's clicking. There's more on the line—more to lose." He looks down at me, his gray eyes inquisitive. "How about you? Am I making you nervous?"

The implication is clear. We were clicking last night. *Hard.*

"Will you make fun of me if I say yes?"

"No," one of his hands flattens on my back, drawing me closer, "because you make me fucking nervous too."

"I do not." I never know when Reese is being serious or just obnoxious, but there's no world in this universe where I make Reese Cain nervous.

"You do," he argues. "I woke up and found no half-naked girl in my bed this morning. Then I texted the last girl that was *in* my bed, to see if we were good and she didn't answer the question." He swallows, and I'm mesmerized by the movement. How delicate his features can be when he's so incredibly strong. "I've been convinced all day that I fucked something up and I really don't want to fuck this up."

Right. Because he let his libido get mixed up in our deal.

"We're fine," I tell him, bending to start cleaning up the colossal mess I made. He shifts to help me, and together we're squeezed in the tight space on the floor tossing packets back into the box. "I told you, I got up early and wanted to try to catch Nadia."

He grabs a handful of wipes, and eyes me, like he thinks I'm lying. Which, fair, that's definitely not the only reason I left. I was in Reese Cain's bed, and I'd been grinding on his very hard erection.

Not a good look for a fake girlfriend.

Remembering my place, I ask, "So how's it going with Shanna anyway, heard anything from her?"

Saying her name draws a grimace. "No, thank goodness. I think she got the message."

"Good." I focus on cleaning up and not the way my chest tightens. If Shanna's out of the picture, then we can wrap this sham up sooner than later and that's probably what he wants. He can get back to his non-committal one-night stands and fulfill puck bunny dreams everywhere.

"It is good," he says with a sense of relief, "but I feel like maybe I haven't done enough to help you with your end of the bargain."

"In what way?"

"Well, we've been to a hockey bar, and you absolutely obliterated everyone last night at quarters, but those are with guys from the team—no one you're interested in actually dating."

"True."

"We need to find a place where you can find a variety of guys, learn how to talk to them, get flirty, show them how amazing you are."

"Did you just say 'get flirty?'" I snort and glance over at him. His face is inches away, those gray eyes earnest and sincere.

"Face it, Sunshine, your flirting needs a little work." He scoops up the last of the packets in one hand and dumps them into the box. He tucks the box under one arm and again offers me his free hand to help me off the floor.

"And you have an idea of where we can do this?" I ask skeptically.

He grins, bright enough to light up the room. "I know just the place."

∽

I have six missed calls when I finally open my phone, all from my sister. After helping me straighten up the mess in the supply closet, Reese invited me to dinner with him and the guys. I begged off, citing a long day and a pile of homework to tackle. The truth is that standing in that tiny storage closet and inhaling his addictive scent made me question my sanity.

There's no other reason I would agree to let him take me somewhere to "get flirty."

I start my walk across campus and press call on my phone. Ruby doesn't even say hello, just launches into, "What the hell do you mean you slept in Reese Cain's bed?"

"Exactly what I said. I slept in his bed—although, for the majority of the night he didn't."

"Explain, and I mean everything. *All* the details."

I tell her what happened. Well, sort of. I start with running into Ethan, to finding out that Nadia screwed up the tickets, and then thinking that Reese had known about it. I tell her that he was a gentleman, offering to sleep on the chair until he fell, and

I was worried he'd injured himself. I leave out the finer details of how this is all just a ruse; fake dating to get Shanna off his back, and in exchange he'll give me confidence lessons.

"Did anything else happen?" she asks, knowing me well enough to assume I'm hiding something.

I look around, making sure no one is nearby, and whisper, "He kissed me."

She sighs, clearly not impressed. "Well, it's not the first time, right?"

No, but... "It was different, and then things kind of escalated."

"Twy," she says, her tone cautious, "did you have sex with him?"

"Oh my God, no!"

"I mean, I wouldn't blame you, it's just..."

"I know," I say, fully aware that sex was part of why my relationship with Ethan ended up disastrous. "It didn't get that far. And again, he was a gentleman and stopped it before it went too far."

But what if he hadn't stopped? Because I sure as hell didn't have any plans to, or at least, my body didn't. I was into the kissing. Because fuck, Reese Cain can kiss with the same level of skill that he can handle a hockey stick. Absolute precision. And then there's his body, which is unreal. Not just the muscles, although those are ridiculous, but the way he moves. He's confident. Determined. Powerful. Since when am I into commanding, muscular men?

I'm not. Reese isn't my type.

Temporary insanity is the only excuse.

"Wow, really?" Ruby says as I cross into Shotgun. "And by too far you mean... a hand job? Blow job? Oh shit, did he go down on you?" She's basically vibrating through the phone waiting for confirmation.

"I'm hanging up," I threaten, trying desperately not to think of Reese between my legs.

"So no oral." She sighs again. "Too bad, with that strong jaw, I bet it's spectacular."

He's good at everything. Why wouldn't he be good at pleasing a woman?

"Goodbye, Ruby," I say, walking up to the teal house.

"Keep me posted!" she shouts before I hang up on her.

Entering the house, it's immediately obvious that Nadia came back at some point. There's a mess in the kitchen sink and protein powder all over the counter. Anxiety fills my chest, not sure if I want to see her yet. I suck it up and peek in her room. Nothing about it has changed since I was there that morning.

Obviously, she doesn't want to see me.

I exhale, realizing that for the first time in years, I don't want to see her either.

∼

It's not until the next weekend that Reese tells me to set aside the afternoon for whatever he has planned. He told me to dress casually, and that he'd pick me up at ten. Casual isn't a problem for me, but I've made one notable change to my wardrobe since the night I slept over. No more athletic bras and boy shorts. If my goal is a boyfriend, I need to at least dress the part. Well, at least under my clothes. Not that Reese seemed to have a problem with it, but... yeah, it's time to break out one of the matching sets Nadia forced me to buy when I was dating Ethan.

Nadia finally came home about forty-eight hours after our fight. We didn't speak, and all she did was shower and change before packing a bag and walking out again. She hasn't blocked me on social media yet, and it's obvious where she's spending all her time: Brent Reynolds' house.

I sit on the front step tying my shoes when I see Reese at the end of the sidewalk. He pauses, watching me for a moment, and I see the muscle in the back of his jaw flex.

"Hey," I say, rising.

"I was wondering where that went." His eyebrow is raised and he's looking at my sweatshirt. Well, *his* sweatshirt. The number fifteen is imprinted over the chest and again on the back along with his name. I'd taken it with me when I'd absconded from his house before dawn. It's soft and has that scent I can't get enough of. *His* scent.

"Oh," I reach for the hem. "Do you want it back? I can chan—"

"Nope." Something dark flickers in his eyes. "Keep it on."

He leads us to the street that runs adjacent to Shotgun, and I see a dark blue, vintage Dodge Challenger parked by the curb. He walks up to it and opens the passenger side door for me.

"Is this yours?" I ask, after he gets in the driver's seat.

"Since I learned to drive," he replies, cranking the engine. It's loud and the car vibrates in a way newer vehicles don't, but the interior is immaculate. Clean, black leather seats, shiny chrome details. "It's the first thing my dad bought with his signing bonus. It was his dream car."

"And he gave it to you?" I run my hands over the dash. "Seems foolish to give a sixteen-year-old boy your prized possession."

He grins over at me. "The caveat was that when I get my signing bonus, I buy him a new one."

"I see now where you get your cocky confidence–from your dad."

The car is as flashy as his persona, drawing eyes as we cut through campus.

"So, what's your dad like?" I ask, noting he takes the turn off campus to a road I know leads away from town.

"As a dad or a coach?"

I think on it. "Both?"

"Before my parents got divorced, he acted more like a dad. She'd do all the mom stuff, take me to appointments, come to school conferences, while he worked with his team. But once they split and I decided to stay with him, he pretty much went full coach mode all the time."

"Well, that kind of sucks."

"I guess," he shrugs. "We both had the same goal, so it kind of worked. I lived and breathed hockey, so it didn't seem strange."

"Do you get to see your mom a lot?"

"Not really. She was ready for warm weather and moved south. Got remarried to an accountant—like the most polar opposite kind of guy from my dad. We stayed where he could keep coaching and the hockey is more competitive. He wanted me to have the best chance of getting a scholarship on a nationally ranked team."

"Makes sense." As a southerner we have hockey leagues, but the culture isn't the same. It's not a way of life like it is up here.

"I go down to see her during the summer, and she'll come up a few times a year to watch my games." He shrugs. "It's not a lot, but we're good."

I can't imagine splitting time with my parents. Both were involved—*overly* involved at times if you ask me. But they'd been high school sweethearts and operated like a cohesive unit. Even when they had disagreements there was never any question they were still in sync. Now there are times where the three of us just feel aimless, like we're floating around without the thing that always tied us together.

We've lost our anchor.

"So," I say, watching the landscape grow more rural, "feel like telling me where we're going?"

He grins, but keeps his eyes on the road. "You'll see soon enough."

"Really? Because we haven't passed anything but farmland for the last five miles." I cut him a look. "You're not driving me out here to kill me and dump my body, are you?

His hands grip the steering wheel. "What's with everyone accusing me of being a serial killer lately?"

"Sorry, I watch too much true crime." I grin, finding his horror amusing. "Although my mom, Ruby, and I all have trackers on our phones so we can search for the bodies if one of us goes missing."

Reese looks over, eyebrow raised. "You've really thought this through."

"I have," I admit. "And I know it seems weird, but there are studies about the psychology behind our cultural obsession with dangerous things. I guess people like to feel like they have some understanding of what could happen, or like, that you can somehow be prepared in a situation so that you aren't a victim."

"Like keeping your phone tracker on." He reaches across the center console, his big hand gripping my knee, and squeezes. "Sorry to disappoint you, but no, I'm not planning on tossing your body out here." I haven't been paying attention to the road or the fact he's slowed down, taking a sharp turn into a gravel driveway. Up ahead is a farmhouse, with a large red barn set behind it. A sign says, "Second Chance Animal Shelter."

"You brought me to an animal shelter? To 'get flirty?' With what? A dog?"

"No." He laughs and turns off the car. "One of the conditions for being part of the hockey team is we have to sign up for campus-coordinated volunteer events." He nods at the barn in front of us. "This is the one I chose."

I narrow my eyes. "I thought today was about me learning to meet guys and building confidence. Instead, you brought me on a volunteer project—to fulfill your obligations?"

"Two birds, one stone, Sunshine."

He opens the door and hops out. I don't move, too stunned to process what kind of trickery Reese Cain has gotten me into. He walks around and opens my door, offering his hand to help me out of the low car. I eye it skeptically.

He sighs. "This is a school-wide event. People from all over campus come to volunteer, so it's not just jocks, but frat boys, science nerds, ag kids, and any other group you're into. Skinny philosophy majors, too." He points to a group of boys walking toward the barn. They're all in black skinny jeans and have shaggy hair. Definitely my type. "Also, don't pretend you're not an animal lover. I saw the picture of the black cat in your house."

I grin. "Bertha. She's my baby."

"I love animals, too. The reason I chose this project is because before my mom left, we would foster dogs. The last one that we took in was George. When my mom moved out, George was the one that was there for me after school and on the nights my dad worked late."

Well, way to soften me up with that story. Jeez. When he offers me his hand again, I take it. He drags me close and I look up into his gray eyes. "So how are we doing this," I ask, "are we here as a couple?"

"I think we have to keep up the act, but I'll give you a little space to mingle." He tugs at one of the drawstrings on the hoodie. "Plus, you've got my name and number stamped on your shirt. I'm pretty sure that's sending a message."

My heart pounds. "I wasn't trying to imply anything. It's just really soft. Like perfectly soft. I can take it off."

"Keep it," he says, tossing his arm over my shoulder and

squeezing me against his hard side. "Never underestimate a man wanting what belongs to another man, Sunshine."

"That's so gross."

He shrugs. "It's biology. The better you understand that deep down, all guys are animals, the better off you'll be."

I've always shied away from any of the volunteer activities at school—partially because my training activities keep me so busy and I'm already doing them for free—but also because I just feel too awkward to jump into a social setting cold. But, as much as I hate to admit it, Reese is right. There are tons of students here from all kinds of groups. We get an opportunity to pet some of the animals at the shelter. Reese drags me to each one, getting down on his knees to greet the dogs and give them a lot of love.

A student photographer roams around, clumping people into groups and taking photos for the university. After posing together, Reese and I get dragged in different directions. There's a little panic at first, not having him next to me for support, but since we're all here for the same purpose, my anxiety quickly diminishes. Of course, people immediately recognize Reese. Why wouldn't they? That poster in his bedroom is hanging on banners outside of the arena and on half the lampposts around campus. He's friendly to everyone, although the emo boys look thoroughly unimpressed.

"Everyone gather around!"

Reese finds me in the group circled around the volunteer coordinator, who passes around a clipboard for us to sign and get a name tag. He's really good at playing the boyfriend. His hands never leave me, touching my lower back, taking my hand in his, fussing with my hair. I guess he had years of practice with Shanna, but he leaves no doubt to everyone involved that we're a couple.

When he wraps his arms around my body and rests his chin on my shoulder, it's hard for me not to buy into it too.

"That guy over there keeps looking at you," he says, mouth next to my ear. His breath is warm and a shiver runs down my spine.

"I think he's looking at *you*," I joke, but can't help seeing for myself. Across the circle I check out one of the guys dressed in black, his hands shoved into his pockets. He's cute, with messy light brown hair. Our eyes meet and he gives me a quick grin.

"See?" Reese says. "Guys always want what they can't have."

For the record, men suck, but I'm here for a purpose and I'm trying not to forget that.

"We've got a lot of work to do," the volunteer coordinator, Henry, says once everyone has signed his clipboard. "We'll divide up into different groups for efficiency."

Reese gets tapped to repair the outdoor enclosure, while I get sent over to a large plastic tub.

"What's this for?" I ask, although when I get closer, I see the industrial sized jug of shampoo.

"It's bath day!" Miranda, another volunteer, says. "First up is Winston."

"I'm more of a cat person," I say, eyeing the cozy cat cabin a yard away.

"The beauty of cats is that they clean themselves," Miranda says. "Dogs? Not so much. We need them nice and clean so that when potential families come in, they're looking their best."

I take off Reese's sweatshirt, hanging it on the nearby fence post, leaving me in an old, threadbare shirt from my high school training program. The neck has holes in it and at some point, I ripped the hem. Not something I normally wear in public, but at least it's not something I'm worried about getting ruined.

The name Winston feels like it should belong to an eight pound, tiny dog that fits in a purse. The dog they bring out? A squat, barrel-chested basset hound mix.

Who, let me tell you, makes it clear he is *not* interested in a bath.

"Okay, Winnie, let's make this happen," I say after my initial efforts are thwarted. Finally, I just bend and pick him up, leg by leg, and heave him into the tub. By the time I get the water running, I'm out of breath. "Damn, you're powerful for an animal with such stumpy legs," I mutter. I manage to get the dog wet by running the hose over his body, while keeping one hand on his collar. "Ready for a shampoo?"

I rest the hose on the edge of the tub, allowing the water to continue to fill the tub, and reach for the soap. Unfortunately, at that moment I spot Reese across the yard.

Oh, man.

He's stripped out of his jacket and is in a tight Wittmore Hockey T-shirt and a snug pair of worn jeans that hang perfectly on his ass. He's lifting heavy two-by-fours, putting his muscles on full display. I'm not the only girl that notices. I hear a "Damn" from a girl putting fresh paper in one of the kennels.

Damn is right.

Winston shakes in the tub, spraying a fine coat of water across my skin. "Hey, sorry pup, I got distracted." But my attention comes too late, because he shakes again, this time knocking the hose off the ledge. The stream shoots into the air and I grab for it, trying to get it under control, but the dog has other plans. His stumpy, thick body makes a run for it.

"Winston!" I cry, as the cold water douses my face. "Help! Please!"

"Hey! I've got you!"

Peering through my wet bangs, I see one of the emo boys grab the hose and fold it in half, cutting off the flow. Miranda captures Winston and drags him back. He's covered in mud. "Seriously, dude?" I say to the dog, wagging his tail at me. "Why you gotta make this harder than it already is?"

"Logan, why don't you assist Twyler? Seems like she could use an extra set of hands."

Her tone is just condescending enough to make it sound like I'm incapable of washing a dog. Which, at this point, is fair.

"Sure," Logan says, pushing his sleeves up and taking Winston by the collar.

I suck in a breath. He's got a tattoo on his forearm. The design is a crown, specific to the New Kings. Similar to one of the ones on my thigh.

"Sorry about that," I say, wiping my face with the hem of my damp shirt.

"No problem, I wasn't into my assignment anyway."

I pour a glob of shampoo into my hand and start rubbing it on Winston's back. "What were you doing before?"

"I was over at the shelter with Captain America." He jerks his chin in Reese's direction. To be fair, in those jeans his ass does rival Chris Evans'. "He's just showing off and making everyone look bad."

I snort. "That's what I call him, too. Mostly to annoy him."

"You're with him, right?"

For some reason, I give a half nod, half shrug. "We work together on the hockey team. I'm the trainer."

"Oh," he gives me a relieved smile and hoses down Winston's back while I lather his legs. "That makes sense."

Wait. I look over at him. "What makes sense?"

"You seem cool—not like the type of girl that would be simping for an athlete."

He's right. I don't seem like that type of girl, but the athletes I know are all pretty great. Sure, they're overly confident and obnoxious at times, but they're also pretty cool. I look across the yard where Reese has reached over one of the wire kennel walls with his long arm to pet a dog. He spots me and waggles his eyebrows at Logan, followed with a thumbs up.

Ugh, that one is definitely pretty great.

I remember why I'm here—to work on my social skills. Logan may be judgmental against jocks, but that's not the biggest red flag.

"So why did you come here today?" I ask, changing the subject.

"Honestly?" He smiles. "My friend over there got a speeding ticket and the options were service hours or an expensive fine. He picked this and a couple of us came with him."

"Hey," I look down at Winston's sad, droopy eyes and wet face, "I don't think the dogs care why you're here."

We talk a little, and I even muster the courage to ask about his tattoo.

"You're into the New Kings?" he asks.

"I'd show you my tattoos but they're, uh, covered up."

His eyebrow arches, curious. "Did you get tickets to the show?"

"Ugh. No." I bite back on my drama with Nadia. I'm still too bitter about it. "We had an away game and I missed out."

"Damn." His face crumples in sympathy. "That sucks."

"Tell me about it."

We talk about our favorite songs and past concerts. Somehow, I manage to get even wetter helping Winston out of the pool, the big oaf dragging half the tub with him and then shaking off before we can wrap him in a towel. Logan captures him, wrapping him up, just as a gust of wind blows through.

"Burr," I shiver, skin pebbling with goosebumps. "I'm not ready for winter."

"Don't you work in the arena all the time?" He looks up from Winston and his smile widens.

"Yeah, and I'm always freezing there too. I'm from the south, we don't get cold weather in Tennessee until at least December.

At least when I leave the arena now, it's warmer outside than inside."

I rub my arms, and Logan's eyes follow the movement, his mouth parting. Oh shit. What a day to ditch the full-coverage athletic bra.

A quick glance down and I see that the thin, wet fabric of my shirt is plastered to my chest. The white lace on the bra is visible as well as the outline of my peaked nipples. Instinctively, I cover my chest. My body may be cold, but my cheeks are flaming hot.

Logan gapes for a moment more, then shrugs out of his hoodie. "Here, you can wear this."

"Thanks," I say, reaching for the jacket, but a six-foot-four wall of muscle steps between us. He's got his sweatshirt, the one I wore today, in his hands.

"Cold, Sunshine?" His eyes are unabashedly zeroed in on my chest, which only makes my nipples tighten. He gently lowers the shirt over my head, engulfing me in his scent.

Before I can speak, he bends and kisses me. Not a simple brush, not a flirty graze. No, a full-on, tongue pushing between my lips, jaw-working kiss.

My knees threaten to give.

He pulls back and winks, leaving my lips burning and my heart pounding, before walking off with a swagger.

I wrap my arms around me and see Logan watching me with a scowl on his face. "Did he just metaphorically piss on you?"

I glance over at Reese's retreating figure, dazed and confused. "Yeah, I think he did."

16

Reese

As captain, I try to be the example of excellence. That means I make an effort to be the first one at the arena, and often the last to leave. While I'm trying to set a tone of the expectations I have for the rest of the team, I also just like being in the gym or locker room before everyone arrives, the room getting loud with voices and slamming lockers.

It's game day, our third and next to last preseason match, and the bus won't be here for another hour. I don't expect to find anyone else here other than maybe Coach Bryant locked up in his office going over last-minute strategy. But the sound of Coach Green's voice in the training room catches my attention—particularly when he says my name.

Curious, I step down the hall and listen.

"I didn't think this was going to be a problem with you, Twyler, which is why I never felt the need to bring it up. You've always been focused and kept a clear distance with the players on a social level." I hear the shuffle of papers. "Hell, the fact you hate jocks was a selling point for agreeing to accept you into the hockey program."

"It's not a problem," Twyler says, her tone firm. "I admit that I've become friendly with a few of the players this year, and that's exactly what you saw in the picture included in the campus newsletter. Two friends at a school-sponsored volunteer project."

"He's hanging on you while you're wearing his sweatshirt. I'm not a teenage girl, but even I know what that implies."

"It means I was cold, and Reese offered me his sweatshirt." Her voice rises. "You know how Cain is—how they all are—they flirt nonstop. It's their only skill besides skating and goal scoring. But you and I both know I am no more Reese Cain's type than he's mine."

Three weeks ago, I would have agreed with her, but now, I'm not so sure. She's always been this weird chick hanging around the training office. Cool enough, but nothing special. Now I know otherwise. She's smart, and yeah, still weird with her serial killer fascination and ridiculous insecurities, but she's cute. No, she's fucking gorgeous.

I may be reconsidering my type.

Green sighs, and in my mind, I can see him stroking that hideous mustache while thinking. "Fine. I believe you. It seemed far-fetched. You and Cain?" He scoffs, and I rankle at his disbelief at the idea of the two of us together. "I know that if Coach Bryant hears about this, he'll tell me to replace you. I have no interest in doing that, so consider this your warning. I can't have my female interns fraternizing with players—especially someone as high profile as Cain. He's got one job this season and it's to stay healthy and get us to the tournament, understand?"

"Yes, sir." I don't miss the sound of relief in her voice. "I promise you that this will not come up again."

"Good," he says. "You're going to be a good trainer, Twyler.

You care about the players and team, but as a woman in a male-dominated sport, keeping boundaries is going to be imperative for the rest of your career."

"Yes, sir," she says again, "I understand."

"Now start packing up the kit for the game. The bus will be here soon."

I duck away before she exits in the hall, not wanting to surprise her. Shit. This is not what I wanted. She made it clear this arrangement couldn't fuck with her internship and that's exactly what it did. And not because of anything she did. But because I had to get territorial.

When I first saw Twyler sitting on her front step wearing my sweatshirt, it triggered an emotion in me that I didn't expect. It took me back to her being in my bed, looking and feeling sexy as hell, and escalated it into something primal. *Prideful.* I liked seeing her marked with my name and number. I wanted everyone else to see it too, which is why, when she gave me two opportunities to get it back, I declined them both.

That selfish act just screwed up the thing that's the most important to her, which makes me a fucking asshole.

Down the hall, I hear Coach Green head out the backdoor. Even though I know I shouldn't, the need to check on Twyler takes over any rational logic and I go in search of her. A shadow moves under the storage room door. The fact that this is becoming our secret meeting place feels ironic in the fact we've done a shitty job hiding our arrangement from her boss.

I open it and step inside.

She doesn't look happy to see me. In fact, she looks fucking crushed. Her eyes are rimmed in red, and I can tell she's trying not to cry.

"You can't be here," she says, focusing back on the medical kit she's packing on the shelf. "I just got a lecture from Coach Green about fraternizing with the players."

"I heard," I admit. "Are you okay?"

"No." Her hands tremor as she places items in the kit. "I'm freaking the fuck out, and you being in here isn't helping."

"I just wanted to check on you."

"I can't be seen with you, and you definitely can't be seen with me—especially not secretly meeting up in a storage closet."

"Twy, I'm sorry, we'll figure something out," I say, reaching for her. The instant my hand grazes her forearm she jerks away.

"There's nothing to figure out. We can't be around each other. Especially not during practice and games. If you need my assistance in a professional capacity, I'll be there for you, but otherwise, please just leave me alone." She swallows and there's a pleading glint in those blue eyes. "This job is too important to me."

"Okay," I say, ignoring the crushing weight that I feel in my chest. Guilt? Regret? Whatever it is, it's not helping either of us. "I'll do whatever you want."

"Thank you."

She turns her back to me before I even get the door open, which I do slowly, checking to make sure no one sees me before I exit.

An hour later, I get on the bus and head to the back, taking a seat next to Reid. Upfront, Twyler sits behind the coaches, Jonathan taking the seat next to her on the aisle. Not once does she look back at me.

"Why do you look like you're about to murder Jonathan?" he asks, fishing his headphones out of his backpack. "Afraid he's hitting on TG?"

"Huh?" I blink, realizing my back is ramrod straight as I watch her over the seat in front of me. "No. Green got on her about fraternizing with the team. He saw a photo of us together at the volunteer event." I run my hand through my hair. "She doesn't want us interacting with one another, at all."

"Oh shit, well, I guess it's okay, right?" He leans back in his seat. "Shanna's off your back. You don't need her anymore, right?"

"Yeah."

That's the right answer, but it's not how I feel. I do need her. That tightness in my chest spreads, and even though I know Jonathan isn't competition, I don't like him sitting next to Twyler. I want to be the one that sits next to her. That kisses her. And hell, more and more I think I want to be the one that fucks her too.

I exhale as the driver starts the bus and pulls out of the parking lot. The big vehicle rocks, but I know that's not what has me completely shook.

I want Twyler Perkins to be mine and I can't have her.

WE'RE PLAYING LIKE SHIT.

No, scratch that, *I'm* playing like shit.

It doesn't help that Rodriguez, from Elan College, is determined to shut me down.

"Get any closer, Rodriguez, and I'll think you have a crush on me," I say, trying to shake him.

The puck zings through the ice; from Reid to Jeff, who eyes the net. It's a distraction, he's sending me the puck, and I sprint, anticipating his pass. It comes smooth and crisp, and I make the connection—

"Fuck!" I swear, watching the puck go wide.

"You kiss your mother with that mouth?" Rodriguez asks, skating by with a smug grin.

"No, asshole, I'm too busy fucking yours."

The insult rolls off my tongue before I have time to think

about it. But hey, it's hockey. Chirps are part of the game. If you can't take a verbal sparring, find another sport. Like baseball.

His fists curl, but Jefferson swings around, pushing me away from further altercation. I'm not one to get into fights. I'm too busy focusing on the win. My brain is occupied with strategy and other than speed, my strongest skill is anticipation. Send me the puck and I'll be there, which is what has Rodriguez so pissed.

I'm faster and smarter than he is.

I've played against him before, but over the last year he's gained twenty pounds of muscle and a shitty attitude. It's made worse by the fact we're playing at their home arena. The whole place is a sea of red and black. Their mascot is a bulldog and their nonstop barking only fuels Rodriguez to be an asshole.

"Don't let him get to you," Jeff says, adjusting his chin strap.

"I'm not." We're down by one, and there are two minutes before we head into the third period. The last thing we need is for one of us to get tossed in the bin. Honestly, Rodriguez having a hard-on for me is exactly what I need. His taunts keep me in the game—keep me focused.

Anything to distract my mind from the dark-haired girl behind the bench.

The ref whistles and the Elan forward, Alton, and I face-off. Rodriguez is a foot behind staring at me like a fucking maniac. Just before the puck drops, he says, "You fingerbang your girl with those hands, Cain?"

It's not enough to distract me, and as I gain possession, I whiz past him, angle the stick, and make the shot. The puck sails past the goalie and lights the lamp.

"Hell, yes!" Axel's voice carries from our goal. It's overtaken by a cacophony of boos—the local fans pissed that I evened up the score.

"Hey," I say, giving Rodriguez a smirk as I circle behind the net. "At least I score."

When I come out the other side, I see a flash of red.

"Cain!" Reid shouts in warning, but it's too late. Rodriguez barrels toward me, his body crushing me into the boards. Chaos surges in the crowd and shouts erupt on the ice. I shove Rodriguez, but Reid is already there, fist connecting with his jaw.

～

It would be easier if Coach Bryant yelled at us when we got in the locker room for intermission. Instead, he's quiet. Too quiet as he surveys the fallout. Reid has been ejected—along with Rodriguez for fighting. Jonah Murphy's knee got tangled up in the scuffle and Coach Green is bent before him, assessing how bad it is.

"Cain," Coach Bryant barks. "Get your side checked out."

"I'm fine," I tell him, after I swallow a gulp of water. "He just knocked the wind out of me."

"It wasn't a suggestion." He jerks his head. "Go."

I stand, doing my best not to wince. Truth is, it feels like I got hit by a sledgehammer.

"Perkins," Coach Green says, distracted by Jonah, "see to Cain."

"Yes, sir." She steps toward the small training room off the locker room. I follow her in and lean against the table.

"Lift up your shirt." When I hesitate, she adds, "We all saw the hit. Let me see it."

How lame is it that I'm into the fact she watches me play?

I lift up the right side of my jersey, revealing the area that got bruised. "Tell me you saw the goal, too."

"I saw it." Her eyes go wide. Not because of my impressive abs, but because I got a hell of a bruise forming. "Jesus, Reese."

"It's fine," I say before she can flip out. "I can still play the third period."

My abs retract before she even touches me, in anticipation of the pain. "Fine, huh?" She rolls her eyes. Her touch is firm but gentle. She's so fucking good at that. "Are your ribs tender?"

"No. I swear it's just a bruise." I take a swig of my water bottle. "I've had worse."

She snorts. "That's not reassuring. Y'all's tolerance for pain makes you keep playing well past the point of reason."

She grabs an ice pack from the cooler and presses it against my side. It's cold, and I jolt before relaxing into the chill on my overheated skin.

"You can go back out, but you need to calm down. It'll help with Rodriguez ejected, but the rest of the team will want revenge." She cleans her hands with antibacterial gel. "I think their goalie has an injury."

"What do you mean?"

"He's favoring his left side, even though he's a righty. My guess is he strained his shoulder. Maybe his wrist. Go for the right. He doesn't have the reach."

"Good catch." I arch an eyebrow. "Thought you weren't into hockey."

"Just because I'm not into it, doesn't mean I don't understand the game." She steps back and gives me a hard look. "Don't do anything stupid out there, okay?"

"I won't," I tell her, easing off the table to go join the rest of the team.

"And Reese," she gives me a final look. "Take the shot when you get the chance. Don't overthink it."

I nod, recognizing that applies to more than just hockey. I had a shot with Twyler and I blew it. If another opportunity comes my way, there's no way in hell I'm going to let it pass.

∼

"Sure you don't want to come?" Jeff asks, shrugging on his jacket. Reid and Axel stand in the doorway, itching to get to the bar.

"Nah, y'all go without me." Truth is that I think I'd pass out if I went to the Badger Den with the guys. I barely got changed, giving up after I pulled on a pair of sweats. It's late, the bus didn't get back until almost ten, but my roommates aren't going to waste a Saturday night. "I'll be here with my ice pack and a pizza."

"Want me to call Ginna?" Axel asks. "She'd be happy to keep you company while you recover."

The answer to that is a hard no. Finding solace in a jersey chaser's pussy is the last thing I want right now. "Pass, but thanks for the offer."

"Your loss, brother," he says, walking out the door with Reid.

Jeff lingers a minute longer, disappearing into the kitchen. He returns with two, ice cold bottles of beer. "One to dull the pain by drinking. One to ice that bruise."

I take them with plans on definitely drinking them both. "Thanks, man."

From the couch I turn on ESPN and order a pizza, trying not to cry when my side seizes from twisting off the cap of the beer bottle. With less than sixty seconds to spare, we won the game when Kirby lit the lamp with a beautiful goal. It was fucking epic, giving the bulldogs an undeniable fuck-you loss at home.

Jonah's knee seems to be okay, just a tweak, but fucking Rodriguez deserved more than just an ejection.

I'm watching highlight reels of professional matches when the doorbell rings, which seems awfully fast for delivery on a weekend. Struggling to my feet, I clutch the ice pack against my side and open the door.

Not only is my pizza steaming hot, but so is the delivery person.

"You're way better looking than my normal pizza guy," I say, looking past the box of pizza to Twyler. She's in jeans that have a row of slashes ripped up the thigh and a tight black sweater.

The image of that soaking wet shirt clinging to her body comes back to me and yep, even in massive pain my dick is ready to go.

I lean against the door and try to look cool, not like I'm barely able to stand without support. "Decide to get a new job so we can be seen together?"

"File this under professional capacity," she says, using the same wording as earlier today. "I came by to check on your bruise."

Her eyes aren't anywhere near where I clutch the ice pack over my ribs. They're hovering somewhere just above the waistband of my sweats.

"I didn't know the training staff made house calls." I step back, giving her room to walk in.

"We don't," she admits, and there's a flicker of something in her eye. She's worried about me.

Huh.

Handing me the pizza, the edge knocks into my side and I release a grunt.

"Oh, shit," her eyebrows furrow, "sorry."

"It's fine, Sunshine."

She rolls her eyes. "Sit down and let me check it out."

I ease down on the couch, and when I move the ice pack, she winces at the discolored flesh.

"Looks worse than it feels," I promise.

"Then it must feel like you got rammed by an elephant."

She's not wrong. "It's part of the game. A little food, a lot of beer, some meds, and a good night's sleep and I'll be fine." To prove my point, I take a swig of my open beer and open the lid on the pizza box. Turning it toward her, I offer, "Want a slice?"

"I wasn't planning on staying." But she glances over at the pizza box and I can tell she's wavering.

"We can even watch a murder documentary." I up the ante, handing her the remote. "Just not the one with the clowns." I shudder. "He freaks me the fuck out."

"Gacy," she says, but then tenses. "Really, I shouldn't be here."

"I think Coach Green would approve of you keeping watch over the team's star player." I wink. "In a professional capacity, of course."

It's a lame way to try to get her to stay, but fuck, I want her to. I just want to hang out with her one way or the other, even if it's just as friends.

"One slice of pizza," she says, diving into the box. "And one show. That's all."

I fight a grin. "Perfect."

"So," she says, with a mouth full of greasy cheese, "how do you feel about cults?"

17

Twyler

This is a bad idea.

I cut my eyes over to Reese and his bare chest and, well... is it possible to get lightheaded from being in the presence of someone so hot?

I can't even blame him for taunting me like this. He didn't know I was coming so it's not like he's doing it on purpose. Although I knew there wouldn't be a party at the Manor tonight because I got a text from Reid asking if I wanted to meet them at the Badger Den. He also tipped me off that Reese would be home. He'd specifically told me he was resting and not going out, thinking that may get me to show up.

The house seemed quiet when I stepped on the porch, but the odds of a few puck bunnies keeping Reese company were definitely decent. I'd made it clear to him earlier in the day that we needed to stop seeing one another. If he wanted to hook up with one—or a dozen—girls, that would be fair.

The first thing I found was a pizza guy walking up the driveway. I tipped him and took the pizza, promising to get it to the person that ordered it.

Then the front door opened to a shirtless Reese Cain, wearing a pair of gray sweatpants that seemed to be holding on to his hips by sheer will.

When I agreed to stay to eat a slice of pizza and watch one episode of "I Didn't Mean to Join a Cult," I meant it. That was two episodes ago and the pizza is long gone. Ninety percent eaten by Reese, but still, I had two slices.

I'd panicked when Coach Green called me into his office this morning. I was embarrassed and terrified I was about to lose everything I'd worked so hard for the past few years. So when Reese cornered me in the storage closet, I was willing to do whatever it took to save my position. Including telling him that we were done.

It's not like he needs me anymore. As far as I know Shanna has left him alone, and his little ploy at the animal shelter worked. Before we left that day, Logan got my number and we've been texting all week, sharing our favorite songs from The New Kings, and getting to know one another.

But after seeing the hurt expression in his eye as I told him it was over, and then tending to his injury during the game, I had a long bus ride home to think about everything. First of all, fuck Coach Green. Would he tell a male intern he couldn't become friendly with members of the team? I don't think so. Reese and I are friends. We work together. Who gives a fuck if we hang out and watch documentaries and eat pizza? How is that different from any other friendship?

The friend in question shifts next to me, adjusting the melting ice pack against his side. The bruise is a mess, but I agree that I don't think it's anything serious. The movement draws my eyes to the hard-packed muscle of his abdomen, and the fine line of dark hair that vanishes under his waistband.

Get a grip, I tell myself. Reese is abnormally attractive. It's normal to get a sweaty, fluttery feeling in your lower belly when faced with a body like his. I'm reacting like any other female would.

I refocus on the screen, where this small man in wire-framed glasses talks endlessly to his followers.

"This guy is a douche," Reese says, fingers absently scratching his lower belly. "Nothing he says makes sense. It's like gobbledygook."

I laugh at the word and the irritated expression on his face. "It must make sense to those people; they can't get enough of it." The camera passes over one of his followers. "That girl said she gave him ten thousand dollars and had to live in her car because she couldn't afford her rent."

He presses pause. "Did you ever see the people that lived over in that community just off campus? Serendipity or something?"

"Oh, yeah." I sit up. "Serendee. Every time I walked past their office or whatever, they tried to get me to come in for a free class."

"Definite cult vibes. All the girls wore those weird, old-fashioned dresses and had the same long hair." He lifts his chin. "You know, Axel used to buy his weed from one guy and he'd show up at parties. He was scary as fuck."

If Reese was intimidated, they must have left an impression. "I heard they got shut down. Tax evasion or something."

"I heard the same thing." His lips twitch. "Guess we'll have to wait for the documentary to find out what really happened."

"You know," I say, leaning back on the couch, "Nadia took a couple of their classes. She kind of bought into it until they pushed a whole celibacy thing."

"Seriously?" he asks, looking away from the TV and over at me. "How are things going with her?"

"Okay, I guess. The other day we had a civil conversation about the grocery list."

"I guess that's a start."

"I just want her to acknowledge what she did was a dick move, you know?" My anger has dissipated, and now I'm just more sad than anything else. He nods and I continue, "She's sleeping at the house a little more—at least when she's not hooking up with Brent Reynolds."

He snorts. "He'll get bored soon. Trust me. We go to the football parties sometimes and I've never seen him with the same girl more than once."

"I know!" I cry, hating how frustrated I feel. "I've told her a dozen times that if a guy doesn't want to be seen with you during the day, he's only looking for a booty call."

Reese's lip quirks. "What do you know about booty calls?"

I roll my eyes. "I know that when a guy calls you to come over after midnight it's just for sex." He grins and curiosity gets the best of me. "Have you ever done that?"

"Sure, a few times in the last year, mostly when we got home from a game too late to go out." He shrugs. "But everyone involved knows the deal going into it, which makes it cool." He gives me a pointed look. "Even Nadia. She knows what she's getting into with a guy like Reynolds."

"I know," I grumble. "She, and all the other girls that think they have a chance with you, choose ignorance."

He shifts, and the couch cushion sinks under his weight, drawing our knees toward each other. "What about you, Sunshine? Any desperate late-night calls from guys asking you for a hookup?"

My jaw drops. "God, no."

"Not even the ex? What's his name? Eric?"

"Ethan. And no." I lean my shoulder into the couch cushion.

"But just to put it out there," warmth spreads over every inch of my body, "I'm not a virgin."

"I didn't assume you were," he says a little too quickly.

I laugh. "You totally thought I was."

"Okay," he admits, a slow grin appearing, "I definitely thought you were."

"I'm just… selective. After Ethan, I decided I needed to do a better job about the people I choose to be in my life." Our eyes meet. "That includes boyfriends. Real or fake."

There's a beat of silence that stretches between us, until he reaches out, brushing his fingers over the curve of my cheek, driving my pulse to thrum erratically. "I know shit is complicated with your internship, but I don't want to only see you in a professional capacity. I'm kind of getting used to having you around."

"I'm getting kind of used to you too," I confess. "You're not as terrible as I thought you were."

He laughs, but there's not a lot of humor in it. His gray eyes darken. "I also don't want to be your fake anything anymore either."

Wait. *What?* "What does that mean?" I ask. "You want this to be real?"

"It already is." He drops the ice pack on the coffee table and scoots closer, jaw tensing at the pain in his side. He's determined to get to me despite that and closes any remaining distance. His fingers tilt my chin, and he lets out a ragged breath. "Tell me you want the same thing."

A million red flags wave, especially the one being held by Coach Green, but I ignore each and every one. "I do."

He presses a slow, wet kiss against my mouth. He doesn't have to deepen it–I'm the one that does that, removing any room for doubt. He escalates, stroking my jaw with his fingers before parting my lips and sliding his tongue inside. I marvel at how each kiss with Reese is better than the last.

He's so good at this.

"Fuck, Sunshine, your mouth tastes so good," he says between kisses. "I've been thinking about it since the night you slept in my bed."

"I've been thinking about it too."

I wrap my arms around his neck and just let go, allowing myself to get lost in him; in the skilled way his tongue strokes against mine, in the way his body is honed into mine, how he touches me with greedy hands.

And damn, the tent in his pants is obscene.

His hands push under my sweater, lifting it to expose my breasts. A thick hum builds in the back of his throat and his mouth drops down, kissing between them. "This fucking bra," he says. "Not that I'm not into your sporty look, but hell, I almost stabbed the eyes out of that kid at the shelter when he was checking you out."

I laugh, mostly from embarrassment. "It wasn't his fault I looked like a contestant in a wet T-shirt contest. If anyone's to blame, it's Winston."

"I had no choice but to make it perfectly fucking clear who you belonged to. That kid was dangerously close to getting his ass kicked." His mouth closes around my nipple, and even through the lace, an unexpected jolt of want surges to my core. The wet heat of his tongue lathes over my nipple and any sense of reason slips from my grasp. Reese's mouth and hands working together? A lethal combination. I haven't had anyone make me feel like this in a long time—maybe ever.

"You make me so fucking hard," he growls into my neck. His words are dirty and desperate, sending pinpricks across every inch of my skin. My clit aches—the want for him growing with every kiss, every touch. "Jesus Christ, Sunshine."

In a sudden move, Reese lifts me by the ass and drops me in his lap. His erection stabs between my legs, and I grind down.

"Just keep doing that," he begs, tongue licking against mine, "your pussy feels so good."

No man has ever talked to me like this—or made me feel like this. I flatten my hands on his ridiculous chest, feeling the hard muscles tense under my fingertips. Rubbing against him, my clit throbs every time his cock hits my core, sending another jolt of desire. Sweeping my hair back, he cups the back of my head, and takes me in another blistering kiss. Between my legs, I feel the build-up, the tickle deep in the pit of my belly and my breath comes faster. I could come like this, no, I'm *going* to come like this, except Reese grips my hips with his big hands and forces me to still.

"I want you so fucking bad right now," he shudders a frustrated exhale, "but my side is killing me."

"Oh my god," I jump off his lap, which is a challenge with the way he's holding onto me. What the hell was I thinking? I came over here to help him, not dry hump him on the couch. "I'm so sorry. Let me take a look—"

"Hey," he grabs my hand and yanks me down to his uninjured side. "No harm done, but this isn't how I want to explore your body. Not feeling like I've got a thousand knives stabbing into my ribs."

"You should've said something."

"It's not really my style to tell the girl I've been chasing for weeks to get off my dick." His arm wraps around my waist and he gives me a slow kiss next to my ear. Reese continues to touch me, like even though we can't do what we want, he still can't get enough of me. Blood continues to pulse in my heart and core. And maybe my ears because I'm not sure I hear him right when he asks, "Were you close?"

Heat blooms in my cheeks. "I'm fine."

His eyebrow lifts, and his hand pushes under the hem of my shirt and lies flat against my belly. Whatever fire has been left smoldering is reignited and without shame, my hips rise at his touch. His fingers tickle as they inch down, thumbing the button of my jeans free.

"Reese," I say, placing my hand over his. "We can wait until you feel better."

"You take care of me all the time," he says, easing off the couch. "Let me do the same for you."

18

Reese

Holy shit.

That's all I can think as Twyler sits on the edge of the bed and I kneel before her. It's almost enough to make me say fuck it and toss her back on the bed and suffer through the pain. As long as it meant I got to bury myself inside of her, I'd take the pain. But I meant what I said, this girl takes care of me, and for once, I can do the same.

Plus, I love eating a woman's pussy, and after all the shit Twyler and I have been through, both of us deserve a reward.

There was no fucking way I was doing this downstairs. Not when my degenerate roommates could come home from the bar, trashed and with girls in tow. Plus, that couch has seen too many hookups and this isn't a hookup. This is the beginning of something.

"Lift your hips," I tell her, reaching for the sides of her jeans. She rises and I ease the fabric over her hips. I leave the bikini bottoms that match her bra, because fuck, I've thought about that white lace plastered against her perfect tits since the day at the shelter. The image had invaded my fantasies night after night and was a feature every time I jerked off. I wasn't messing around about that little shit ogling her. He's lucky he still has eyes.

I run my fingers down her thighs, finally getting a good look at her tattoos. They're matching, a crown on each side, surrounded by designs. "Is this for your band?" I ask, recognizing the imagery.

"Yes." I trace the shape of the crown with my fingertip, but she pushes me away. "I'm ticklish."

I grin and kiss her kneecaps. "I'll try to remember that."

Spreading her thighs, I take my time, pressing kisses along her soft skin. When I reach her pussy, I lean forward, teasing her through the fabric.

Who am I kidding? I'm teasing both of us. My cock aches worse than my side.

I run my finger under her panties, along her clit. She's so fucking wet. Twyler whimpers, arching her back into the bed. I meet her eyes. "You good?"

She nods wordlessly.

I make quick work of her panties and spread her legs wider, bringing my mouth to her core. She's drenched, probably still turned on from the hump fest on the couch downstairs. I know I am. There's something about the slow build of this thing, the challenge of winning over Twyler, that has made everything so much hotter.

Flattening my tongue over her pussy, I lick in slow, teasing strokes. Her hips rise and fall against my mouth, her fingers pushing in my hair. I groan as they tighten, pulling at my scalp.

Looking up, I see that she's no longer watching me, her eyes are closed. She sighs, and her lips part, making my cock throb. Slowly, I lick along her slit, tasting her as I work my way to the hot bud. I flick my tongue against it, sucking her clit until her legs tremble by my ears and her hips rise, chasing my tongue.

My dick is barely constrained against the flimsy sweats I'm wearing, and I feel the wet precum oozing off the tip. If she doesn't come soon, then I'm probably going to go off in my pants, because this is the single most erotic moment of my life. The tension and weeks of slow-building want. I've never been with a woman like this before. Shanna decided she wanted me, and I went along with it. The puck bunnies are easy pickings. But Twyler... this woman made me work for it.

And it makes me harder than a rock.

"I'm coming," she whispers, and fuck *yes*, I can feel the orgasm shudder through her body. Her pussy pulses and she curls her fingers into my hair as the explosive shockwaves take over. Her breath is low and quiet, in no world is Twyler a screamer. My little introvert would probably curl up and die first, but that's part of what makes her sexy. She's just who she is, nothing about her is for show, and I fucking love that about her.

When every muscle in her body loosens, I place my hands on the mattress and slowly lick my way up her body; from her belly to her lace-covered tits, until I reach her mouth and I kiss her again.

"Ruby was right," she says after I help her back into those sexy panties and we both settle up on the pillows.

"About what?" I ask, trying to follow.

"She said you'd be good at oral. That you have the mouth for it." She curls against me. My side hurts like a mother, and my dick throbs, but just having her next to me is enough.

"Yeah?" I'm not above fishing for compliments. "Well, it wasn't all me. You did a bang up job receiving."

"See, that's the funny thing. Ethan tried going down on me a few times, but I didn't like it." She ducks her chin. "I thought it was just me."

"Definitely not you," I run my hand down her stomach and cup her between the legs. "Your pussy is fantastic. He's just a fucking loser that doesn't know how to please a woman."

She presses her nose into my side, hiding her face. "God, you're so weird and you have a dirty, awful mouth."

"Nah, I'm just hot and dirty for you."

"I noticed." Her eyes dart down to my erection trying to burrow out of my pants. She reaches out and says, "I can—"

"As much as I want you," Jesus, my balls hate me right now, "and I really fucking want you. I'm pretty sure that if you touch my dick, Sunshine, I probably *will* crack a rib." I thread my fingers with hers. "When I finally can have you, I don't want anything holding me back."

She looks startled by my admission, but it's the God's honest truth.

"But understand, I'm going to make you mine." I brush my fingers over her cheek and then make the heroic decision to put a little space between us. "Can you hand me that laptop?"

She leans over and grabs it off the bedside table. Jesus, her ass. I almost reconsider my decision to wait until I'm all healed up.

No. No. I have more restraint than that. Plus, I'm too fucking selfish.

"What's that for?" she asks, handing it to me.

"Would it be strange post-sex behavior if we watched the rest of that documentary? I really need to figure out what the fuck happens to these people. Do they drink the Kool-Aid or just lose all their self-respect and money?"

"It may be strange, but it's my kind of strange," she says,

leaning back against my pillow. "You'll be addicted to true crime just like the rest of us."

I doubt it. There's only one thing I'm addicted to and she's right next to me.

～

"So what's going on with all that?"

I'm in the middle of a set of reps, a fifteen-pound weight in each hand. It's half the weight I normally lift, but I'm still letting this injury heal. On an exhale I grunt out, "All what?"

"You and TG," Axel asks, racking his own weights. His tank has the sleeves cut out, revealing his tat-covered arms. "You usually can't keep your eyes off each other at practice, but neither of you have even glanced at the other today."

He's right. I haven't looked at her once, but every fiber in my body, particularly my cock, knows the location of Twyler and her hot little body when we're in the same room. We agreed not to do anything to raise Green's suspicions. Including making eye contact.

It's for the best. I've been desperate for her since our status changed from fake relationship to on the downlow. We stayed up late watching her crazy cult show and talking. And making out. Just kissing. I can't remember the last time I was content to just fool around with a girl and not take it further. Fuck, it was perfect.

But it's been three days, and the bruise on my side is finally healing. If I don't get inside this girl soon, I may actually explode.

"She did me a solid by helping me out with Shanna. Now that she's backed off, there was no reason to keep up the act." I allow my gaze to drift over to where she's working with one of the guys. "It was never anything real."

I'm a hockey player, not an actor, but the bullshitting I do on the ice must have taken root, because Axel seems to buy it. He follows my gaze and says, "She is pretty cute."

My reaction is instantaneous. "No."

He laughs and runs a hand through his blond hair. "What do you mean, no?"

"Stay away from her, man." I rack my weights and grab my towel off the bench. "We're not supposed to mess around with her. Remember Green's warning."

"What Green doesn't know won't hurt anybody." He looks back over at Twyler and I see the interest in his eye. "She wouldn't be the first girl we've both had a go at."

It's a good fucking thing I already put down the weights because Axel is dangerously close to getting hurt. I turn and push into his space. My voice is low when I say, "As your captain and friend, I'm telling you to back the fuck off. That girl is off-limits."

Axel's jaw tics, like he's considering his options, but we both know he doesn't have any. I pulled rank, and for Twyler, I'm not afraid to go a step further. He must come to the same conclusion because he gives me a slow grin and holds up his hands. "No worries, man. She looks a little too timid for my liking anyway. The kind of girl that gets attached."

There's no reasoning with a manwhore like Axel. I spent the last five months working my way through the puck bunnies, but he's the kind of guy who has spent the last three years cutting a wide swath across all segments of the female population at Wittmore. The best thing for him is to think she's more trouble than she's worth.

Once he refocuses on his workout, I exit the gym, needing to cool off before I do something stupid. The pent-up need to be with Twyler isn't helping. I'm tense all the time. Entering the locker room, I grab my phone.

OneFive: Meet me before class?

She responds faster than I expect.

InternTwy: Where?

OneFive: Student Center. Bottom floor. Room 110.

She responds with a thumbs up and I feel the pressure lift off my chest. I've never had the need to see a girl like this before. I don't know if it's the weeks-long build up, or the added secrecy, but I know I'm not going to stop until I get to her.

∼

Room 110 is a small office in the student center reserved for one-on-one athletic tutoring. There's an online sign-up form and I made sure to block off the next thirty minutes.

I've just taken off my jacket when Twyler walks in. She closes the door and looks around at the set up. Although I haven't turned on the overhead lights, the home screen on the two computers on the far wall provide enough of a glow to take in the rest of the room: a study table, a leather couch, two computer areas and a flat screen on the wall.

"God, you guys are so spoiled. No wonder you're a bunch of entitled pricks."

"Right?" I laugh, reaching behind her to lock the door. In a fluid motion, I take the backpack off her shoulder and pull her toward me, wasting no time getting my mouth on hers. "God, your mouth. It's so fucking delicious."

I'm already hard. Fuck, I've been hard for weeks now. The last thing I want is for Twyler to think I'm just a dick chasing her pussy, but there's no way she doesn't feel me pressing into her lower belly.

"How are you feeling?" she asks, breaking our kiss. "How's the bruise?"

Green is the one that's been following up on my injury. I sat out Monday practice and took it easy at morning skate.

"A little sore, but better." I kiss along her jaw. "I had a good nurse."

"I'm not a nurse," she says, but her head falls to the side. I suck her ear and grab a handful of tit, while grinding into her. "But I'm glad you're better so I can finally do this."

Her fingers push at the hem of my shirt and splay over my abdomen. She likes my abs and I don't hate it. I work hard on my body and having a girl like Twyler, a girl who's hard to impress, be into it? Yeah, it does an ego good.

She continues to explore, bending to kiss the skin just below my belly button, and my stomach caves. Falling back, the edge of the table cuts into my ass. I'm so hot for this girl I could come just from her touch. I swallow and reach down, squeezing the bulge outside my jeans.

"This may have been a bad idea," I mutter, trying to gain some control. "You keep doing that and I'm going to come in my pants."

"You know," her fingers gently glide over the indentations of the muscles leading down below the waist of my jeans, then move to my belt. "I can fix things other than bruises and sprains."

Any coherent response is caught in my throat because my brain short-circuits when she unzips my pants and takes my cock in her soft, warm hand. I don't miss the way her eyes widen, and she mutters, "Is there anything about you that's not perfect?"

She drops to her knees.

"Sunshine," I say, voice hoarse, "I didn't bring you here to—"

Her mouth lowers to the head, tongue darting out to lick the bead of precum glistening at the tip. Holy shit. I thought Twlyer's mouth was good for kissing, but watching her pink lips circle around me? Fuck. Me.

She squeezes the base of my cock with her hand and continues to play with the head, tasting and teasing along the ridge. I don't know if she's intimidated, or afraid to take me down, but it doesn't matter. It's goddamn glorious. Twisting my fingers in her hair, I groan and fight the urge to rock my hips.

Those blue eyes look up at me and she asks, "Is this okay?"

"Fuck, yes. Better than okay," I say, gliding my thumb over her pink cheek. "Harder works too. I won't break."

A line slashes between her eyes and asks, "What about teeth?"

"Uh," my foggy brain tries to follow, "what about them?"

"Ginna said something in the bathroom at the Badger Den about you liking—"

Pressing my fingers under her chin, I force her face upward. "I like you. I like your mouth. My cock likes whatever you want to do to me, because it's you, Sunshine." I rub my thumb over her wet, puffy bottom lip. "But let's keep the teeth in check. I'm pretty sure Ginna was fucking with you."

"Oh." She scowls. "She's such a bitch."

For a second, I think the spell may have been broken, but Twyler grips the base of my cock with renewed vigor. Competitive, huh? She wets the tip with her tongue again, but this time follows it up by swallowing me down. I almost black out watching my dick vanish between her lips.

Winding my fingers back in her hair, I cup the back of her head. Not to guide her—but to anchor us together. My hips rise, fucking slowly into her mouth, and there's no doubt in my mind that my girl is into this. With each thrust she takes me in a little deeper, adding a sexy little pump with her fist. The tickle builds in my lower belly, then spreads to my balls. I nudge her, "Babe, if you don't want me to—"

I pull out, but she clamps down, jacking me against her tongue and sucking me hard. My body seizes and white-hot pleasure zips up my spine. The pent-up explosion happens without warning, just a deep-throated groan. The result fills her mouth, and she looks alarmed for a second, before swallowing it back.

"Christ," I mutter, pulling her off her knees. I wrap my arms around her. "Thank you, I really fucking needed that."

"You're welcome," she replies with a laugh.

I wipe off my dick on an extra shirt in my backpack, then stuff myself back in my jeans. Twyler pulls at her hair, trying to tame it, but it's always a little wild—and now, knowing the reason it's messed up is from my hands being in it? It's sexy as hell.

Once we're straight, I pull her to me and push a lazy kiss into her mouth. "You go first. I need to catch my breath."

"See you later?" she asks.

"We're having a team bonding night. There's a big NHL game on tonight so we're going as a group to watch at the Den."

"Oh right, I heard y'all talking about that."

I grin. "I love it when you say 'y'all.'"

I watch her go, and then take a deep breath. She's only been gone for a minute when the door opens. Brent Reynolds sticks his head in.

"Oh, hey. I saw some chick leave and thought the room was empty." He winks. "I assume you're done?"

"Yeah," I say, reaching for my backpack and jacket. "That was just my tutor."

"She's hotter than mine," he says with a laugh, flipping on the lights. If he suspects something he doesn't say it, just dropping his books on the table. "So hey, I've been meaning to talk to you."

"About what?"

"Shanna Wentworth."

I hitch my backpack over my shoulder. "What about her?"

"We've been going out some and I've been thinking about keeping her around."

"And what? You want my blessing or something?" I laugh. "Go for it. You're definitely her type." I pause. "I thought I heard you had something going on with that girl Nadia."

"Nadia's definitely fun, but that kind of ran its course. I passed her on to the guys." Unaware of how gross that sounds, he shrugs. "I'm thinking more long term. Shanna's girlfriend material. She looks great on camera. The head of PR for the team loves her."

"Sounds like a match made in heaven. Why do you need to talk to me?"

"I guess I was just wondering what really happened with all that?" He sits down and crosses his arms over his chest. "Did she get clingy? Have a crazy streak? Something I should know about?"

"Nah, Shanna's solid. We just had different goals, I guess." I rest my hand on the door. "Sounds like you two may be more aligned."

"Great," he says, giving me a grin. "Thanks a lot."

A short guy with glasses and a briefcase walks in the door. The tutor, I assume.

"Well, good luck," I say, more than happy to put some distance between the quarterback and myself. It's not until I'm out the door that I add, "You're going to need it."

19

Twyler

I'm almost late to class.

Professor Kent is already setting up at the podium, and I quickly slide into the open seat next to Nadia. Even though we're barely speaking, neither of us moved our seats during our shared class.

"Hey," I say, giving her a tight smile. This is what we do now. We greet one another, and ask basic questions, but personal stuff has been off the table for a while.

My heart is still pounding from rushing across campus and from what just transpired between me and Reese.

I gave him a blow job. In the middle of the day. On campus.

What is this life?

I'm not embarrassed about it, but I am a little shocked at myself. Maybe even a little proud? Reese makes me think and feel and do things that I'd normally be too hesitant to even consider. His confidence is contagious.

Keeping this relationship a secret isn't nearly as easy as I thought it would be. I did my best to ignore him during his workout this morning, but ultimately, it proved impossible. His presence is commanding. He's a natural born leader. And holy shit, he's so hot. From that cocky grin to the ripped muscles that line his lean body. And now I get to touch them.

I fan my face and try to settle in my seat, giving my attention to Dr. Kent, who is speaking to a TA. This week we're moving to the eighties. Hair bands and new wave. An image of Duran Duran fills the screen at the front of the classroom, and I make note to tell my mom. She loves them.

My heart rate finally slows, and I glance over at Nadia. Her eyes are narrowed and she's watching me.

"What?" I ask.

"You look... different."

Her scrutiny makes me fight the urge to wipe my lips for any lingering evidence that Reese's cock has just been in my mouth. I can't help but notice she's got dark circles under her eyes. Too many late nights out, I guess.

"Nothing's different," I say, lifting my shoulder nonchalantly. "I had to run across campus to get here on time. I'm out of shape."

"No, it's not that." Her mouth purses and her eyes skim over me. "Something's definitely different."

This may be the most we've said to one another in weeks that doesn't involve toilet paper or a spider in the kitchen. The urge to confess everything builds on the tip of my tongue and I swallow it back. We've never kept secrets even if that meant me telling her the horrific truth about Ethan, or her oversharing about her sexcapades with half the Wittmore athletes.

I asked Reese to promise not to say anything, to anyone. No one can know. Not even our friends. But I know Nadia. She's like a dog with a bone. A gossip bone. She's not going to give up until I reveal something.

"Reese and I broke up." The lie sits like a stone in my belly.

"Okay, class, today we start our section on the eighties," Professor Kent says from the front of the room, "the era of big hair, eyeliner, and keyboards."

Nadia's hand shoots out and grabs my forearm. "Did he dump you," she whispers, "because I'll—"

"No," I tell her quickly, and quietly. I feel like shit for lying because Reese deserves no one's wrath. I offer a portion of the truth. "Coach Green saw a photo of us together and gave me the riot act about dating a player. He made it clear that if he caught me with him or anyone else from the team, I'd lose my internship."

She sits back in her chair, eyes blinking. "Wow."

Kent continues to talk, the slide show flipping through images. My focus is split between Nadia and the professor, although it's kind of hard to ignore David Lee Roth in those bright, ball-hugging spandex pants.

"Are you okay?" she asks. I don't miss the sincerity in her voice.

"It was never serious," I reply without looking over. "I told you we were just having fun."

She must buy it, because she quiets, and we both redirect our attention to the lesson. I'm thankful that the topic is fun and interesting, it helps keep my mind off of everything. When class is over, I don't rush out like I have been doing. I take my time and wait for Nadia. As we fall into step she says, "I'm really sorry about the tickets. I knew how important it was to you and I let a guy distract me."

Hearing the apology loosens something in my chest. "Thank you, I really appreciate it." I step aside and lead us out of the way of the flow of students. "I apologize for judging you—because I was. I let my own hang-ups about guys bleed over into not supporting your decisions."

Her hands grip the straps of her backpack. "You weren't wrong about Brent. He's a dick."

"Oh no." I cringe. "Do you want to tell me what happened?"

"I saw him outside the coffee shop last week and when I went up to say hello and give him a kiss on the cheek, he totally brushed me off." She shrugs. "All he wanted was a fuck buddy. Someone to come over after dark and leave before morning."

"God, that sucks." My heart aches for her because I know deep down that she wants something real.

"Apparently all athletes are asses."

Not all of them, I want to say, but don't. I'm the one forcing Reese to keep our relationship quiet. He'd probably shout it from the rooftops if I'd let him.

"Twyler, hey."

I look up and see Logan walking over.

"Logan," I say. "How are you?" His sleeves are pushed up and the crown on his forearm is visible. Nadia takes it in immediately and grins at me. "This is my roommate, Nadia."

"Nice to meet you," he says, then turns to me. "Did you see the video drop?"

"What video?" I already have out my phone, searching for New Kings. The band is notorious for going online in the middle of the night and dropping news. It could be a new song, a tour announcement—almost anything. I'd been in a rush to get to early practice and then was occupied with Reese after. I hadn't checked any of my accounts.

"A few fans posted videos of the new tour. They've added Heartbreak to the set list."

"Shut up." My eyes widen and fuck, I find the video. The song Heartbreak is notorious in the fandom. It's a little obscure and never got any radio time, but it's my favorite. I listened to it on repeat during my dark days.

I press play and he leans over, pressing his shoulder to mine.

We watch together and tears spring to my eyes. "Oh my god, it's amazing."

"Right?"

"I can't believe I'm going to miss it." I instantly feel guilty for saying it and look to tell Nadia it's okay but she looks more stricken than I feel.

"I'm so sorry, Twy."

"It's okay." I nudge Logan with my elbow. "I know someone who will bring me back a T-shirt and a video."

He grins. "Absolutely."

Logan takes off, heading to class, and I don't miss the huge smile on Nadia's face.

"So, Logan. He's a cutie."

"He's okay," I say, non-committal. A month ago, Logan would have been my dream guy. But today… well, things have changed.

"Just okay?" She looks over her shoulder and watches him walk off. "He's into you."

I snort. "Probably because he basically saw my tits in an accidental wet T-shirt contest."

"A what? Okay," she links her arm in mine, "I'm officially skipping class so we can catch up. You and I stop talking for a couple of weeks and you break up with the hottest guy on campus and meet another, equally adorable guy? What kind of sorcery is this and how do I get some for myself?"

∼

OneFive: What are you doing?
InternTwy: Watching a show about a cold case.
OneFive: Of course you are.
InternTwy: How's the Den?

OneFive: I feel like I'm babysitting a group of horny fifteen-year-olds having their first drink.

InternTwy: You're not actually their dad, you know that, right?

OneFive: It feels like it.

OneFive: I'd rather be feeling you up right now.

InternTwy: Now who's acting like a horny fifteen-year-old?

OneFive: Me, Sunshine. I'm horny for you and it's fucking killing me.

"Who are you talking to?" Nadia asks.

I lower the phone and adjust the dumb grin on my face. I hate lying to Nadia, especially with our new-found peace, so I just shrug.

"Is it Logan?" she asks eagerly. She's in the chair across from the couch doing homework. "Or wait. Is there another hot guy you haven't told me about?"

Avoiding the question, I ask, "Are you bored? I'm bored." I turn off the TV. Who am I kidding? I've watched three different shows about this cold case already. No one's solving it unless there's a miracle. "Want to go do something?"

"I always want to go do something, Twyler, you know that." She grins, slamming the laptop shut. "What are you thinking?"

Thirty minutes later we walk into the Badger Den. Coach Green can't demand that I avoid the team in a public place. The Den is a Wittmore institution, it makes perfect sense for me to come here with a friend. The place is packed with hockey players and fans coming to watch the game on a dozen screens. That and the girls that love to hang out with them.

Neither of us took much time on our appearance or dressing up other than changing out of our pajamas and into actual clothes. My hair is twisted up in a bun, the best I could do last-minute.

I push through, thinking about how far I've come since the last time I came here with Reese. I'd been so nervous. Not just about being with him, but in general. Putting myself out there. The farther I get away from Ethan, the more I realize how much he affected everything in my life. I don't want to be that person anymore.

"TG!" Reid calls over the crowd. He rushes over and gives me a hug. I don't miss the can of Busch Light in his hand. "I wondered if you were coming."

"I'm not on the team, Reid."

"Sure you are." He sees Nadia and nods. "Nadia."

"Hey, Reid."

A few other guys come up to greet us and I say hello. My eyes are skimming the room for Reese, but I can't see him over the crowd.

My phone buzzes in my pocket and I pull it out.

OneFive: So you're horny for me too, huh?

So he can see me. Another message pops up before I can respond.

OneFive: Because I can't imagine another reason you'd show up here.

"Come on," Reid says. "We've got room at our table."

Nadia goes first, following Reid's broad-shouldered body as he pushes through the crowd. Most people are watching the game, but as the back booth comes into view, Reese's gray eyes are pinned on me, making little to no effort to pretend otherwise. My gaze drops to his mouth and my skin heats, thinking about how good it felt when he was between my legs.

This may have been a terrible idea.

There isn't actually room for the two of us, not with four massive hockey players already crammed in the booth, but Reid forces Kirby to shift over, leaving a sliver of space next to him. Across the table, Reese and Jeff make space, but the two guys are so big that whoever ends up sitting there will basically be in

Reese's lap. I pause, determining the best route to take, the one I should or the one I want.

Nadia leans in and whispers, "I got your back," and squeezes in next to Reese. I don't miss the dirty look she gives him. From the way his eyebrow raises, he doesn't either.

"So, how's the bonding going?" I ask, cupping the glass of beer Jeff slides down to me. I take a sip. Thankfully, it's not Reid's pick. "Everyone BFF's?"

"Someone made the rookies all take shots when we first got here" Kirby says, eyeing Reid, "so they're all wasted."

"Hey! It's tradition," Reid counters. "Matching shots for your jersey number."

"You made up that game." Reese rolls his eyes. "Just because you got wasted on shots on your first night out with the team, doesn't mean it's a tradition."

"Are you serious?" I ask, looking over at the group of guys. "Emerson is number eighteen. You want him to take eighteen shots?"

Reid shrugs. "If the number fits."

"Conveniently, Reid's jersey number is seven," Jeff says, tipping his beer back and taking a swallow. "And even then he blacked out by the sixth shot."

"No regrets." Reid grins and looks between me and Nadia. "You girls want in? I can go get a round."

"No thanks," I say, "I'll happily leave that tradition to the real teammates."

A knee brushes mine and I shift, trying not to cramp anyone's space, but then I feel the firm spread of fingertips clamp down. I glance up and Reese is staring up at the TV watching the game, but I don't miss the curve of his lips.

I've never been with a guy this touchy, like he can't get enough of me and I'm all he wants. It's weird and new and amazing. Our eyes meet over the table and a flicker of heat licks up my spine.

I look away and try to focus on the rest of the table, but I'm distracted by his presence. My phone buzzes in my pocket and I discreetly check.

OneFive: Meet me in the back?

I don't need to think twice. He's right. I came here for a reason.

InternTwy: Five minutes.

Luck is on my side and there's a dramatic play on the screen. Everyone jumps up, shouting. "What the fuck, Ref!" Reid curses, flipping off the screen. "Did you see that?"

I slip out of the booth, mouthing to Nadia that I'll be back.

With all of the attention on the game, it's easier for me to slip down the back hallway. The bathroom is empty; thank goodness Ginna isn't in here again. And after smoothing out my hair and washing my hands I step back outside, peering down the hall to see if Reese is there.

He's not, but someone is. Someone worse than a puck bunny. It's Ethan.

"Hey," he says, "I thought I saw you walk back here."

"And you followed me?" I ask, wondering what he's doing. No, wondering what he's doing *here*. "What are you doing in a hockey bar? This isn't your scene."

"I didn't think it was yours either." He shrugs. "Joan's brother is visiting and he's a big fan." So he's making concessions for Joan and her brother. Interesting. "Saw your hockey player back there. Why is he sitting with Nadia and not you?"

There's something in his tone. Ethan does this whole thing where he slowly sets a trap and waits for the other person to step into it. "We didn't come together. It's a team thing. Nadia and I just popped in for a bit."

"Right." He laughs to himself. "Sure. I understand."

Against my better judgment, I ask, "What do you understand?"

"It finally happened."

"What happened?" My head starts to spin.

"You turned into her—Nadia. A jersey chaser. And what better place to do it than from inside the locker room." His eyebrow arches. "Tell me, do you fuck all of them or just one at a time?"

"Oh my God," I glance around, making sure no one else heard. "Why would you say that?"

"Because, Twyler," he steps close and I catch the scent of his body spray, "you're a sheep—always looking for a leader to follow. When you lie with dogs and all that..."

"Shut up, Ethan."

But he's just getting started, even with the whole disaffected attitude, I see the glimmer in his eye. All he wants is to get under my skin and fuck, mission accomplished. Bending down, close enough that I can feel his breath on my ear, he asks, "Do you cry when he fucks you too? Because a big alpha male like that must like it rough." His fingers graze my throat. "Or have you finally learned to like it that way."

I jerk away, choking back nausea. I push past him and take the first route of escape I can find; the back door. Cold air slaps my face and I try to breathe but I can't. Anxiety and panic claws at my chest.

I do the thing I know best, I run.

20

Reese

"Cain!" Axel cries. "Settle a bet for us."

I'm on my way to meet Twyler when he stops me near the bar.

"Pete thinks that McDavid is going to pass Gretzky, but I think it'll be Ovechkin. He already passed Gordie Howe—"

Peering over Axel's shoulder, I see Twyler waiting for me. She's not alone though. My eyes narrow to get a better look down the poorly lit hall. She's talking to some guy.

"McDavid is the better skater," Pete argues. "Everyone knows that."

"Yeah, but without a solid line to back him up, he can't fulfill his potential. Ovechkin on the other hand…"

Half listening, I try to get a better look down the hall. I've never seen this guy before. He's not a regular at the bar—definitely not the athletic type. He has piercings on his eyebrow and lip, and dark, shaggy hair. It's not that kid Logan that she's become friendly with, but he's got the same vibe.

I know one thing; I don't like the way he's smiling at her.

I start to move around Axel, but his hand clamps around my forearm, trying to get me to settle the bet. "Dude," I tell them, "no one knows if it'll be Ovechkin or McDavid, or some unknown that hasn't made it up the ranks, but we'll probably find out in the next two seasons if they pass Gretzky's high score."

Down the hall, this guy has moved closer to Twyler. His fingers graze her throat and I see the panic in her eyes.

I jerk my arm free. "Oh, hell no."

Pushing past Axel, I charge down the hallway. Twyler is gone, but the guy that was talking to her isn't.

"Where is she?" I ask, pushing open the bathroom door. It's empty.

"Who?"

"Don't fuck around, man." I square up to him. "Where's Twyler? I saw you talking to her just a second ago."

"She left," he jerks his thumb at the backdoor.

"She left," I repeat, then tilt my head. "What did you say to her?"

He shrugs. Fuck he's cocky for a skinny guy. "Nothing that wasn't the truth, but typically, Twy can't handle the facts."

He starts to pass me as though the conversation is over, but I clamp a hand over his shoulder, dragging him to a stop.

"Hands off me, asshole."

I drop my hand, but we're not finished. "Why did she leave?" Because there's no way she'd take off without telling me or Nadia. "Tell me what you said to her."

"You know," he says, raking his hand through his hair, "you should be thanking me."

"For what?"

"For getting her ready for you. She'd never be able to handle a bunch of jocks if I hadn't broken her in first." He smirks. "You're welcome."

White hot rage licks at my spine, but it doesn't cloud my mind enough to not spit out, "You must be Ethan."

"She talks about me? Not a surprise really. Girls never forget their firsts, right?"

"You little fuck." My arm snaps out, grabbing him by the shirt. He's so skinny I could snap him in two without breaking a sweat. My elbow snaps back, swinging into a punch, and I'm glad when I see the panic fill his eyes. My swing misses–not because of my aim. No, someone's got a grip on the crook of my elbow and drags me back.

"Hey! Cap! Cool it, shit." Reid's got a tight hold of my shoulders. I fight against him, but he's strong.

Ethan puts some distance between us, brushing down his shirt. "I always knew you guys were just a bunch of psycho roid-ragers covering up your violent tendencies under the guise of athletics." He eyes me with superiority. "Thanks for proving it, asshole."

"Let me go," I say to Reid. "I'm not finished."

"Can't do it," Reid says, voice tight. "Even if he deserves it. Coach'll flip if you go down for fighting."

He's right. I'll get in a fuckton of trouble. Although, I'm pretty sure it'd be worth it.

"What's going on?" Axel comes around the other side. His voice has that easy drawl that he uses to taunt forwards on the ice. He takes one look at my furious expression and then another down at Ethan who seems to realize he's not just outsized—he's outnumbered. "Why are you picking fights with hipsters?"

"He said some rude shit about Twyler." My fingers curl into fists.

"TG?" Axel says, suddenly interested. "What's a little fuck like this have to do with our girl."

"I knew it," Ethan shakes his head, but I don't miss the smug smirk on his mouth. "I knew she was fucking all of you. God, what a whore."

"What did you say?" Axel steps between us, knuckles cracking. "I know I didn't hear that right."

In a blink, the whole scene unfolds in front of my eye. One of us destroys this little shit. Like fucking destroys him. We all get tossed into jail. Coach has to come bail us out. The season and our careers are ruined before they even get started. All over a pathetic, abusive, little shit. Taking a deep breath, I tell him, "Get the fuck out of here."

"What?" Axel looks at me in disbelief. "You're going to let him just—"

"Yes." I look at Ethan. "You get the fuck out of our bar or I can't guarantee you don't get a beatdown the next time." He seems to realize I've just given him a free pass and starts to walk back to the bar. Reid loosens his grip and releases me. I turn to them and say, "Escort him out."

"Where are you going?"

"To find my girl."

∽

Twyler linked up our phone tracking systems after we took our relationship underground. Not so we could find each other, but rather, in her words, "If I go missing or turn up dead, they'll figure out pretty quick you were my secret boyfriend. This protects both of us."

This is what it's like to fall for a girl obsessed with true crime.

And fuck, I definitely think I'm falling for her.

Outside the bar, I quickly look at the app, and see that Twyler is already up at Shotgun, her little icon moving in the direction of the teal house.

I break into a jog, running out of the business district, and back onto campus. She's walking up the sidewalk leading to her porch when I catch up.

"Twy," I call out, "wait up."

I expect her to keep running. Maybe even to shut me out. The things that asshole said to me—if he unleashed the same toxicity on her? She's probably in a full-blown panic. But she slows her gait, walks up her front steps and opens the door. When she steps inside, she doesn't shut me out.

I follow her in, closing the door behind me, and find her in her room, curled on her bed, her arms wrapped around a pillow shaped like a cat. That prick called her a whore and accused her of sleeping with the team. No wonder she's upset.

"Can I come in?" I ask, hovering in the doorway. If she says no, I'm not sure what I'll do.

She nods, and I hear the sniff. Dammit, she's crying. That goddamn bastard, the urge to track him down is barely outweighed by the desire to stay.

"Fuck, Sunshine," I say, sitting on the edge of the bed. I lay a hand on her head and stroke her hair.

"He's such a dick," she says. "It's like he has some radar that tells him exactly when to show up and fuck with my life."

Her cheeks are streaked with tears, but she looks more pissed than sad. My heart aches seeing her like this. It took so long and so much work to get her to drop that shield. I won't let him fuck that up. Without asking, I curl up next to her and wrap my arms around her body, holding her tight.

"Sorry I ran. I know you hate it when I do that."

"Keeps me in shape." I crack a smile, but it's halfhearted.

"You had every right to get away from that bastard, although next time, I'd rather you come find me."

"I panicked."

"I know." I rest my head on her shoulder. "I also know he needed his ass kicked."

She cranes her neck to look at me, eyes wide. "Did you?"

"Almost. Reid stopped me mid-swing." I take a deep breath, maybe my first one since leaving the bar. "But I couldn't. Letting my temper get the best of me would hurt the whole team." I cup her face and wipe a tear off her cheek. "And it would bring up a lot of questions about why I was fighting with your ex that neither of us want to answer."

"Thank you," she says. "He's just... god, he's the fucking worst."

I have a million questions. How did she end up with this prick? And why did it take her so long to get away from him? How does he still have such a hold on her? I don't believe she still loves him. Not after hearing what he said about her. I don't want to pry, but it feels like a weight holding her down.

"I'm hoping we scared him enough not to bother you anymore." I press a kiss on the back of her neck. "But if you want to talk about it—him—I'm here because..." God, why does this feel so important to say? "I like you, Twyler. A lot. And I want to be here for you."

She's quiet for a long beat, and as her breathing evens out I'm sure she's fallen asleep. But then she speaks out, voice quiet. "I haven't told many people about my relationship with Ethan. Nadia and Ruby know, and mother has enough details that she worries about me. My dad was already gone when I got involved with him and he was probably the only one that I would've listened to." Her heart pounds in her chest and I can feel it against my body. "I was vulnerable, and with a guy like Ethan, he probably saw me coming like a lamb to slaughter."

I tighten my grip around her waist.

"I do have a therapist, and she helps, but even then, it's a struggle to put it into words."

"Take your time," I tell her. "And only if you want to."

She shifts, rolling to face me. We lie face to face, my hand shifts to her hip. Biting down on her bottom lip, she exhales and says, "Going to college wasn't a given for me. Even before my dad died, my parents had been questioning if I was ready for the responsibility. I had a pretty bad track record of making not-so-great friends. According to my therapist I'm attracted to 'toxic' people." She adds the finger quotes for effect and rolls her eyes.

"You're not the first teenager to make stupid decisions in high school, babe."

"These weren't your standard adolescent dramas. My parents would have been thrilled if I'd been sneaking out and going to parties. That they knew how to deal with. But the depression and isolation," her blue eyes flick to mine, "the self-harm. That freaked them out."

The thought of her hurting so bad she'd inflict injury to herself… I just want to take that pain away. "I can see that they'd be overwhelmed."

"But it did get better. I got help. I stopped the self-harm. I threw myself into the sports training at my school, and got my shit together academically. I got into Wittmore, but unfortunately one bad habit followed me to college. I just had some kind of radar for toxic people." She looks up at me with those bright eyes. "You know, I met Ethan the first day I moved into the dorms. I was looking to shake off my past self and take some chances. In hindsight, I was incredibly vulnerable, reeling from my dad's death and being in an unfamiliar place. Ethan probably picked up on that the instant he saw me."

"Because he's a goddamn predator," I mutter.

"I thought he was edgy, and sexy with the piercings and

tattoos. He wasn't into sports or anything mainstream. Just the polar opposite of the jocks I spent all my time around in the program."

"You mean hot, sexy, muscular guys with a dedication to their body and sport?"

That earns me the smallest flicker of a smile and a massive eye roll, and the tight spot in my chest loosens. "Smug, cocky, self-absorbed, testosterone-fueled jocks. Yes." Her hand flattens against my abdomen, and I know she's into my body even if it kills her to admit it. "Ethan was broody and struggled with his own bouts of depression. I felt like we understood one another and that maybe I could help him. Instead, I got tied into his personality pretty quickly. Everything revolved around his moods, his approval, his criticism… it became both important and impossible to meet his standards."

"So he's a pretentious dick."

She laughs. "Pretty much."

I tuck a strand of hair behind her ear. "And he got off on making you feel like shit."

"Apparently so." Her entire body stiffens. "He hated the fact I was working with the athletic department, he called it 'basic' and tossed around all his theories about how institutions are just making a profit off the backs of student athletes—"

"He's not entirely wrong about that," I admit. It's one reason strong players draft so early. We're taking a risk every time we go on the ice. One college injury may end a career before it begins.

"—but," she continues, "things really escalated when I got assigned by my program to intern with the hockey team."

"Let me guess, he hates us the most?"

"You got it." She smirks. "Hockey is just 'sanctioned aggression.'"

"Does that mean if I kick his ass, they'll look the other way?" I ask, regretting that I didn't do it when I had the chance.

"Because I can go pick up Axel and Reid and we'll happily test that theory."

She shakes her head. "It would only prove his point, that you're just a bunch of aggressive cavemen."

"I can live with that."

"I'm sure you could." She sighs. "I just lost sight of myself when I was dating him. I thought him being a dick was just 'honesty,' and the shitty way he commented on my hair or clothes, or body was just him being 'real.' Ruby hated him, and I thought she was just being controlling. My mom tried to straddle the line because she knew if she voiced her disapproval, I'd just dig in deeper." Her eyes turn downward. "Ethan wasn't content just being a controlling gaslighter. It got worse when we started having sex."

My mind goes back to his comment about "breaking her in" for the team and that quick heat of anger comes back. I lift her chin until her eyes meet mine. "Tell me he didn't force you." Because I *will* murder him.

"Force, no. Pressure, yes." She wipes at her eyes. "But it wasn't even that he was just... rough. He was inconsiderate of my feelings and body." She swallows thickly. "The last time we were together we were just hanging out in my dorm. Nadia was out and we were watching a movie. Everything seemed fine and we started making out." Her fingers twist in my shirt. "He wrapped his hands around my throat. I freaked out. I don't know. I think I didn't trust him, and I just wanted him off of me. The last thing I remember is his eyes changing. Like, a switch flipped."

"What do you mean the last thing you remember?"

"I woke up on the bed. Alone. Bruises on my throat. I passed out and he left."

Blood pounds in my ears. He choked her out and left her there? Unconscious? That's why she freaked out when I tried to touch her neck. "Did he do anything else?"

"*No.*" She shakes her head. "My clothes were still on. I think he scared himself and took off."

"Jesus Christ, Twyler."

"Nadia came home and knew something was wrong. She tried to get me to report it, but he'd just fucked with my head so badly that at the time I thought I'd asked for it somehow. Over the two years we were together he stripped away so much of my identity that I had no idea who I was or what I thought."

"Sunshine, I am so fucking sorry this happened to you."

"It gave me the guts to break up with him and cut him out of my life for good. I eventually told Ruby, who looped in my mom. Things got bleak for a while, but I was stronger than before. I had friends and family and the resources to get back on track."

"And you gave up on men—other than through work."

"Pretty much." Her shoulder lifts in a shrug. "It wasn't hard. None of the jocks were interested in me. It was a safe place to hide." She smiles. "Until you ran into me at that coffee shop."

"No regrets, babe." I take her hand and bring her knuckles to my mouth, kissing the ridge. "I really, *really*, want to go beat his ass for hurting you and making you doubt yourself." I catch her eye. "You're amazing, Twyler. Kind, smart, tolerant of all the bullshit we put you through for your job..." She laughs and I run my thumb over her cheek. "You're beautiful."

Her skin turns pink. "Thank you for saying all that, but I don't need you to beat anyone up and risk your position as captain or even as a member of the team. He's a loser and not worth it."

I don't agree. At all, and the only thing keeping me from going off and tracking his scrawny ass down is the girl in this bed.

"You're worth it." My eyes dart to her mouth and I repeat what I said earlier, "I like you."

"Still?" Her expression is incredulous. "Even after dropping all that trauma on you?"

"Even more, maybe," I confess. It may scare her off after all of that. She may not want to be with anyone yet. This started off as a game—*safe*. I understand that better now. But my feelings have only intensified.

"I like you, too," she admits, twisting her fingers in my shirt and pulling my face down to meet hers. "A lot."

21

Twyler

It's not the first time I've been in bed with Reese Cain, but it's the first time he's been in *my* bed, and I just revealed to him how my entire life is one giant dumpster fire.

Yet, he's still here.

I'd gone to the bathroom, washed my face, and changed into a soft pair of shorts and my favorite stretched-out T-shirt. When I come back, I see he's kicked his shoes off and is stretched out on the bed waiting for me.

"If you need to go back to team bonding night, it's okay. I understand."

"The other seniors can handle it. I'm done playing dad for the night." His eyebrows rise. "I'm firmly in supportive secret boyfriend mode."

I ignore the "boyfriend" comment and crawl in the bed, sliding under the covers. His feet hang off the end, and it's a double, so with his broad shoulders the two of us barely fit.

Barely.

"Thank you for coming after me. I promise one of these days I'll stop running."

"Doesn't matter, Sunshine. If you run, I'm pretty sure I'm just gonna keep chasing you."

Telling Reese about Ethan feels like taking off shackles that I've been wearing for the last two years. It's liberating. And it makes me bold.

"You can stay if you want." I push up on my elbow. "Like overnight."

"Yeah?" His eyes dart down to my chest and warmth spreads through me. Unlike Ethan, Reese never makes me question if he wants me.

"It can be your turn to do the walk of shame."

"It'd be my honor," he says with a grin, already removing his jeans. He drops them next to his shoes and reaches for his shirt behind his neck, pulling it off.

Mercy, his body.

I already know that Reese is touchy, but he wastes no time getting under the covers with me. He crowds into my space, pulling me close, and for the first time in my life I don't fight against it. I trust him. Resting my head on his chest, I hear his heart thumping against my ear.

"Can I ask you a question?"

"Sure."

"Can I kiss you?"

I lift my chin. "Please."

He inches down until our lips touch, the kiss bringing on a rush of emotion. I don't ask what Ethan said to him. It doesn't matter. It's all lies, and I know that now.

He doesn't get to make up my truth.

With each kiss, each lick and taste of his tongue, the feel of our shifting and tensing muscles, as my walls lower. Reese knocks them down, brick by brick until I'm laid bare. For once, I don't feel vulnerable. I feel *alive*. My body aches with the need for connection, both emotional and physical.

"I don't want to rush you," he says between kisses, palm kneading my ass.

"You're not." I take a breath. "I want this."

I push him on his back and climb over him, grinding down on his thick erection until we both groan. His hands move under my shirt, big and calloused, cupping my breasts.

"God, your tits," he says impatiently, stripping off my T-shirt and tossing it aside. He lowers his face to lathe his tongue across one nipple. "How are they so perfect?"

How is *he* so perfect? I want to ask as I run my hands over his ridiculous abs. He rolls us over, flattening me on my back. Hovering over my body, he runs a finger down the center of my chest, circles my wet and peaked nipple then down my stomach. With a yank, he unties the string holding my shorts up, and pushes them down.

"Let me get you ready," he says, spreading my legs apart. He pushes two fingers against my clit then drags them down to my opening. "Fuck, you already *are* ready, Sunshine."

That doesn't stop him.

His tongue is warm, and he works slow, driving me crazy with every lick and suck. It's excruciating, and I feel the tingle in my clit, signaling my orgasm. But I don't want to come on his mouth. I know exactly what I want.

"Reese," I beg, pulling at his hair. "I need you inside."

He grins, giving me one last torturous lick before easing off the bed. His erection pushes at the flap of his shorts, and he yanks them down, freeing his cock. Bending, he fishes a condom out of his wallet and climbs back in bed, until he's kneeling between my legs. I can't keep my eyes off him or my hands away from his chest. I trace the muscles and thread my fingers through that fine hair under his belly. He grunts and the tight muscle in the back of his jaw tenses. I know that muscle. I've seen it on the ice. When he's focused on keeping control. When he knows what he's after.

Right now, he's after me.

Lifting my ass, he angles my hips and runs his cock over the slick heat of my core. My legs tremble and he ruts against me, eyes meeting mine. "You sure?

"Absolutely."

He still doesn't rush, running his hand down my body as he lines up with my entrance. Lowering himself, right as he pushes in, he captures my mouth in a searing kiss. It's meant to be a distraction for the way he invades my body, but I feel everything. The way my body stretches taking him in, the sweet intimacy of being so close to this man.

Breathing hard, his body stills. "You sure you're not a virgin? Your pussy is tight as fuck."

He's so filthy. "It's just been a while."

"Yeah, well, I hate to tell you, but this isn't going to last long. Not with the way you're gripping me."

I exhale, forcing myself to relax. I've waited for this, and I don't want it to be over before it starts. I know my body isn't just out of use, it's carrying all that baggage Ethan left me with.

"That's better," he says, as my muscles loosen. His hand pushes the hair off my face. "You're so fucking beautiful."

No one has ever told me that, outside my parents. Ethan couldn't compliment me, and the way Reese says it, the dark intensity spreads warmth through my body.

Slowly, the cords of his neck taut, he moves. The tiniest rock of his hips. He kisses my jaw, and collar bone, taking care to stay away from my throat. His massive hand pushes at my inner thigh, spreading my legs wider, and he sinks in, filling me even more than before.

I moan, loving the way he's inside of me, and when he

punches his hips again, this time he doesn't stop. His mouth latches to my breast and he sucks, sending fire straight to my clit. I meet him, thrust for thrust, until my breath quickens, and his strokes move faster. The orgasm hits me like a detonated bomb.

For a split second, it's just me and Reese. There's no outside world, no pain and suffering, just our bodies in sync. When he plunges into me one last time, his forehead buries into the crook of my neck, and I feel the groan that follows deep in my core.

Kissing me, he rolls off, taking his heat and strength with him to clean up. When he returns, he wraps his arms around me, dragging me against him.

This whole thing may have started out fake, but it sure as hell is starting to feel very real.

∽

"When are we going to talk about Reese Cain?"

My neck heats and I take a sip of iced coffee hoping it'll cool me off. One look at Nadia's questioning face, and I know it's pointless. Still, I try.

"What about him?"

She rolls her eyes at me. "I know he almost beat Ethan to a pulp the other night. And I know he came back to our place and spent the night. I'm pretty sure I heard him sneak out before daylight—you know, because the hinge on the front door squeaks." Her eyebrow rises, giving me a chance to deny any of it, but I stay quiet. That only propels her to keep talking, "But I am absolutely positive that I saw a used condom wrapper in the bathroom trash can that wasn't put there by me."

"Oh." Well, shit. Looking around I see a pack of sorority girls. Two guys that are so tall they have to be on the basketball team, and various other individuals waiting to cross the street. If we're going to talk about this, it can't be here. "Follow me."

I hope she's going to tell me no, that she needs to get to class, but I know better. Nadia will happily show up late or skip an entire class for good gossip. I take her down a small walkway between two buildings and sit on a brick wall.

"Okay, Twy, spill. What's going on?"

"Remember how I told you that Reese and I broke up?"

"Yes."

"Well, the truth is that we were never dating in the first place. We agreed to pretend see each other until Shanna got off his back and in return, he helped me gain a little confidence with guys."

She blinks, like she's trying to process everything I just said and is failing spectacularly. "I'm so confused right now."

"It started off fake." I tell her how at first this was just a charade. A stupid deal we made with one another and how we both benefited from the arrangement.

"But then..." she prompts.

"But then Coach Green called me into this office and gave me the warning. That did happen. He caught us hanging out as friends and thought it meant more. We called it off to protect my job." I pick at a thread on my jeans. "Except by then we'd started to like hanging out together, and instead of stopping, everything escalated."

"So you went from fake dating Reese Cain to for real fucking him."

It's more than that, I want to say, but this is Nadia, queen of the one-night stand. I don't feel the need to justify anything to her. "Pretty much."

She crosses her legs. "Does that mean he's your boyfriend now?"

I think back to how he said he was in boyfriend mode last

night. He'd also just called himself the team dad. I'm not staking a claim on the overuse of hyperbole.

"We haven't had that talk yet, but part of our deal was not seeing other people."

"Your *original* deal," she says.

"Right." It's true we hadn't updated that part, but it didn't feel necessary. We like each other and I'm willing to see where this goes without putting a label on it. This way, I don't feel like I'm lying as much to Coach Green.

She runs her fingers through her hair and groans. "I want to be pissed at the two of you for sneaking around, but I get it. Your job is important to you. And he stuck up for you last night with Ethan, so I have to give him credit for that." She grins. "Although kicking his ass would've been epic."

"Trust me, he wanted to."

Her smile wavers. "How is it that you end up with the hotshot athlete that you didn't even want and I'm stuck as a late night booty call?"

"Hey, I tried to get you to seriously consider Reid, but somehow you ended up with Brent Reynolds instead."

"I know." She twists the rings on her finger. "I have a problem."

"Well, when you're ready to do something about it, I'm here for you." I check the time and see that we're going to have to rush to get to class. "Please don't tell anyone about me and Reese. Coach Green can't know—no one can know. Not the players or anyone else. I'll lose my internship for sure."

"I won't," she says, wrapping her arm around and pulling me in for a hug. "I won't tell anyone that you got railed by Reese Cain last night." She winks. "*Twice.*"

"So enough about me," I say, ready to change the subject. "What's the deal with Brent? Is that still going on?"

I've been working on not being so judgmental, especially

when it comes to Nadia. I still worry about her though. Chasing jerseys never seems to work, but as long as she's having fun, who am I to question?

"Here and there, but it's football season, you know they're busy." She knocks her elbow into mine. "Kind of like Reese. Who would've thought we'd both be banging star athletes?"

What's going on with me and Reese feels like more than banging, but I don't say that. Reese also told me that he ran into Brent, and apparently, he and Shanna are seeing each other now. I expected Nadia to bring it up, but she hasn't.

So yeah, Brent is busy, but not enough to stop the booty calls or keep him from trying to lock in a budding socialite. "Anyone else caught your interest?"

"There are a few guys on the team that are fun. This one guy, CJ, is pretty cool. He's injured and unable to play this season. Brent said he needed some cheering up." She curls a lock of hair around her finger—something I know she does when she's unsure. "I don't mind."

"Huh."

She cuts her eyes at me. "What?"

"I'm not judging, I promise. It just seems weird he's okay with you seeing other guys on the team."

"He didn't outright say it. I figured I'd test it out," she admits. "See if maybe he'd get jealous."

"Did he?"

"Not really, but like I said, he's busy. He's the quarterback and CJ is injured. They're best friends and I don't mind giving him a little attention while Brent's busy." She pauses outside the building, hair spiraled around her finger. "He's kind of depressed. Worried that he's not going to recover in time for the draft. He's stressed out and if I can help, I will."

Oh Nadia. This girl *never* learns. "Well, for the record, I think you can do better than a football player."

"You got another hockey player lined up for me or something?"

"No, I'm out of the matchmaking game, but there are some nice guys. Like Reid, you guys have fun together even if you don't hook up."

"True," she admits, "but a girl has needs, Twy, and not all of us have a Reese Cain sneaking in and out of our room."

∽

The following week is a blur. Classes are getting harder with more papers and tests rolling in. Practice is busy—the more games the guys play, the more injuries start to emerge. The final preseason game is in two days and then the team heads straight into the season. There's no time for anything preventative to slip through the cracks and the pressure is building on both the team and trainers.

I'm grateful for the distraction. It was hard enough staying away from him before, but now that I know what it's like to have his powerful body hovering over me, and *in* me, it's impossible not to think about him all the time.

"This weekend we're playing our final preseason game against our toughest competition, Mason U," I overhear Coach Bryant say to the team in the locker room while they dress for practice. I'm crouched next to Pete, wrapping his ankle. "We managed a W for the first three games, but they sure as hell weren't all pretty. If you pull that kind of sloppy play with Mason, they'll wipe the floor with you and then come back during the season and swipe our spot in the championship."

Bryant goes into the specifics of what he wants the team to achieve at practice. My neck prickles and I glance over my shoulder. Reese is watching me and just before he pulls his jersey on over his head, he winks, sending a warm heat spreading across my body. I turn away before anyone notices.

"How's that?" I ask Pete, checking to make sure the tape is secure. "Too tight?"

"Honestly it could probably be tighter," he says, wiggling his foot, or trying to. Increasingly, Pete is having me secure the tape on his ankle tighter and tighter, and I'm worried about his mobility.

"Are you sure you don't want Coach Green to refer you for a scan? If it's bothering you that much, it could be something bigger." He slides his skate on, clearly dismissing my concerns. "Otherwise, we may need to start loosening the tape. I don't want you to end up with a problem on the ice."

"Nah," he says, pulling on his sock. "It's just how I like it. Thanks, TG."

Bryant finishes up, and the guys all head out to practice. Coach Green stops me on the way to grab the water bottles. "How's your tape supply?"

I investigate my kit. "Almost out."

"Go grab two new rolls for practice. Between Pete and Haskell, we're running through the tape faster than they go through beer on a Friday night."

"Yes, sir."

"Then you can grab the water bottles and get them set up. I have a feeling Bryant's about to run them ragged."

I nod, and head down the hallway to the supply closet. I've got two new rolls of tape in my hand and am trying to decide if I should mention Pete's over-taping to Coach Green, when the door opens. Fully dressed in pads, helmet, and practice uniform, Reese looks even bigger than normal. He quickly steps in and shuts the door behind him. The cocky smirk on his mouth tells me everything about why he's here.

"No," I say, making an attempt to step back but there's no room. "Absolutely not."

"What? I have an injury that needs looking at."

He's full of shit, but fine, I'll play. "What injury?" My eyes dart down. "And don't say it's that."

He laughs. "No, Sunshine, my cock works perfectly fine, but my lips are really dehydrated." His hands move to my hips. "And I think you're the only one that can help me."

The thing about Reese is that he's difficult, no, *impossible* to say no to. Not with that sexy, confident grin and those playful gray eyes. I mean, that's what got me into this in the first place, right?

But I want to kiss him too, and we're so busy that it's been a challenge to get time alone. His house is off-limits. Mine is located in a high-traffic area. I look up at him and sigh. "One kiss."

"Thank you." He bends, mouth slanting over mine. He doesn't waste time, pushing his tongue between my lips and sweeping it inside. His jaw is strong, everything about him is strong, and it's so easy to get caught up in him. He pulls back, licking his bottom lip. "There. So much better."

"You're an idiot," I say, fully aware of the stupid grin plastered on my face. "Go."

He exits, and I gather a few more things before heading back out. Looping my kit over one arm, I grab the caddy that holds the water bottles in both hands. Reese is down at the end of the tunnel, pushing open the door, when he sees me.

"I've got it," he says, coming back to help me.

"I'm good," I tell him, although I know that I can't open the door and carry all this out at the same time.

"Twy," he says, taking the container from me. He lifts it easily with one hand and opens the door with the other. The cold air of the arena slaps the heat off my cheeks, and he takes the bottles over to the training table. Coach Green watches from the bench.

"Thanks, Cain," I say, voice even. "You didn't need to do that."

"You looked like you were struggling." He tugs at his gloves, eyes flicking up to where I can feel Coach Green approaching. "Just being helpful."

He takes off before my boss makes it to us, slapping his helmet on his head and grabbing his stick.

"Everything okay, Perkins?" He gives me a long look.

"Yep," I focus on arranging the bottles, and not how I'm caught between the two most amazing things in my life. "Everything's perfect."

22

Twyler

"Two more, please."

"Seriously?" I watch the woman add two additional waffles to the tower of food on Jefferson's plate.

"Thanks, Shirlene, you're the best," he says, giving her a wink. The cafeteria worker beams back. "And yes, TG, I'm a growing boy. My body needs the fuel."

If Jeff gets any bigger both his ego and body will struggle to fit through the door.

"I'll just take one," I say, holding up my tray. Shirlene drops the waffle on my plate next to two slices of bacon and a banana. "Thank you."

Crossing the dining hall, Jefferson carries his tray in one hand and eats one of the waffles with the other. One of the perks of being a training intern is access to the athletic dining hall. Groups of athletes cluster around the tables, usually divided by sport. The women's softball team sits up near the window, and the football players occupy a long table closest to the cereal bar.

Brent Reynolds holds court at the end, three demolished plates of food sitting in front of him.

The hockey team has staked out a section right in the middle and Jefferson drops his tray and sits at an open seat at the end. I scan the table for an empty spot and whaddaya know… there's an empty chair next to Reese. He doesn't look up at me when I approach, but grabs his backpack out of the seat and moves it to the floor. Ah, no wonder it was empty.

"Hey, TG," Reid says, holding up a piece of toast. "You watch that new documentary on Dahmer?"

"Dude, you know the rule," Kirby says. "No talking about cannibalism while we eat."

"You were seriously just talking about the rash on your balls." Reid rolls his eyes dramatically and looks back at me. "The four-part one?"

"I did," I tell him, pouring syrup on my waffle. I take my time, filling up every little divot. "And, honestly, the whole thing is just really sad. Those poor kids." I shift my gaze to Kirby. "Do you need to go to the clinic? I can make you an appointment."

"Or you can just wait for the health department to follow up," Axel adds. "But it may spread to your cock by then."

"Shut up," Kirby says, although I see the unease in his eyes. "I just need to air my balls out a little longer after I shower."

Reese leans over and punches Kirby so hard on the arm that his fork jerks and snags his lip. "Jesus!" he touches his lip. "You could've hurt me."

"You're right. I could have." Reese narrows his eyes. "Stop talking about your balls in front of Twyler." Pete coughs and Reese sighs. "And everyone else. It's fucking disgusting."

"Cap's right," Murphy agrees. Kirby touches his lip and mumbles something about girls shouldn't be invited to the table if they can't handle the talk.

"Sorry about that," Reese says, resting his hand on my knee

under the table. Despite the cooler air, I'm wearing shorts and a hoodie after working with the guys in the weight room. "You don't have to ruin your morning by eating with these degenerates."

"I don't mind," I say quietly, making sure the other guys aren't listening. "It's pretty much the only way I can see you during the day." I cut off the corner of my waffle and grin. "Even if I have to listen to Kirby talk about his balls."

Even if Coach Green wasn't watching me like a hawk, the matchup against Mason U has completely consumed the team. If the guys aren't on the ice, they're in the weight room. If they're not in the weight room, Coach Bryant has them watching film. The guys are exhausted, physically and mentally. The time we have together has shrunk, and is a pretty good indicator of what will happen once the regular season starts.

It's going to suck.

This is one of the solutions, having meals together with the team. It's loud and the guys are obnoxious. No one around us pays us the slightest attention. I think I've become another fixture to them—just another part of the team—the girl to come to when you have a boo-boo.

With Kirby shut down, the guys fall into talk about the alumni dinner coming up. It sounds like Coach Bryant encourages the guys to bring a date, hoping that it'll make them behave better. I barely listen because Reese's thumb is rubbing small circles over my inner knee. I try to ignore him, but that's impossible. Even before I got into this situation with him, he was a force to be reckoned with.

His fingers inch up my thigh, and although it's a tiny, almost insignificant touch, a zing of electricity shocks my core like I've been struck by lightning.

Unaware of my suffering, Pete asks Reid, "Who are you bringing to the dinner?"

Reid doesn't answer right away, spending way too long on a piece of bacon. Finally he admits, "I asked Darla."

"You didn't," Reese says, fingers curling. "I thought that was over."

Reid sighs. "I did too, but she texted me the other day and one thing led to the other…"

"You mean she sexted you," Axel says. "And you folded like a shitty hand of cards."

He shrugs. "What can I say, she gets me. It's easy and she likes dressing up."

I glance at Reese and wonder if he ever wishes he was back with Shanna. She had no reservations about being seen in public with him, but the slow drag of his fingers up my thigh makes me think that his ex is far from his mind.

"How about TG?" Axel asks "You bringing a date to the alumni event?"

My fork stops mid-air. "Uh, I don't know if I'm supposed to– I'm just there as support staff."

Reese and I haven't talked about the alumni event since we first made our deal. The arrangement had been that we'd reassess our relationship at the one month point–this week. We'd also decide how to handle the fundraiser when we got to it. Well, it's here and I still have no idea what to do.

"Wait," Reid says, looking at me with wide eyes, "does this mean you're going to wear a dress?"

Every person at the table swings to look at me. Or it feels that way. "I wear dresses," I say, feeling my cheeks warm. "Sometimes."

Reid grins, eyes flicking over to Reese. "I can't wait to see it."

I feel Reese's eyes on me before I look at him and when I do, the dark intensity in his eyes makes me sweat. I don't know if Reese wants to see me in a dress or not, but I know that look. He definitely wants to get me naked. Under my hoodie, my nipples tighten, and I lick my bottom lip. When I dare a glance at him, he's watching me, eyes dark and zeroed in on my mouth.

Heat spreads across the back of my neck.

"You know," I say, cramming my last piece of bacon into my mouth, "I forgot I have an appointment with my advisor before class."

"See ya, TG," Reid says, barely glancing over from his conversation.

"Bye," I say. I don't breathe again until I'm outside and inhale the cool fall air.

My phone buzzes.

OneFive: Tutoring Office?

Followed by...

OneFive: Unless that appointment thing is real.

OneFive: Which I'm pretty sure it's not...

InternTwy: On my way.

How he beats me to the student center, I'll never know. A secret passageway only jocks know about? He enters the office and once I'm sure no one is watching, I follow him in.

The door is barely shut when he pushes me up against it and secures the lock.

"That was a fucking nightmare," he says, fingers gripping the zipper of my hoodie and lowering it down. "Sitting that close to you and not being able to get my hands on you." He licks my mouth. "I don't like it."

"Wait," I press my hands to his chest, eyes wide, "if you weren't touching me in there who was? Kirby?"

"I'd fucking kill him," he growls, capturing my mouth with lips that taste like syrup. Nimbly, he pushes my hoodie off my shoulders and shoves his hands up my shirt. "Sometimes I hate these fucking hoodies, you know that? They cover everything." His head dips down and he buries his face between my tits. "But then I'm glad no one gets to see these but me."

His words are a sweet relief, knowing that my need for him matches his desire for me. This thing… it never feels one-sided. Not when I can feel the hard length of his erection drilling against my stomach.

My hips grind into him, seeking friction, and a big hand grabs my thigh, hiking my leg around his hip. I moan when his length hits me across my core. Reaching between us, he tugs my panties aside and glides the tip of his cock over my throbbing clit.

I cling to him, burying my face in his chest, wanting him to fuck me.

Suddenly he lifts me and turns me around, bending me over the study table. His fingers hook into the waistband of my shorts. He pauses, leaning over to ask, "Is this okay?"

"Yes," I say, only wanting to feel him inside of me.

He lowers my shorts and panties and I hear the crinkle of a condom wrapper. His hand flattens over my lower back as his cock presses against my entrance. "Jesus, you're so wet," he says, followed by a low groan. His arm wraps around my waist and in one quick move, he punches into me at the same time he pulls me against him.

A gust of air leaves my lungs as the sensation of fullness spreads through me. I grip the edge of the table and fall into the spontaneity of this moment. How vulnerable I am, how utterly desperate he makes me feel, but also how safe. Ethan always made me question myself, picking at my insecurities until I could barely function. Reese draws me out, pushes me into new things, and over and over lets me know how much he's into me. His confidence is infectious.

There's no doubt how much he's into me right now, not with the way he's holding onto me. His hand slips between my legs and he rubs my clit, drawing me closer to the edge. I let go—of the worries, the complications of the two of us being together, of my past fears. I let go of it all, and let the orgasm shatter over me.

My body squeezes him, and his breathing turns short and erratic, hips flexing into my backside. He tightens his grip around my waist, pulling me closer until we're almost standing—two bodies flesh to flesh—then releases a long, muffled groan against my shoulder and comes.

"Fuck, Twy." He turns my head and presses a sloppy kiss to my mouth. He looks into my eyes. "How the hell does it keep getting better?"

I have no answer. Not when he pulls out and cleans us both up. Not when we kiss goodbye and sneak out of the room one by one, going our separate ways across campus like it never happened.

Because he's right. This thing between us only keeps getting better and I never want it to stop.

∼

"You coming over soon?" he asks, the same bass pounding in the background of the phone that I can hear echoing down the street. The party up at the Manor is in full swing and I'm pretty sure every cluster of people walking past my house is headed there. The guys won the game against Mason—a shutout—and with the full season starting next week, there was no way they wouldn't celebrate.

"Still waiting on Nadia," I tell him. She agreed to go with me as a buffer since I'm uncomfortable showing up there alone. "She was supposed to be back an hour ago."

"You think she's bailing on you?" The noise behind him grows more muffled.

"I don't know. She's been a lot more reliable lately." I scroll through my texts with her. "She said she was meeting up with Brent around six and that she'd be home by nine." It's already ten after ten.

"She's still seeing him?" he asks. "I thought he'd moved on."

"He may have, but she hasn't."

"Sure you don't want to come without her?" I hear the frustration in his voice. "I can sneak you up to my room and we can just celebrate alone."

"Tempting, but…"

I may just be feeling paranoid, but I can't shake the idea that Coach Green is watching us, or rather, me. Like he's waiting to catch me and Reese in a compromising position. I'm willing to go to the party as just another student—with a friend—but alone? I can't risk it.

My phone buzzes.

"Hold on," I check the notification. "Oh, it's just Ruby."

She's attached a video with the message: *Is this Nadia?*

"Hey, let me call you back."

"Okay, but if you're not here in an hour, Sunshine, I'm coming down to get you."

We hang up and before I can press play on the video, Ruby calls.

"Did you watch it?"

"No, not yet."

"Put me on speaker." I do and she adds, "It's not good, Twy. I'm worried."

"Okay, chill," I say, used to my sister's overdramatics. I press play and at first, I'm confused. The image is blurry, but I can make out Nadia's long, curly hair. She's sitting on a bed, and although her back is to the camera, it's obvious she's topless. She leans over and that's when I notice the guy in the bed. He's also bare-chested—but his face is cut from view. She kisses his chest, the movement exposing her thong.

"Where did you get this?" I ask, thumb over the exit button. Whatever it is, I'm not comfortable watching it.

"It was posted on the live stories, and just wait…" Nadia shifts, seconds away from flashing her chest, when a sticker appears across the screen.

To watch a live feed go to lonelycams #nadia

"I checked the link and it's behind a paywall," Ruby says. "Twy, did you know she was doing this?"

"No," I say, looking at Nadia's expression. It isn't clear with the grainy lighting, but she's my best friend. I know her and something about this feels wrong. "Is it just me or does she look like she doesn't even know the camera is there?"

"I don't know," she says. "It's hard to tell and Nadia has a history of—"

"She doesn't have a history of selling herself online, Ruby."

"I know. I'm sorry. I told you, I'm worried."

"It's okay," I say, crossing the room to grab my shoes. "I'm going to figure it out."

"What are you going to do?" Her voice raises. "Twy—"

I hang up and immediately press another number. Reese picks up on the first ring.

"On the way?" he asks.

"No, something came up." I search for my keys. "I need to go find Nadia."

"Babe, I'm sure she just flaked. Just let me come down."

"She's in trouble." My voice shakes when I say it. "I think. I don't know. Ruby sent me this video of her and I'm going to go look for her."

"Now?"

"I just need to make sure she's safe."

"Okay," he pauses. "I'll get my keys."

"Your keys?"

"I'm coming with you."

"It looks like it's a house off Miller Avenue." My eyes are glued to Nadia's icon on the app tracking feature. It hasn't moved in the last four hours.

"That's where the off-campus football players live," Axel says from the backseat of Reese's car. "I've been to a few parties over there."

"Does Brent Reynolds live there?" I ask.

"Yeah, he's one of them."

When Reese picked me up, I'd asked him why Axel was crammed in the back of the sports car. He'd simply replied, "He was the only one that wasn't shit-faced."

"Son of a—" a string of curses comes from the back seat. He's watching the video, getting angrier with every second. "There's no fucking way she agreed to this."

The truth is that I don't know what's true. Nadia has put herself in some pretty high-risk situations before, but my gut is telling me something isn't right.

"You didn't have to come," I tell them both again. I've been saying it since Reese arrived at my door.

"Yes, we did," Reese answers unequivocally. "You definitely weren't going into whatever situation this is alone." His hands grip the wheel. "And something tells me if I show up at an off-campus football house asking questions, I should probably bring backup."

The closer we get, the tighter the knot gets in my belly. Nadia is notorious for going off grid. I'd begged her more than once to keep her tracker on if she met some guy in the middle of the night. She rarely did—in fact, for some reason she'd do the opposite. Go dark the second she left. The fact she left it on tonight... well, that's triggering my spidey-sense. Something's not right.

Reese stretches his arm across the center console and rests his hand over mine, threading our fingers together. Despite Axel being in the car, I let him reassure me. Fuck the rules.

"There are other movies on this account," Axel says, the screen lighting up his face. His blond hair dips in front of his eyes and he brushes it back. "All paid access. All the same angle—making it impossible to know if the girl is aware of the camera. Whoever this guy is, he never shows his face." He grunts. "Seems shady as fuck."

I take a deep breath and tell him to take the next right. He slows the speed as we get closer to Nadia's icon.

"That one," Axel says, leaning between the seats. "I came here for a party right before the semester started."

He points to a one-story brick house. It's nice, which isn't surprising. Brent is the quarterback and that comes with some nice perks. The lights are on, but there are only a few cars out front—a big white pick-up and a smaller sports car. Definitely not a party.

"I know they didn't have a game this weekend," Reese says, pulling his car up to the curb in front of the house. He turns off the car and looks at me. "Stay here, okay?"

Um. No. "Not okay. I'm coming."

"Twy," he frowns, "we have no fucking idea what to expect in there."

"Seriously, TG," Axel says. "Reynolds we can deal with, but he's not the one in the video. We have no clue what's going on."

"She's my best friend." I look between them. "I'm coming."

Reese sighs and brings his hand to my face. "If shit goes sideways, you get out of there, understand?"

Axel and I hang back as Reese knocks on the door. Both guys are in their hockey jackets, and Axel has a split lip from taking a hit with a stick during the game. Nothing seems to faze him—probably part of being a goalie.

The door swings open and Brent takes up the entire opening. A baseball cap covers his head and he's wearing an old Wittmore football T-shirt.

"Cain." His eyes ping between us. He jerks his chin at Axel. "Rakestraw. What's going on? Thought you guys were having a party tonight?"

"We are," Reese says, shoving his hands in his pockets. "We heard that a friend of ours may be here."

"Friend?" His forehead wrinkles. "No one is here, but me."

Fucking liar. I step next to Reese. "Where's Nadia?"

He looks down at me, lips curving slightly. "I thought you looked familiar. You're Cain's tutor." The way he says "tutor" drips with sarcasm. "Sorry, babe, I don't do homework on Saturday night."

I have no fucking clue what he's talking about and don't care. "Is Nadia here? She texted me and said she was coming over here hours ago."

He casually rubs the back of his neck. "Eh, I think she's busy. I'll tell her to call when she's finished."

"Well, tell her it's an emergency," Reese says. "Twyler needs to talk to her."

"Look, man," Brent starts, but Reese pushes past him. Axel goes next and I follow. The living room is to our left and a cluttered office to our right. There's the faint scent of sweat and body spray, like the locker room, plus an added layer of something oily, like incense.

"We know she's here," Axel says. "Her phone tracks to the house. Whatever the fuck is going on here is starting to look shady as hell, Reynolds."

I'm tired of waiting. "Nadia!" I call out. There's a hallway that leads to the back of the house. "Is she back there? Are those the bedrooms?"

"Dude, you can't just barge in here," he says, more to Reese and Axel than me. "Call your little bitch off."

"My what?" Reese's voice turns deadly. He pushes at his jacket sleeves and balls his fist. "What did you call her?"

"You heard me," Brent says, turning his cap around. "You need to leave."

Thank God for Axel's reflexes because he jumps between them before Reese makes contact.

"Reynolds," Axel says, his voice level. "I don't know what the fuck you've got going on in here, but we aren't going to be satisfied until we locate her friend. The next step is to call the police." His eyes slide to the coffee table littered with beer and alcohol bottles. I don't miss the baggie of white powder either. "I don't think you want that."

"Call the police." Brent shrugs and then folds his massive arms over his chest. "You think they're going to arrest the quarterback of the football team? My coach'll handle it."

"They'll care when they find out someone is running a live porn cam out of here." I look up at him. "I need to know she's okay."

Brent, all six-two, two hundred and twenty-five pounds of him, makes no attempt to move from between me and the back of the house. "Nadia's a big girl, sweetheart. No one is forcing her to do anything she wouldn't do on her own."

Sounds like a confirmation to me, and I get tired of waiting. I push past him, shouting, "Nadia! Are you here?" but he doesn't let me get far, clamping his big hand on my shoulder and dragging me back. That's when Reese explodes.

"I swear to God, you touch her again, and you'll lose that million-dollar arm, Reynolds." Reese's voice is strained, his gray eyes wild. Brent drops his hand. "Twyler, go outside."

"But—"

"*Go.* I promise I'll bring her out, but I can't deal with this asshole and keep you safe at the same time." His eyes plead and I realize the situation is one second from escalating. I step back and he jerks his head at Axel. "Go find her."

Axel doesn't hesitate, pushing past us both. Brent doesn't move, seemingly aware that he crossed a line when he touched me. I go out on the porch, pacing as I hear more shouts from inside.

"Is this what you're doing, McMichael?" Axel yells. "Holding girls hostage and filming them?"

McMichael? Before I can process the name, Nadia rushes outside in only her bra and a pair of shorts. She's frantic, eyes wide and rimmed in red. I open my arms and she falls into me. "Oh my God, Nadia, are you okay?"

A sob escapes and she shivers against me. "I was so scared. I kept telling him I wanted to leave."

"Brent?" I ask, holding her tighter as a tremble runs through her body.

"No. CJ."

CJ McMichael. Axel steps out of the house, expression hard as stone. He takes off his jacket and wraps it around her shoulders. "You two get in the car."

"What happened in there?" I ask, looking behind him. "Where's Reese?"

Voices rise inside the house, and I see Reese chest to chest with another guy I don't know. He's huge, bigger than any of the other guys. His leg is in a cast.

"I know you think you're Teflon, but you're not," I hear Reese as Axel pushes us toward the car. "Especially you, McMichael. This is the shit that'll follow you for the rest of your fucking life and no franchise will touch you."

"Is that CJ?"

She nods.

"Get in the car," Axel says. "I'll get Reese."

I walk her to the car and help her into the backseat. Looking back, I see Axel and Reese exit the house. Reese's gait is jerky and his jaw is angry and tight. He looks over his shoulder more than once like he's considering going back in. Thank God, Axel keeps him moving.

"I'll sit in the back," I tell Axel when they get close enough. He nods and slides in the passenger seat.

Reese approaches, hands cupping my face. "You okay?"

"Yes," I nod, although the harsh truth about what just happened is slowly hitting home. "Are you?"

"Fucking McMichael," he growls. "I knew he was a prick but..." he exhales and presses his forehead to mine. "How is she?"

"I'm not sure, but thank you for coming out here with me."

"Don't thank me. They're both going to be lucky if this doesn't get out." He presses a kiss to my mouth. "Come on, let's get you two back home."

23

R eese

"You good?" Axel asks when I walk back onto the porch of the teal house. The car ride back was tense, no one speaking other than a few whispered words between the girls in the backseat. Back at the house, Twyler's been closed up in Nadia's room. I can't bring myself to leave without checking on her one more time.

"Yeah," I nod, still trying to get my temper under control. "Thanks for coming with. That could've been a huge shit show."

"Could've?" He laughs darkly. "Fuck, I don't know what those guys are thinking."

It's hard to rattle Axel. Nerves of steel are required when a slapshot is hurtling at your face a hundred miles an hour. I'd told Twyler I picked him because he was the most sober. Truth is, there's no one I'd rather have by my side in a dicey situation.

"McMichael is benched for the year," I say. "He's fucking desperate, that's what he's thinking." His shot at the NFL is dwindling the longer he's off the field. "But Reynolds? He's just an idiot."

"Well, you know I've always got your back. On or off the ice." He looks over my shoulder through the open door to the house. "So, you and TG, huh? For real?"

"Yeah." I'm not afraid to admit it. "It's for real."

"Nice. She's a cool chick. Cute and funny. I like her for you." He grins. "I fully approved of your puck bunny phase, but it never suited you."

"Please don't say anything." I run my hand through my hair. "Green can't find out or she'll lose her internship. She already got a warning."

"Your secret's safe with me," he says, then lowers his voice, "but Nadia needs to report this shit, because I don't think that clown is going to stop any time soon."

"Me either." I exhale. I'd offered to stop at the hospital or the police station, but all she wanted was to come home. "But that's her decision to make."

We agree to meet up in the morning before practice and Axel heads out. When I go back inside, Twyler is closing Nadia's bedroom door.

"How is she?" I cross the room and wrap my arms around her waist, pulling her to me.

"Tired. Scared. I don't know the full story, but it seems like this is something CJ has been pressuring her to do for a while. Tonight, she went over to just hang out with Brent and he was there. They ordered pizza and talked her into staying." She grimaces. "It wasn't until she stood up to leave that she realized she felt dizzy. She thinks they put something in her drink."

"Jesus Christ."

"I know."

"Is she going to report it? Because we can back her up." I tilt my head. "Axel, too."

"I don't know. I'll talk to her about it in the morning."

"Good." I kiss her forehead, then slowly travel down to her nose, cheeks, until I finally capture her lips. "I know you're tired. I'll head out."

Her fingers wind in the front of my shirt. "Stay."

"You sure?"

She nods. "I want you here."

She pushes up on her toes and curls her hand around my neck, pulling me down. I kiss her, feeling a rush of intensity. "Whatever you want," I tell her, meaning it. If tonight proved anything, it's that I'm all in with this girl.

Leading me into her room, she closes the door behind us. Silently, we undress; me kicking off my shoes and pants. Twyler peels off her clothes until she's down to just her bra and panties. My cock jerks at the sight of her. I wrap my fist around the base and stroke to the tip.

She's nervous. I see it in the tremble in her hand, and the tightening of her throat as she swallows. Exposing herself like this isn't easy. I know that. But fuck, Axel's got it wrong. She's not cute. She's fucking gorgeous.

Tired of staying away from her, I yank my shirt over my head and close the distance. Pressed together, I lift her hair and kiss the smooth skin on her shoulder. My cock drills into her belly, hard and relentless, but I will it to behave. I've wanted my mouth and hands on this girl all fucking day. My dick can wait.

Gently, I kiss under her ear, trailing my lips to her jaw. I look down at her; so small and sexy. I could lift her up and toss her on the bed, but that's not what I want to do, not yet.

I tilt her chin, forcing those blue eyes to meet mine. "Trust me?"

She nods.

"Can I kiss your neck?"

She tenses infinitesimally, but nods.

"Say the words, Sunshine."

"Yes, I trust you."

My heart pounds, threatening to crack through my ribs, because I know how monumental this moment is. Lifting her hair, I start with the softest kiss, barely grazing the skin. I know this is hard for her—that she trusted another asshole with her body, and he violated her—but I want her to know I'd never hurt her. Never exploit. And I take my time, pressing tiny kisses from her ear to her neck.

"We good?" I ask, gently rubbing my thumb down the column of her throat.

"Yes." She exhales and her head tilts, exposing a wide swath of skin.

I lick and suck, methodically, exploring every inch as her body melts into mine.

Meeting her mouth again, I say, "Thank you," before licking her lips and kissing her hard.

Her hips grind against me, and I run my hands down the soft expanse of skin on her back. My thumb brushes over the clasp of her bra. The strip of lace and satin falls to the floor.

"I hate not being able to touch you all day," I tell her, flattening my hands over her tits. Her nipples pebble and she looks up at me with that wide-eyed gaze that makes me feel lucky that she's let me past the gates. "I see you during practice and want to push you up against the lockers and fuck you right there." Taking a nipple in my mouth I suck until her nails claw into my shoulders and her breath catches in her throat. "I want to pull you into my lap on the bus and let you ride me all the way home."

My hand drops to the edge of her panties, and I push my fingers beneath the fabric. I brush against her clit, rubbing her until her hips buck forward.

"But most of all…" I kiss down the flat expanse of her stomach, all the way to her thighs. I press my lips against the tattoo on her left thigh and then the right, skimming my thumb over the design. I feel the ridge of scarred flesh underneath, the reminders of her self-harm. "I want the whole goddamn world to know you're mine."

I bite her hip, dragging my teeth down to the edge of her panties. Hooking my fingers in the waistband, I yank them off, eyes trained on her pussy.

I want her to know that she belongs to me. That no man will ever touch her or hurt her again. I want to say these things, but that's not who we are outside of this house. But inside? Now? I'm going to claim her as my own.

"You're mine, Sunshine." I lick her clit. "Tell me you understand that."

"I do," she says, voice caught in a shudder. My mouth is on her clit, sucking the hot nerves between my lips. Her knees tremble and her fingers twist in my hair, pulling my mouth against her pussy. She's close, but I'm feeling selfish.

"Hold on, baby." I give her pussy one last kiss and stand. "Please don't come until I'm inside of you."

Wrapping my arms around her, I lift her up and carry her to the bed. Laying her flat on her back, I stand over her for a long time, taking in every last inch of her. She's perfect. Perfect hair. Perfect eyes. Perfect mouth. Don't get me started on her tits and pussy because I could survive on nothing else for days.

"You're teasing me," she says, squirming under my gaze. "Come here."

I don't resist, climbing over her, sliding my arm under her back to lift her toward the headboard. Her hands flatten on my chest, exploring the hard muscle. I don't feel solid, like I could melt under her touch. Like this girl liquifies me, turning me into something hot and volatile. Combustible.

The only thing that'll make me feel whole again is being

inside. Fumbling with the drawer in her bedside table, I grab a condom, and quickly roll it on.

Her thighs fall to the side, inviting me in, and I settle between her legs. With one hand by her head and the other stroking a long path from her chest to her belly, I push in with a groan.

Her pussy is still crazy, deliciously, tight.

"Fuck," I breathe, jaw clenching to maintain control.

Who the fuck am I kidding? I lost control the first time I kissed this girl.

Her hips rise and her legs coil around my waist, allowing me to sink in deeper. I chase that feeling, wanting to be caught in a stranglehold. She meets me thrust for thrust, breath for breath, until my balls are full, aching with the need for release. I press my forehead to hers, crushing her to the mattress when she cries out against my mouth, the orgasm rushing over.

The quiver of her pussy around me is all it takes to send me falling after her.

Falling *for* her.

There is no fucking doubt in my mind, it's as clear as the lamp light signaling a goal, or the post-coital bliss glowing off the girl beneath me.

I'm in love.

~

IT'S NOT unusual to wake up in the Manor to the sound of two of my roommates fighting over the Xbox or the last frozen waffle. Once Reid and Jeff got in an actual physical altercation over who left wet clothes in the washing machine for three days, making the house reek of mildew. I jumped out of bed and scrambled downstairs, almost taking a hit from Reid's fist as he went after Jefferson.

Spoiler alert: they were Axel's clothes. He left them in there and then went to spend the long weekend at the Kappa sorority house.

And although I'm not particularly pleased my girl isn't in the bed next to me, the sound of soft female voices in the living room is a hell of a better way to wake up in the morning.

I'd laid awake long after Twyler fell asleep, thinking about our relationship. It wasn't just sex brain talking when I told her that I wanted her to be mine. This girl is everything I want. I can't get enough of her. I want her in bed and out. I want to see her wearing my name and number on her back—in public. I want to hold her hand and kiss her whenever I want to.

Because I can't keep going on pretending like this isn't a thing.

I love her and it's time we figure out how we're going to move forward.

It's not going to be easy, but I'm willing to talk to Coach Green about it–even Bryant. He made me captain for a reason–I'm levelheaded and show good leadership. I can juggle a girlfriend working with the team just as much as I can keep a bench full of knuckleheaded hockey players in line.

Sitting up, I search the room for my discarded clothing. I've just found my shirt in the corner, behind the desk, when I hear Twyler say my name in the other room.

"Reese said that if you want to file a report, he and Axel will both make a statement."

"I'm not filing a report," Nadia says.

"What? Why?"

I move closer, standing next to the bedroom door where I can hear better.

"Because I don't want to." There's a pause. "Brent didn't invite me over. He hasn't asked me to come over in weeks, but every time CJ texted me, I hoped that Brent would be there and, you know, some kind of spark would happen."

"Hoping to see one guy doesn't mean you were agreeing to be filmed having sex with another." Twyler's voice is firm.

"I knew what CJ wanted," Nadia says so quietly I have to strain to hear her. "He'd been begging me to make a video for LonelyCams for weeks. I told him no, but he was just really persistent. He wouldn't let it go."

"Last night you said you didn't agree to it."

"I didn't." She sniffs. "But I also didn't walk out of there when I should have. It's my fault. I went to the house. I ate the food and drinks. I didn't fight back or try to leave."

"Because he drugged you!" Twyler's voice rises.

"Twy," Nadia says. "You know what it's like to have shitty stuff done to you by a guy. There are shades of gray and I don't want this out there. Everyone already thinks I'm a stupid, slutty jersey chaser. I don't want to be a victim on top of that."

Twyler sighs, and I step away from the door, realizing that my eavesdropping just makes me another asshole invading Nadia's personal life. I also don't miss out on the fact that although I've always gotten consent from the women I was with, I can't say for certain we were always on the same page.

I'm pulling on my jeans when the bedroom door opens, and Twyler steps in wearing the hoodie she stole from me weeks ago. A feral possessiveness licks up my spine.

"Hey," I say, drawing my eyes away from the sweatshirt to the defeated expression on her face. "Everything okay?"

She shrugs. "Nadia doesn't want to file a report. Which is her choice."

I wrap my arms around her and pull her to my chest. "You're a good friend."

"I just hate that all of this is happening to her."

"I know, Sunshine." I press a kiss to her forehead. "Nadia's tough and she's got your support. Maybe she'll come around."

She leans into me, and I know now is the time to talk to her. To lay my cards on the table, but I've also got practice in an hour and I've got to get home for my gear. Something tells me it's going to take more than a few minutes to convince her to give me a shot.

"So listen," I say, tilting her head up where I can look her in the eye. "I was hoping maybe we could meet up later today." My phone buzzes on the bed. Probably one of the guys reminding me about practice. I pick up and scan the message. "What the fuck?"

Her eyebrows lift and she peers around me to see the phone. "What?"

"It's Brent." I frown at the text. "He wants us to meet him."

"Why the hell would we do that?"

The phone buzzes again—another message but this time it's a photo. I open the screen and peer at the grainy image. Despite the quality, I recognize that it was taken last night—the camera angle coming from the direction of Brent's house, capturing me and Twyler next to my car, caught in an embrace.

The message that follows is to the point: *We need to talk*.

24

Twyler

The bright yellow truck stop sign glows against the gray sky. Nightfall comes faster now, and although I don't mind the cold, I'm not a fan of the shorter days. I hate leaving the house before daylight and coming home after the sun sets.

I pull into the driveway, past the eighteen-wheelers, and spot Reese's Challenger parked near the diner. Thankfully, practice was only watching film, because neither Reese nor I had the attention span to do much more. Both of our minds were occupied with why Brent asked us to meet way out here near the highway to talk.

"Hey," he says, meeting me at the car. His hands are shoved in his pockets and it makes his shoulders seem even bigger. "Find it okay?"

"Yeah." I look around. "Could he have picked a crappier place?" It's all truckers and travelers. No students. I feel like the location choice must be as much about Brent not wanting to be seen as it is about our secret.

"We have no idea what he wants or knows," he says, before we go in. "I think we need to hear him out before we say anything, okay?"

I nod, but my stomach churns. Reese and I are both recognizable in that picture. Coach Green will easily be able to recognize us. Somehow Brent knows our secret.

Reese opens the door, holding it for me to enter first. The scent of fried food wafts out along with the strains of classic rock. Two men sit at the counter and a solo guy sits in a booth by the front window. Reese strides in, shoulders squared to where Brent waits at booth in the back. There's a plate with a hamburger and fries sitting in front of him.

It's easy to see why Nadia was attracted to him. He's undoubtedly handsome with a strong jaw and straight nose. Clean-cut with a Tom Brady vibe. The kind of guy a franchise could make their poster boy.

Too bad he's a total asshole.

When we approach, he gestures to the empty seat across the table. I slide in first, next to the window, and Reese follows. I'm used to being around confident men. There's no way to play college or higher-level sports without a healthy dose of egotism. It's just part of the game. I try not to feel closed in, but it's impossible not to feel small surrounded by two, hulking athletes. Both leaders on their teams. Both with something to lose.

It's like an alpha male face-off.

"Want something?" he says, nodding to the waitress behind the counter. "This place is a shithole, but the food is amazing."

"We're not here to eat," Reese says, his hand tangling with mine under the table. "What's this all about?"

Brent pops a fry in his mouth. "Obviously some serious shit went down last night, starting with the fact you barged into my house uninvited—"

"My friend was in danger!" I bite back.

His eyes dart to Reese, some bro signal for him to control me, but Reese just shrugs and says, "She's right. Nadia has made it clear that she didn't want to be on camera and told CJ repeatedly."

"He said, she said." Brent dismisses, but he does lower his voice. "Look, I'll be the first to admit that it was stupid as fuck for CJ to film and post those videos. He's been feeling down about his injury, and his prospects for the NFL. I felt sorry for him." He shoves two more fries into his mouth and keeps talking. "Nadia's easy. That girl will do anything I ask her to do. I figured she'd give him a blow job or ride him a few times and he'd blow off steam." His eyes meet mine. "I didn't know about the videos until he'd already put them up and I had no fucking idea he was doing it without consent."

"Why would we believe that?" I ask. "You literally just admitted to passing girls around like candy."

"I don't really care if you believe me or not," he shrugs and picks up his burger. "But what I do know you care about is that no one finds out that the two of you are fucking."

"Why do you assume that?" Reese asks, casually, leaning back.

Brent takes a huge bite, chewing and swallowing before he replies, "Because your girl Shanna got her panties in a twist when I told her I saw you sneaking around with your tutor."

"We weren't sneaking—" I start, but he rolls his eyes and I stop.

"Babe, I know the look of a guy who just busted a nut, so don't bother pretending like you weren't."

I should be used to crass jock talk by now, but from the heat burning my cheeks I'm obviously not immune.

"Shanna showed me a picture of the two of you together and told me that you're the team trainer. It didn't take long to find out that you two aren't allowed to see each other and that's why you're keeping it a secret." He smirks at me. "No one's firing the Captain over here. You're the one at risk of losing your job."

"That's a bold assumption," Reese says.

"Is it? The look on your faces tells me I'm right." He licks mustard off his thumb and leans back, throwing an arm over the back of the booth. "Normally, I wouldn't give a shit about who you're fucking, but after last night, I need a little leverage."

"Let me guess," I say sarcastically, "you want us to keep quiet about CJ running an amateur porn studio out of your house."

"Yep. I'll make sure he removes all the videos and deletes them too. Not just the ones of Nadia. But you have to agree to keep quiet about this. I don't want to hear a fucking whisper about this on campus."

"And if we don't keep quiet?" Reese asks. "Or Nadia decides to report it?"

"She won't," he says confidently. I don't miss the smug uplift of his lips. "I told you, she'll do anything I ask her to do. *But* if I find out anyone says a word, that photo goes straight to Coach Bryant and every other member of the hockey staff, including your student advisor and the head of the athletic department."

"Send it," Reese says, nonchalantly. "Because fuck you and your blackmailing ass. We may be breaking a few rules but you two were breaking the law."

Reese is right. I know he's right, but it doesn't stop the panic from building in the back of my throat. Everything I've worked for is about to crumble.

"Wait." I grab Reese's arm. "Can we talk first?"

He looks down at me, and there's real confusion etched on his face. I give him a pleading look and he relents, "We need a minute."

"Go for it," Brent says, then waves over the waitress. "Can I add a slice of pie?"

Reese's gait is agitated as I follow him out of the diner door and back into the parking lot. Once we're outside his fingers thread through mine and he drags me around the side of the building.

"You're not seriously considering this are you?" he asks, running his hand through his hair.

"Considering what? Keeping the secret we've been hiding for weeks now? Which has been for a very specific reason." My voice bounces off the brick wall of the building. "Or not going to the police which is exactly what Nadia wants?"

His jaw tightens and his gray eyes blaze. I expect an argument, but I sure as hell don't anticipate what comes next.

"Even before he asked to meet up, I was ready to figure out how to go public. I want to be with you, Twyler. All of you, all the time. I want you to be my girlfriend." His hand rests on my shoulder and he gently slides it up my neck. A reminder of how sweet he was to me last night—how careful he was with my fears. "This isn't how I wanted to tell you, not back behind some shitty truck stop diner, but..." he swallows, "I love you, Twy. And I'm not willing to let anyone else dictate this relationship any longer. Especially not a fucking asshole like Reynolds."

I blink. "What did you say?"

"I love you." His hand cups my cheek. "And I'm ready to go public—fuck the consequences."

A flood of emotions runs through me. Happiness? Yeah, I mean, this incredible, sexy, supportive man just declared his love for me, but... fuck, there's something else, this nagging self-doubt that's so hard to shake. He loves me now? Now that he's toe-to-toe with another alpha jock? Someone is walking out of here a winner, and I know Reese hates to lose.

"Do not get lost in your head, Sunshine. Push whatever negative thoughts are invading your brain aside. I'm serious." He pulls me forward and places a kiss on my forehead. "I love you and you don't have to say it back, but it's been on my mind to say since I realized you were the most kick-ass girl I've ever met, and I don't want to ever let you go."

I want the whole goddamn world to know you're mine.

"I don't want to let you go either," I say, a rush of conflicting endorphins running through me. "I love you too."

"Thank Jesus." He lifts me up and kisses me on the mouth. There's no reason for this kiss to feel different from the last but it does. When we pull apart he asks, "Does that mean I get to tell that asshole to go fuck himself?"

I grimace, nose wrinkling, and feel him stiffen.

"Can we wait?" I ask.

He lowers me to the ground. "Wait for what? You know we can't hide this forever."

"I know." He's right. Every day it gets harder to sneak around, and as long as anyone knows, we're at risk of being exposed. "I just don't want Brent Reynolds to be the one that pushes me into talking to Green."

"So you want to make a deal with him?" he asks warily.

"No. I just... I want to do this on my terms." I squeeze his hand. "What he's doing to us is no different from the bullshit he's been pulling on girls like Nadia. Forcing women into compromising positions and making us risk our reputations if we don't play by his shitty, manipulative rules."

"Son of a bitch," he mutters, rubbing the back of his neck. "You're right."

"Make the deal," I tell him, "but it's only temporary. I want to tell Coach Green because I want to come clean too. I hate lying to everyone and I really hate sneaking around. We're not doing anything wrong. But I also don't think that buying us a little time is a bad thing. It'll force him to take and keep the videos down, and in the meantime, we can work on Nadia to make the report."

"And you'll tell Green?" The muscle at the back of his jaw tenses. "Because I'm serious, Twy, I'm tired of hiding this."

I nod.

It's time to come clean, but not without a little ammunition of my own.

~

Two, long, anxiety-filled days pass before Professor Purvi is available to meet with me during office hours. But now that I'm sitting across from my advisor, that urge to bolt is strong. What if she tells me something I don't want to hear? Or I have to make a decision between my internship and Reese?

I hate feeling out of control, and everything about this situation feels like it's slipping through my fingers.

Professor Purvi flips through a thick file of papers on her desk—the standards and rules for working as an intern. She pushes her long, dark hair over her shoulder and closes the file. "I've triple-checked the criteria and there's nothing in here that says it's against the standards of your internship to date a player."

"You're sure?"

"Like I said, the university can't dictate a student dating another student. It would be different if either you or the player in question held a position of authority, but since you're both enrolled students at Wittmore, there doesn't seem to be any conflict."

"And do you have any problem with it?" I ask. "Ethically?"

"With you dating a hockey player?" She snorts. "No more than dating any of the other guys on campus. At least the varsity athletes have a measure of accountability around them." She leans forward, resting on her elbows. "But in all seriousness, professionalism is important in a situation like this. Your internship comes first, especially one as coveted as varsity hockey. You're being assessed based on your performance and you'll need those references moving forward. The sporting community is tight-knit. Any job you apply for in the future will want a referral from Coach Green."

"He's made it clear he doesn't approve and has warned me about getting involved with any of the players."

"It's possible he's just looking out for you and being protective." She rests her hands on the file and leans forward. "But I don't think I have to tell you that you'll have to work twice as hard in this field simply for the fact you're a woman. If some of these coaches have a reason to accuse you of being a distraction, they'll pounce on it."

"That's been my fear." I sigh, leaning back in my seat. "I'm a hard worker. I do everything Coach Green asks me to do and then some. I get along with all the players and show no favoritism to the guy I'm seeing. In fact, I do my best to ignore him most of the time."

She grins. "I'm sure he likes that."

"He's been respectful of my situation, but neither of us are comfortable hiding it anymore." I don't go into the situation with Brent and CJ. I'm still holding out hope that Nadia will file a report, but I also want to be prepared for it by getting my business together. "We'd both feel better getting this out in the open."

"Then you should." She smiles gently. "I can attend the meeting with you, if you'd like."

"No," I exhale. "Thank you, but I think this is something I should do on my own."

The plan is to tell Coach Green as soon as I get to the arena, but the meeting with Professor Purvi started late. By the time I get there, the guys are already on the ice. Pete is sitting on the bench wrapping his ankle.

"Let me do that," I say, dropping next to him on the bench.

"It's fine," he says, securing the end. "Coach is already pissed I'm not out there."

"Wait." I grab his foot and push my fingers under the tape, making sure there's enough give. There's not. "You need more flexibility in your ankle."

"Pete!" Reid shouts. The guys zip up and down the ice, running shooting drills. "Get your ass out here!"

"See?" He grabs the roll of tape from me, and pulls off a long strip, wrapping it around two more times. He tosses it back and I catch it. "Thanks, TG."

Before I can respond he's gliding off, merging in with the others. I'm about to call out for him to come back when Reese skates up and grabs a bottle of water.

"How did it go?" he asks, squirting a stream into his mouth.

"Fine," I focus on the bottles. "I'll tell you later."

"But everything's okay?"

"Yeah," I give him a small smile, "I think so."

He grins back and my stomach flips, both out of fear of being caught and the memory of hearing him say "I love you." He hands me back the water bottle and his fingers graze mine. I'm so gone for this guy.

He skates off, shoulders squared, stick sweeping out to make contact with the puck already in play. He's so natural at this, able to flip one switch to the other. Juggling work and my social life has never been a strength—to the point that I avoided it for a long time. My eyes are still trained on him, but a breakaway down the ice draws my attention away.

"Somebody block him!" Axel shouts, eyes wide as Pete comes barreling toward him as he chases the puck. His gait is awkward, fast, but out of control. He's lacking the smooth finesse that I know he's capable of. Panic fills Axel's eyes as Reid hustles across the mouth of the goal, body rigid as he checks Pete, knocking him away from the goalie. The two players slam full speed into the wall, rattling the boards. Pete crumples to the ice, followed by a string of curses.

"What the hell, man?" Axel shouts, abandoning the goal and skating over, looking ready to get in a fight with his teammate. Reese is already in the middle of it, arms wide, keeping the guys apart. He drops to his knee and I lose sight of him as the others huddle around.

"Get the kit," Coach Green orders, taking off toward the injured players. My heart pounds, and I grab the medical kit, following him out to the ice.

"Jesus Christ," I hear Reid shout. "He wouldn't stop! I had no choice."

"Everyone move back!" Coach Green muscles through the players. They make a small gap and I skirt in behind him. Reese rises off the ground, moving back with the rest of the team. Reid stays, bent on one knee, his face red and flustered. Pete is leaning against the board, wearing a pained grimace. Coach Green carefully unlaces Pete's skate and eases it off, revealing the thick tape. Coach asks, "Can you wiggle your toes?"

I know the answer to that is no. He barely had any flexibility.

"Perkins, hand me the scissors."

Still standing, I open the kit and rummage around until my fingers make contact with the hard metal scissors. "Here," I say, handing them over. Coach Green carefully cuts through the tape, but my stomach lurches when I see the way his ankle juts to the side, twisted unnaturally.

"Fuck," Pete says, eyes wet. "Is it broken?"

"I fucking hope not," Green mutters, inspecting his foot. The skin is white, but his toes are a purplish red. "You've just about cut off the circulation." His gaze shifts up to me. "Did you wrap this?"

"I—" My words die in the back of my throat. I *didn't* do it, but

I should have. I was late and even then, when I saw it, I didn't stop him. I knew he was pushing it too far and was going to get hurt.

"It's not her fault." A strong hand lands on my shoulder, heavy and reassuring. Reese adds, "Pete wrapped his own ankle."

Staring down at that ankle, bile rises to the back of my throat. Coach Green was right after all. I was distracted. I did let it affect my work. I was late, dealing with this relationship drama. I didn't tell Coach Green the risks he was taking and what he was asking me to do.

"Perkins!"

I blink, jerking away from Reese's touch. "Yes, sir."

"Go call the emergency number and get an ambulance down here."

"Yes, sir," I repeat, dropping the kit on the ice. One last look at Pete and the anguish on his face and I understand now why Coach Green was so adamant about me not getting distracted. It was never about me and Reese. It was always about putting the team first.

As I rush away from the consequences of my actions, I realize that doing both is impossible.

25

Reese

I wait until after dark to show up at the teal house. Before I walk up the path, I draw my hood up over my head, hopefully cloaking my face. After Pete was carried off the ice by the EMTs, Coach Bryant sent us to the weight room for the rest of practice. I'd tried to text and call Twyler after I left the arena, but she never responded. Anything past three of each just feels like stalking.

I knock on the door and wait, determined not to walk away without talking to her about what happened. I know she blames herself for Pete's injury. He's been over-wrapping that ankle since the beginning of the season despite her telling him to take it easy. It's not her fault he's a stubborn bastard who refuses to listen.

The door opens, but I deflate when Nadia is the one that answers.

"Hey," I say, peering around her into the small house. "Is Twy here?"

"She is." Her hip props against the door jamb. "But she doesn't want any visitors."

"I just want to check on her after what happened today." And find out what her advisor said, because before Pete went down, she'd been happy, like she had good news. "Can you tell her I'm here?"

"She's pretty rattled." Her arm stretches out and she grips the opposite side of the door. A clear indicator she's not willingly letting me pass. "I think she just needs some time to process everything."

I don't blame her. The first time I heard someone's leg snap was at hockey camp in the fourth grade. I can still hear the howl of pain when that kid went down, grabbing his leg and crying for his mother. Pete took it a lot better than that ten-year-old, but I saw the look in his eye. Fear. Not just about the pain, but for his future.

"I just want to make sure she's okay."

"Reese, honey, and I mean this in the nicest way possible…go the fuck home. She'll call you when she's ready."

My eyebrows raise, because even though I knew Twyler was upset, I didn't think she'd shut me out. "Okay," I say, not feeling okay at all. I thrust a hand in my hair. "Will you tell her I came by?"

Nadia looks sympathetic as she starts to close the door in my face, because I don't know where else to go. Right before the door shuts, I hear a voice and my heart skips a beat. "It's okay, you can let him in."

Nadia frowns, but jerks the door back open. She looks between us. "I'll be in my room."

I don't move until Nadia's closed behind her bedroom door, then I cross the threshold and yank down my hood. She's got her arms wrapped around her waist and she steps back, just out of my reach. Ouch. Okay.

I take a deep breath. "I didn't get to see you after practice."

"After Pete went to the ER, Coach Green called me into his office."

"Oh, shit." This was her biggest fear, telling Green about the two of us, but she's eerily calm. "Okay, how did that go?"

"I explained everything that had been going on. Pete's need for tighter and tighter wrapping. My warnings about mobility. I'd documented it in his file." Her eyes are cast down and hands are shoved in the pockets of her hoodie. "I admitted that I'd been distracted by personal stuff for the past few weeks," she finally looks up. "I didn't tell him about you."

"Oh." I'm confused. "Why didn't you tell him? That was the plan."

"Because I proved him right. I wasn't able to juggle my relationship with you and my obligations to the team. My advisor told me today that it was okay for us to date. There are no rules, but she also reminded me how important this position is to me. How it was imperative that I act professional if I want a good review and recommendation once I graduate."

"No one is going to question your dedication to your internship, Twy."

Her chin lifts. "Would you seriously consider staying together if I took focus away from your game? If it risked you getting drafted next year?"

"Maybe, but that isn't a problem for me." Fuck, I've been killing it in the preseason.

"But what if it was? Isn't that why you broke up with Shanna? Your goals didn't align?"

Shanna? "What are you saying?"

"*Our* goals don't align, Reese. This program means everything to me. When I was in my darkest place being able to devote my time and energy to the sports training program is what got me through. When my dad died, it helped me find a place to belong. When Ethan pulled the rug out from under me, it's where I found balance and strength." She inhales. "I know you understand this. You give everything to your sport. To your dreams. You made hard decisions because you refuse to compromise." She taps her chest. "*This* is my sport—just without the million-dollar paycheck and adoring crowds."

I swallow. "What are you saying?"

"I'm being forced to choose," her voice wobbles, "and it's not you."

She may as well have taken out a gun and fired a bullet in my heart. "You're serious about this."

"I've been clear from the beginning that my internship is my priority. It's my future, Reese."

Bam. Another round fired. "And you don't see me as part of your future?"

A tear builds in her eye, but she brushes it away before it falls. "I'm sorry, I don't."

∽

"What the fuck, Cain?" Kirby shouts. "That was a perfect pass!"

"You call that perfect?" I skate around the goal, eyes trained on Kirby. When I get close, I bump my shoulder into his—hard. "It was way outside. You need to work on your fucking accuracy."

"It was right in the crease!" He shoves me back. "You go blind all of a sudden? Jerking off too much? Maybe it's time you found a girl to fuck instead of your ha—"

Crack!

I see red, and twenty-one years of well-honed restraint goes down the drain in a split second. No, fuck that. It isn't a split second. It's four miserable days since Twyler dumped my ass and I've been spiraling ever since.

"Cain!" Coach Bryant shouts over the sound of the team dragging me and Kirby off one another. "Off the goddamn ice."

"But Coach—"

"Don't make me tell you twice, son." He gives me a hard look, like he's daring me to cross a line. I jerk my head in a nod and skate off the ice, throwing my stick over the board and yanking off my gloves. I've just tossed my helmet down the tunnel when I notice a familiar face sitting up in the stands.

Son of a bitch.

I drop down on a bench and unlace my skates, taking deep breaths in an attempt to calm down. When I can't avoid it any longer, I climb up the stairs, and meet him.

"Hey, Dad," I rub the back of my sweaty neck, "how long have you been here?"

"Long enough."

Jesus. It's one thing to make an ass out of myself in front of the guys and Coach Bryant. But my dad? Shit. "Was this a planned visit?" I ask, nodding down at Coach. "Or did he call you?"

"I was on my way down for the alumni event. Ben suggested I stop by and watch practice." His eyes track the play down on the ice. "Want to tell me what's going on?"

What I don't tell him is that I'm hungover. For the third straight day. And that I skipped two classes and everything is falling apart. "It's been a bad week."

"I heard about Pete." He leans forward and rests his elbows on his knees, clasping his hands together. "Green says his ankle should be okay with surgery and PT."

"He's still out for the season."

"It happens," he shrugs. "He's young and will bounce back."

I grunt, not convinced. Dad was young. He didn't bounce back. But Pete's not the problem anyway. I felt nothing but relief that Coach Green said he'll make a full recovery and will probably be back on the ice by next season. No, Pete was the catalyst, not the problem.

Down by the bench I see Twyler's dark ponytail bob as she carries in a heavy cooler of water. Jonathan runs up behind her and takes the extra weight. I drag my eyes away and stare at my hands.

"Oh, boy," Dad says, following my gaze, "it's true."

"What's true?"

He nods down at Twyler. "This spiral is about a woman."

Did Coach tell him that? I swallow the lump that builds in my throat every time I think about her.

"She's cute."

Gorgeous. I shake my head. "Well, she's not mine, that's for sure."

"What the hell did you do?"

"Me?" I bark out an incredulous laugh. "I didn't do anything. Hell, no. It was her decision." He gives me an expectant look. "She had to choose between her internship and our relationship." I nod down to her. "You can see which one she chose."

I'm not happy about it. Fuck, I've been drowning my sorrows for days, but Twyler called it. I'd never give up hockey. Not for anyone. And I shouldn't ask her to do the same thing.

And she wasn't wrong about Shanna either. She'd given me an ultimatum and I walked because our goals weren't the same. Who am I to do the same to Twyler?

Next to me my father hums, watching Axel argue with Emerson in front of the goal. Axel's pointing to the area outside the crease, where Kirby's been applying pressure all practice, hammering the goal with opportunities to score, including the one I missed. He and I approach playing differently, and it's been hard for us to find a good groove. It's also hard for the defenders to block.

"You see that?" he asks, pointing down to the ice where Emerson's been hovering in front of the net all practice.

"Yeah, they've been fighting since the season started."

"Refusing to compromise is usually about fear. It feels safe to stay in one place, but it can leave you vulnerable to your opponent. Being inflexible and resistant to compromise will limit his options." He lifts his chin. "That kid needs to make a choice, choose a path, get out of the goal, put some pressure on the forward. Change up the dynamics or he'll never get what he wants."

As if my dad's some kind of hockey whisperer, Emerson finally gets the guts to go after Kirby, leaving Axel alone to defend the net. The result is an impressive deke, and he clears the puck down to the opposite end where Reid is waiting.

Dad stands, clapping his hands, shouting out to Emerson for the good play.

"Don't limit your options, Son. Not on the ice or with anything that's important to you." He glances over at me. "That was a lesson I didn't learn until it was way too late."

It's not unusual for my father to use hockey as an allegory to real life. This is the man who took me aside before my first date, handed me a box of condoms, and explained that wearing one is like a goalie protecting the crease. It's the last line of defense between an unwanted pregnancy or STI.

This talk about compromise has me thinking about when my mom left. I wasn't privy to the inner workings of their relationship, but I know one thing: my father didn't fight for her. He let her make her decision and she never looked back. Although I don't regret my decision to break up with Shanna, neither of us was willing to make a compromise for the other.

Down below, the players maneuver on the ice, and I realize

that the same principle that applies to the game – being willing to adapt and make choices that benefit the team—applies to me and Twyler.

If we're going to make this, or any relationship work, one of us is going to have to step outside of our comfort zone.

26

Twyler

"You've got this."

It's mid-afternoon and the coffee shop is packed with students grabbing caffeine to get through the rest of the day. Nadia and I managed to snag a small table in the corner. I'd brought her with me for support, but I'm pretty sure I'm going to bail.

"It's too soon."

"No," she says, taking a sip of her mocha, "it's the perfect time. It's why there are all those sayings like, 'If you fall off a horse get back on,' or my personal favorite, 'the best way to get over someone is to get under someone new.'"

"I want to ask Logan to the fundraiser," I say, wiping the condensation off the side of my ice coffee, "not get under him."

"Not yet." She winks.

This is the fundamental difference between me and Nadia. She's already moved on from the situation with CJ, like it never happened. In fact, when I got home last night from practice, she was already at a party with some guy from the baseball team.

"I'm just not sure it's a good idea." Across the café, Logan steps in, hair disheveled and cheeks red from the wind. He looks around, eyes brightening when he sees me. He waves, gesturing that he's going to get in line. I nod back. "Reese and I are definitely over, but I'm not sure I'm ready to get involved with anyone else."

"You're inviting him to a school-sanctioned event. It's not a commitment of any kind. You need a date and he's a nice guy who will look hot in a suit and make you look good to your boss. He checks all the boxes." She stands, grabbing her coffee. "Don't let your breakup with Reese send you into another two-year hibernation."

She's right. I agreed to fake date Reese in the first place so I could actually have a social life and get the courage to meet guys and go on dates. The last thing I want is to go back to being invisible. If one thing can come from this disaster, it would be for me to use the skills he taught me.

"Go get him," she says, slipping out the back door.

Thankfully, before I can talk myself into following her, Logan walks up. "Hey," he says, pulling out the chair. He shrugs out of a charcoal gray coat and hangs it on the back. "Sorry I was late, some guy in my Econ class wouldn't stop asking questions."

"Let me guess, second career?"

"Yes!" He shakes his head. "How did you know?"

"It's just something I've noticed." I watch Logan dump a packet of sugar into his coffee. "Older students—the ones that are paying for their own classes–definitely seem to want to get their money's worth."

"Same. I get it, but sometimes I just want to leave class early," he grins, "and hang out with this cool chick I know."

"Well," I say, hoping my cheeks aren't too red, "Nadia and I needed to go over some stuff for our history of rock class anyway."

"Oh, you got in that class?" He settles back in his chair. "I've heard it's really interesting."

"I've enjoyed it, but so far no New Kings." I smile. "Guess they're too contemporary."

"Have you ever heard their cover of Elvis' Suspicious Minds?" he asks. "It's epic."

"Oh my god, yes, it's so good."

Logan is easy to talk to—at least about our favorite band. It's not a hardship. I can fangirl about them for hours. I feel the tension of the week loosening as we discuss our favorite songs and the playlists for the concert. "I still can't believe I didn't get tickets."

His cup hovers in front of his mouth. "Have you tried the resellers?"

"Yeah, way out of my price range."

"I wish we'd known one another when they went on sale. I totally would've bought you one." He sets his cup back on the table. "And to be honest, I'd definitely rather go with you than my roommate Trent."

His comment is easy enough–transparent enough that I finally blurt, "I have a confession."

"Oh yeah?" He leans forward, resting his elbows on the table. "What have you done, Twyler Perkins?"

"I may have invited you to coffee for ulterior motives."

"Now I'm definitely intrigued."

"That may just be my way of tricking you into thinking what I'm about to ask you is interesting." I take a deep breath. "I have this fundraising event—an athletic alumni thing—this weekend. I have to go as part of my internship, but I can bring a... guest. I wondered if you'd be interested in going."

Clutching his cup between his hands, he asks, "What about the hockey player? Is he going to be there?"

"Yes," I say, not sure I'm following. "All athletes involved in varsity sports are required to attend."

"He just made it pretty clear at the animal shelter that he was into you." Right, the marking his territory thing. "I like you, Twyler, and I'd really like to spend more time with you, but I don't want to have some six-foot-two hockey player on my ass."

Six-foot-four.

"Oh no," I say quickly. "That is not a thing. I promise. We're just friends. Not even that."

A small smile lifts his lips. "Yeah?"

"Yeah," I say, trying my hardest to feel it in my bones. To will it to be true. Logan is great. He's the right kind of guy for me. He's my type, not off-limits, and definitely not a distraction. "What do you think? Free food? Limited drinks? Weird old guys reliving their glory days?"

"Well, when you put it like that..." he says, tilting his head in consideration, "...sure, I'm in."

I grin, feeling a mix of pride for pulling it off and nerves, wondering if I'm doing the right thing. It's one thing to try to move on, it's a whole other to attempt to do it in front of the man you're trying to get over.

∼

The knock on the door comes just as I've pulled my dress over my head. My hair is done. Makeup, as Nadia calls it, on point. The lace-up back of my dress needs tying, but I leave it, rushing out of my room to open the door for Logan.

Except it's not. Logan, that is.

Reese stands on my front porch, looking like a fucking GQ model, in a dark gray suit and tie that match his eyes.

"What are you doing here?" I ask, completely rattled. Have I lost my mind? Did our wires get crossed? No. *Hell no*. He never asked me to go with him and even if he did, I wouldn't–couldn't have–said yes.

While my brain is having a seizure, his gaze sweeps down my body, taking in the red formal dress I'm wearing. The knot in the back of his jaw pulses and he swallows, so slow, that for a second, I think he may choke.

"Reese," I repeat, "what are you—" My eyes dart behind him. "Logan!"

Reese recovers and grins, turning to my date. "Hey, man, how are you?"

"I'm… good." Reese offers his fist, and although Logan looks at it warily, he bumps it, as though it would violate some bro code not to. Questioningly, he looks to me.

"I don't know what he's doing here," I say, quickly. "I promise."

"Me?" Reese asks innocently. "Oh, I'm just picking up my date." He peers over my head. "There she is."

Behind me, Nadia strolls out of her room in a skin-tight, black dress. The front plunges into a deep V-neck, revealing more cleavage than I could ever muster. She rests one hand against the doorjamb, while easing her foot into a five-inch heel. "Hey, Reese. Hey, Logan." She takes them in. "You guys look great."

"So do you," Reese says, giving her a wink.

Something in my brain breaks. "You're here for Nadia."

"Yep." Something mischievous twinkles in his eye. "I asked her to be my date for the fundraiser."

"You…" I take a deep breath. "Logan, can you excuse us for a minute?" I don't wait for him to respond, grabbing Reese's arm and dragging him inside. "Be right back." I grin apologetically at my date before shutting the door in his face.

"Okay, what the hell is going on?" I spin, hands on my hips, looking between them.

"I needed a date," he shrugs, "and Nadia needed to prove to CJ and Brent that she's okay. So, it seemed mutually beneficial."

Ah, another deal. "Nad, is that true?"

She looks at Reese and then back at me. "Pretty much. The last thing I want is for those two to think they ruined me." She grabs the bodice of her dress and lifts her tits up higher. "Fuck them."

I look at Reese and he's the picture of innocence. I've spent the week avoiding him–making sure that I was completely focused on practice and my work with the team. It'd been a challenge for sure, and more than once I'm pretty sure I caught him staring at me. But seeing him now, how he makes my chest close up–I know I made the right decision. I mean, I've barely even spoken to my date. Reese is too consuming.

"Whatever," I say, turning to head back to my room. "Let me get my shoes."

I grab them off the floor and when I come back out, Nadia's on the porch with Logan. Reese is still in the living room. "Hey," he says, pointing to my back. "You forgot the back."

"Shit," I mutter, reaching around and feeling the strings. "Let me get Nadia."

"I can do it."

The back of my dress is designed like a corset, with a crisscross of straps that ties down at my lower back. I start to tell him no, but I can't do it by myself.

"Sure, okay." I turn, exposing my back to him. He lifts my hair and drapes it over my shoulder. Goosebumps run down my arms.

"Jesus," he mutters, "this looks like witchcraft."

I laugh, happy for a break in the tension. "It's kind of like lacing a skate–just make sure it's tight."

"Hm," he hums, tackling the laces. "So, Logan, huh?"

"Like you, I needed a date." His touch is so gentle—precise—and a shiver builds in my spine thinking of the times those hands made me feel so good. "I figured why let all those confidence lessons go to waste."

Row by row, I feel Reese tighten the strings. I find my breath caught in my chest, terrified to move, until his fingers brush against my lower back tying the ribbon into a bow. "There. I think I got it."

"Thank you," I turn to face him and there's no mistaking the dark heat in Reese's eyes. I feel the same in the pit of my stomach. Is this what Romeo and Juliet felt like? Star-crossed lovers? Whatever it is, it hurts, and I'd do almost anything to take that pain away.

Almost.

"You guys coming?" Nadia calls.

Her voice breaks the spell, and I grab my purse and rush out the door.

We've got a party to attend.

~

THE FUNDRAISER IS HELD in the athletic complex, in a huge room just for events. It's located on the sixth floor and the wall-to-wall windows provide a fantastic view of campus, including the football stadium and hockey arena.

"Who knew this was up here," Logan says, taking in the room. There are long buffet tables filled with food, and several bars tucked into the corners. Massive screens hang on the walls, displaying images that showcase Wittmore's athletic teams through the ages.

"Yeah, the team had a promotional meeting up here before the season started and we were invited as part of the support staff," I explain. On that day, it had been photographers and journalists attending, but tonight the room is a gathering place for men and women of all ages. It's not hard to discern that many are former athletes; a lot of them possess the same confident aura as the guys on the team.

Logan and I drove here alone—thank goodness—giving me some much needed space from Reese. I'm still processing that he asked Nadia to be his date, and although his reasoning makes sense, I'm a little pissed.

Okay, I'm more than pissed. I feel betrayed.

I'd tried to explain to Logan how surprised I was to see Reese, but he waved it off. Apparently, the shocked expression on my face was enough to convince him that I had no idea what was going on.

"Holy shit." The curse is followed by a long whistle. "TG?"

I turn and spot Reid gawking at me. I fight the urge to fidget with the satin fabric of my dress. "Told you I wear dresses."

"Yeah, but you didn't tell me how hot you'd look." He punches Axel, who's whispering in the ear of the girl hanging on his other arm. "You see this?"

Axel pivots and his jaw drops. "Fuck, TG—"

"Nope." I hold up my hands, narrowing my eyes at them. "Don't be a creep. Either of you. I'm still the same girl you proclaimed was like one of your twelve-year-old brothers."

"I take it back. Every word," Reid chimes in, more amazed than inappropriate. "I've just never seen you in anything other than jeans and a hoodie. You clean up good, Perkins."

"Likewise," I admit. I take in Reid and Axel in their fitted suits. Outside of practice, I've never seen them wear anything other than jeans and T-shirts either—and for Axel, the shirt is always optional. Tonight, they both look impressive and mature.

Even Axel's shock of blond hair and the tattoo creeping out of his collar doesn't detract. I rest a hand on Logan's arm and introduce him. "This is Logan."

"Hey, man." Reid extends his hand for a handshake. They make small talk, which isn't as awkward as I thought since hockey isn't Logan's thing, but he keeps up. "Oh shit," Reid grumbles, "Coach is waving us over. Probably another lecture on not embarrassing him."

They head off and I turn to Logan. "Sorry about that. It's like working with a bunch of untrained puppies." I watch them gather around Coach Bryant. "All in all, they're pretty harmless."

Logan takes my hand. "For the record, I agree, you do look hot in that dress." He pushes a curl of hair behind my ear. "Stunning, actually."

The compliment makes my cheeks flush, but it also brings a warring conflict in my chest. Isn't Logan what I've wanted? Why I agreed to Reese's help in the first place? I hate the confused, weird way this whole thing makes me feel.

I conceal all of this from Logan by suggesting we grab some food before the guys wipe out the buffet. We load up our plates, and I purposefully avoid the tables at the back of the room. They're occupied with a myriad of athletes, accompanied by dates.

Brent is a central figure, with Shanna draped over his arm in a shiny, sparkling dress. They exude the air of a perfect couple. And when I spot Nadia and Reese seated with the rest of the hockey team, I get the same vibe. There's a certain kind of woman that is required to support a leader like Reese. I know she's not genuinely dating him, but her time chasing jerseys has finally paid off. Like Shanna, she knows exactly how to behave and act in this environment. She can be here for Reese and not have to split her attention between his goals and her own. That's what he deserves.

And exactly what I can't give him.

I lead Logan over to sit at a table with Coach Green and his wife, Janie. Jonathan's there with his boyfriend, Rich, and there are a few other trainers that work with the other teams. This is where I belong. Logan helps me scoot in my chair and I put on my best effort while we eat.

"Hey," I say to Logan after the plates are cleared, "I'm going to the restroom."

He stands with me. "I'll grab us another drink."

I smile. "Thanks."

I've just stepped out of the bathroom stall when Nadia walks in. We approach the sinks at the same time. I turn on the faucet, and she drops her purse on the granite countertop.

"You and Logan seem like you're having fun," she says, fishing out her lip gloss. "For a skinny guy he sure fills out a suit."

"He's a nice guy." Her eyes meet mine in the mirror and I blurt, "You and Reese look good together."

"Well, a sack of potatoes would look good next to him," she mutters, opening her mouth into a circle. "But you should've seen Brent's face when we walked in–" She stops abruptly, eyes widening. "Are you crying?"

"No," I lie, grabbing a tissue off the counter and dabbing my eyes. "Absolutely not."

"You are. You're crying." Panic fills her eyes. "Fuck no, that is not what's supposed to happen."

"I know he's not mine to claim. I just... God, Nadia. Reese? Really? Do you like him?"

"Twy." She drops her lip gloss and spins, grabbing me by the arms. "First of all, there is no reality where I'd go out with Reese Cain for real. He's your ex–and that is a hard no for me. He's also too fucking functional, and you know my type is hot and messy."

I chuckle, because it's true. One of the reasons it hit me so hard is that it took me by surprise.

"You do know the real reason he invited me, right?" she asks.

"Because you know how to make small talk, have killer tits, and will look perfect in the press photos next to the captain of the hockey team," I guess. At the end of the day, Nadia is everything that I'm not. Confident, sexy, beautiful...

"Um, no." She rolls her eyes. "He invited me because his coach said it was mandatory for the players to have a date and it would look bad if the captain didn't follow through. You weren't going to go with him and he sure as fuck didn't want to open the door for another girl to get the wrong idea." She squeezes my hand. "Babe, he's locked down. For *you*. And he wanted to make that absolutely clear by bringing the one person who understood that."

Her statement swirls in my head. He didn't bring another date because he's waiting for me? Even if it's true, I'm not sure it matters.

"It hurt seeing you with him," I admit.

"It hurt because you're still in love with him," she says gently.

"I may be, but nothing has changed. Nothing will change and we both need to get over it."

Me. So *I* can get over him.

She snorts.

"What?" I ask.

"Men like Reese don't get over stuff. They see an obstacle and figure out a way to bulldoze over it, or smash through it."

"He's more rational than that. He understands my decision. My job comes first—just like his does." She makes a face, like she doesn't believe me. But I'm not relenting. "I thought you supported me being here with Logan anyway."

"I do support you." She drops the lip gloss back in her bag and runs her hands through her hair, fluffing it. "But I also know that trusting other people, men in particular, to be there for you when you need it the most is something that's hard for you." She rests her hand on my arm. "I just think that if you gave him a chance, you may find out that you can trust Reese."

She walks out and I follow her, feeling unmoored by everything going on in my life. Maybe I can trust Reese, I think, reentering the main room, but the bigger question is, can I trust myself?

27

Reese

"Did she ask about me?" I ask Nadia, swaying to the beat of the music. I have to admit the girl is beautiful and fun. I can see why she's popular with the jocks. But she's not the woman I want to be holding right now.

No, the girl of my dreams is across the dance floor with another guy. His hand is wrapped around her back, and he's holding her close. She keeps smiling at him like he's said the most hilarious things. I've had a tight, rage-inducing feeling in my chest since Logan walked up to the teal house. I'm not acutely familiar with the sensation, but I know what it is: jealousy.

"She asked me if I liked you."

"Did she now." My eyebrow shoots up. "What did you say?"

"That you're not my type."

"Please," I give her a grin, "I'm everyone's type."

She laughs, and not in a flattering way. "Seriously though, how do you fit a helmet over that massive ego?"

"Ah, well, it's not a helmet. It's a specially designed 'ego containment unit.' Comes with extra reinforced padding." I spin her around. "League approved."

"You're ridiculous," she says, rolling her eyes. "No wonder Twyler likes you."

"*Liked*," I say, emphasizing the word. "Throw me a bone; you know her better than anyone, how do I win her back?"

She's silent for a moment, and I'm pretty sure she's not going to answer me. Fair. Twyler's said from the start that Nadia is fiercely loyal. Just when I decide to let it go and figure it out on my own, she says, "Losing men isn't new to Twyler. She's accustomed to having her heart broken. At this point it may feel more normal than having someone stick around."

"You mean Ethan."

"Partially." She glances across the hardwoods to Twyler and Logan. It's obvious they're both uncomfortable dancing, but they seem determined to try. "She was devastated when she lost her dad. They were super close, and he was her rock when she was struggling. She tried again with Ethan, putting her trust in the wrong person. When that went badly, I think she learned it's easier to either not try at all or to—"

"Run."

She chuckles. "That's my girl—she's fast, right?"

"Crazy fast for someone with such short legs."

"Yeah, well, I think she discovered it's easier to find an excuse to walk away first. At least that way she'll have control over her heartbreak."

"I don't know how to fix this," I admit. "And it's super fucking frustrating."

She gives me a sympathetic smile. "She needs to know you're not going anywhere." She directs us across the dance floor.

"Come on, let's go cut in. If that skinny kid's going to be her new boyfriend, I need to get to know him better."

"Over my dead body," I mutter.

She smirks. "That's the attitude."

We weave our way across the dance floor and as the song changes, Nadia releases me, walks up to Logan, and taps him on the shoulder. "Come on," she says. "I'm here to prove I don't give a shit that my booty call is here with another girl."

Logan isn't a fool. He sees me standing there, waiting for my chance. He looks at Twyler who gives him an apologetic, but resigned look. Before he can argue, Nadia grabs his hand and whisks him off.

"Dance with me?" I ask, holding out my hand.

"I'm not sure it's a good idea," her eyes dart around, searching to see if anyone is watching. I don't give a fuck who's watching, and wrap my arm around her body, pulling her to me.

Fuck, yes. Finally. This feels right.

"You're oddly good at this," she says, her limbs stiff as I maneuver us around the floor.

"When I was in middle school, my dad became obsessed with the skill and grace of figure skaters. Hockey players are known for their brawn, and twelve-year-old boys in particular are fighting against hormones and uneven growth spurts. He signed the whole team up for classes at a local dance studio hoping to build a little finesse."

"I don't know if it worked on the ice, but you definitely have surprising moves on the dance floor." She's still tense, eyes peeled like she's waiting to get busted by Coach Green. I can sense she's waiting for the right moment to make a break for it. "Reese, I really—"

I let her talk the other day when she ended it. Now it's my turn and I cut her off.

"I want to make something clear," I say, tightening my grip

on her hand. "I invited Nadia with me tonight for the reasons I said before, but also because if you wouldn't come with me, I wasn't going to ask anyone else."

"You should do what I'm doing, move on."

"Impossible, Sunshine." I flatten my palm over the crisscross of straps on her lower back. "I need you to understand that I'm not finished with you. *We're* not finished with one another, and when you're ready to sit down and come up with a way to deal with the obstacles in front of us, I'm ready."

"You're wrong," she says with a tremor in her voice, although her jaw is tight with determination. "There is no solution other than for us to go our separate ways. I need you to accept that."

My fingers lift to her chin, then slowly stroke down the column of her neck. "We are abso-fucking-lutely not over," I declare, meaning it one hundred percent, "and the sooner you meet me in the middle, the better."

The song ends, and I release her before I do something incredibly stupid like kiss her in front of her date and boss and everyone else in the room. That urge to claim her is stronger than ever, but I won't force her. All I can do is let her know my intentions.

If Nadia's right, I need to show Twyler that I won't be another man that abandons her; emotionally or physically. So even though it kills me, and goes against every fiber in my being, I allow her be the one to walk away.

※

It's a beautiful late fall day. The kind where the sun shines through the yellow and red leaves, giving everything a colorful glow. Perfect for sitting outdoors with friends or doing homework before the cold weather pushes everyone indoors for the next six months.

I find Logan lounging on the amphitheater steps, engrossed in a paperback.

"Hey, man." I drop next to him, taking my backpack off and setting it at my feet "Good book?"

"Hey." He squints up at me, eyebrows furrowed, then down at the book. "I guess. Required reading for my lit class."

I was already aware of that, and where to find him, thanks to one of the guys on the team.

"Listen, I'm not going to bullshit you," I say, getting straight to the point. I've already wasted enough time. "I'm not giving up on Twyler."

"Yeah, I gathered that the other night." He closes the book. "I guess the big question is how does she feel about it?"

"I've made it clear how I feel." I shift my gaze across campus, observing all the people milling around between classes. "And I'm willing to wait for her, even if that means she wants to date other guys for a while."

He sighs, running his hand through his hair. "Well, if it's any consolation, I don't think I'm going to be one of those guys."

I turn to him. "What? What happened? You two looked like you were having a good time at the fundraiser." I narrow my eyes at him. "Did you fuck it up?"

"It was fun. More than I thought I'd have with a bunch of jocks." He grins sheepishly. "No offense."

"None taken." I press on. "So what happened?"

"Nothing exactly, but I could tell she was preoccupied all night. I'm pretty sure you're the reason behind that."

I grimace. "Shit. That's not what I want."

"You just said you want her."

"I don't want her distracted by me—that's the whole reason she won't go out with me in the first place." He chuckles at me. I narrow my eyes and demand, "What?"

"That sounds like a load of crap."

"What do you mean?" This guy. I bench press his body weight and he's sitting here laughing at my pain. "She specifically broke up with me because our relationship was distracting her from her job."

"Dude," he says, standing up, "I'm sure you've dated way more girls than I have. But what she told you is nonsense. She didn't break up with you because she's distracted. She broke up with you because she's scared."

"Shit," I mutter. "That's exactly what Nadia told me."

He slings his backpack over his shoulder. "Well, good luck, man. She's a great girl. I just want her to be happy and if you make her happy, I hope it works out."

With my mind reeling, he walks away. "Hey," I call, jumping up and following him. "You mean that about making Twyler happy?"

"Absolutely."

I grin and clap him on the back. "Then I think there's something you can help me with."

∽

"Want me to add five more?" Jeff asks.

"What?" I ask, dragging my eyes from the door. I see he has two five-pound weights in each hand, waiting to add them to the bar. "Oh, yeah, do it."

We've been in the weight room for thirty minutes, but there's no sign of Twyler. Coach Green is here and has been working with one of the rookies on the mat. It's possible she's in the back, but I resist the urge to go find her in the supply closet.

She and I have been orbiting each other since the fundraiser, both existing in the same space, but never colliding. I want to prove to her that I'm okay with her attention being on her job, the same way I'm focused on mine. Our first regular season game is this weekend and all I want is to cap off my senior year with a trip to the Frozen Four. That starts on Saturday.

But even with my focus on the game, she's never far from the forefront of my mind. Especially today. I have something to ask her.

"Jonathan," Coach Green calls out, and the equipment manager emerges from the locker room. "Can you grab me a bandage from the supply closet? They're in the red drawer. Perkins marked everything."

That blows that theory.

Maybe she had something for class. Or she's sick?

"Dude!" Jefferson taps on the bar with this fist. My eyes draw up to my friend's annoyed expression. "Are you lifting or staring into space all day?"

"I'm lifting," I grumble, gripping the bar and lifting it over my head.

The next day I'm even more determined to see her. I show up early for morning skate, iced coffee in hand. The coffee shop doesn't open until later, so I made a pot before bed and let it cool overnight. A literal ice breaker.

Using my keycard to get in, the building is quiet, but I know she likes to arrive before the team. Music comes from the training room and my heart thuds. I know that once we finally talk—once I make my gesture, this will be it. I reach around the door and knock.

"Morning, Sunsh—"

I stop short, the ice sloshing in the cup, when I see a guy sitting at the desk going through player files.

"You're not Twyler."

"I'm not." He gives me a friendly smile.

"Who are you?" I take in his WU collared shirt and joggers.

"I'm Cameron," he offers his hand. "And you're Reese Cain,

captain of the team, senior and forward. It's an honor to be assigned to work with you and the team."

I don't shake his hand, mine are full, the cold drink sweating against my palm. "What do you mean 'assigned?'"

"Temporarily—for now at least." He shoves his hands in his pockets. "The person that had this internship told our advisor she needed some time off."

"Time off? For how long?"

He shrugs. "I really don't know. I'm a semester behind so I wasn't eligible for an internship when they were assigned last spring. When this opportunity came up, my advisor had me fill in."

I stop fully listening after his first sentence and turn back down the hall. I get out my phone and shoot off a message.

OneFive: Where are you? Everything okay?

There's no response before I get on the ice or after.

Quickly, I change and head off campus, over to the teal house. Banging on the door with my fist, I'm disappointed when it's Nadia that answers.

"Is Twy here?" I ask, peering around her.

"She's probably at the arena," Nadia replies, grabbing her backpack. Then her eyes widen. "Hold on, isn't today an early practice day?"

"Yeah, and she didn't show. Yesterday either." I look past her, for what? No clue. "Some substitute intern was there saying he was filling in for a while."

A deep line creases Nadia's forehead. "That doesn't make sense."

"It sure as hell doesn't. She's not responding to my texts either." Now I push past her, entering the house. Nothing looks out of place in the living room. I head to her bedroom. "Did she sleep here last night?"

"I don't know. I stayed out." She catches up to me and grabs my arm. "Reese, you can't just barge in there."

"She'll get over it," I say, eyes scanning the room. It looks just about the same as the last time I was here, but there's one noticeable thing laying over the back of her desk chair: my hoodie. "What's missing?"

She sighs and steps in and inspects the room. Opening the closet door, she points out, "Her duffle is usually on the floor."

"She left?" I ask.

"You can't jump to conclusions," she counters, but a hint of concern colors her expression. This isn't normal behavior for Twyler—skipping practice, bailing on her internship, packing a bag mid-week.

Something akin to fear builds in my chest. All the things she told me about spiraling after breaking up with Ethan. The depressive episodes in high school.

"Did you check her tracker?" She opens her phone. "Are you still connected?"

"Oh, genius!" Damn that tracker. It might actually be useful. My stomach sinks, however, when I realize the truth. "She turned it off or blocked me."

"Me too," she admits, "but not until yesterday afternoon." She holds up the phone, revealing Twyler's history. Her little dot blips an hour south, then vanishes.

"Where's that?"

"It's not where she's been," Nadia says, her fingers moving across the phone's screen. "It's where she's heading."

In an instant, everything clicks, and my decision is made.

I'm going to find her.

28

Twyler

It's been two days since I went into Coach Green's office with vague excuses about why I'd be absent for the rest of the week.

One day since I got in the car with a small bag of belongings and drove home, showing up on my mother's doorstep without any warning. It was dark and I'd hoped that the lack of daylight would hide the fact I'd been crying. My mother's no fool, but she also knows that pushing me will only send me on the retreat. Once I promised I wasn't hurt or having some kind of breakdown she gave me some space.

Mom didn't pretend to be happy to see me in the middle of a school week, but my cat Bertha hasn't left my side since I got home. It's as good an excuse as any to stay on the couch, curled up in my favorite blanket, watching a solid stream of true crime documentaries.

"I'm going to head to the store, do you need anything?"

"We could probably use some more chips," I say, looking at the empty bag on the coffee table.

My mom stands in the doorway, keys clutched in her hands. "One bag or two?"

There's an underlying question here that isn't about chips. She really wants to know how long I'm planning on staying. The truth is that I don't know. I can get away with keeping up with my classes online for a few days, but I have some big decisions to make and only a few days to make them.

Reese's declaration to me on the dance floor sent me on a spiral. I'd barely been able to keep it together for the rest of the ride home or when Logan kissed me on the front porch of the house.

Yeah, Logan kissed me and then asked if I wanted to go to the New Kings concert with him.

It wasn't until I said no to a chance to go see my favorite band with a really great guy, who happened to also be a pretty good kisser, that I realized everything in my life was upside down.

I needed space from Wittmore, my internship, but most of all, Reese.

My mom is gone no more than four minutes when my sister comes in the door. It's this thing they do when they're worried about me, communicating about me not being alone. They're worried I may fall back into old habits and do something harmful. I get the fear, but I hate the babying.

"Hey," Ruby says, grabbing the chip bag off the table and sitting on the other end of the couch. She looks into the empty bag. "Seriously? I work a nine-hour day with a group of kids I'm certain are spawned straight from the devil and you don't leave me a single chip."

"In my defense," I say, keeping my eyes on the TV, "I had no idea you were coming over."

She kicks off her shoes and draws them under her body. "Oh,

is this the one where four people were in the house together and one died and there's zero evidence who did it."

"Yep."

"Have you gotten to the part about the cache of sex toys?" she asks casually.

"No!" I press pause on the remote and whip my head toward her. "Don't be a spoiler."

"Sorry." She holds up her hands innocently. "I figured you'd already seen it."

I turn back on the show and do my best to ignore her, but she's restless, shifting around until I finally look over and snap, "Okay, what's going on? Why are you here?"

"Me?" She shrugs. "I just wanted to hang out with you while you're in town." She pushes her feet out, crossing the imaginary boundary line on the couch. Her toes brush against Bertha, who stretches lazily and gives her a side eye. Thank you, Bertha. "So, how long are you going to be in town?"

Again, I pause the show. "Mom made you ask me that, didn't she?"

"She didn't make me. I'm wondering. She's wondering." She pins me with a look. "Fine, tip-toeing around it isn't working. What the hell are you doing home in the middle of a school week?"

"I needed a break to figure some things out." I scowl at her. "Everything's under control."

"Mmhm," she hums. "And is that why you didn't tell Nadia you were leaving?"

"You talked to Nadia?" Well, that rankles me even more. "Did you call her?"

"No," she says matter-of-factly. "She called me. Worried, by the way. She said you just took off, left your classes and your internship. No one knew where you were!"

Bertha startles at her loud voice and I run a hand down

Bertha's head to settle her. "I emailed my teachers and had a meeting with Coach Green. He knew I needed a few days off."

"Isn't the first game of the season this weekend?"

"My advisor found someone to cover for me." I press play on the TV, but she reaches out and snatches the remote out of my hands then turns it completely off. "Hey!"

"Twyler, what's really going on?" She sighs. "You can tell me or Mom, but she's going to find out."

"Somehow I've fucked everything up."

"That sounds a little melodramatic."

"Oh yeah?" I launch into everything–all of it. What really was going on with Reese. The warning from Coach Green. How I was so distracted Pete got seriously hurt from my negligence. The fundraiser and Nadia and Logan. When I finish, she stares at me unblinking, so I go ahead and add, "There's something else."

"Okay," she says warily.

"Logan invited me to the New Kings concert, and I said no." Her mouth opens, but no words come out. "Say something," I tell her, pulling at the fringe on the edge of the blanket.

"I'm just processing." She rubs her eyes. "Reese Cain told you that he loved you."

"Yes."

"And another guy, one that you like, asked you to go see your favorite band and you said no."

"Right."

"So you have basically rejected two perfectly acceptable guys, one that has declared his love for you, for no reason."

"I mean… basically, but it's more complicated than that."

"I don't think it is." She tilts her head. "Do you love Reese?"

My heart pounds just at the question and my stomach hurts because I miss him so much. "You know my instincts on relationships aren't great. I thought I loved Ethan, too. What if this is just another way for me to sabotage my life? Because there is nothing wrong with Logan. He's great, but of course I want the guy that makes me choose between a man and my job."

Ruby opens her mouth to speak, but I cut her off.

"Being a trainer is everything to me, Ruby, you know that. It's the thing that got me through high school and Dad dying and all the stuff with Ethan. I'm good at it. It's reliable. Guys come and go—but this job is my future, and I can't risk losing it."

"Oh, Twy." She scooches across the couch and pulls me into a hug. Normally, I'd fight it, but I'm too worn out. I just want this achy-hollow feeling in my chest to go away. "Jesus, you're a hot mess."

I could get mad, but a laugh slips out instead. That's followed by a rush of tears that I've been holding onto for days. For once my sister doesn't judge me, she just lets me get it all out.

"Better?" she asks when I finally pull away.

"Not really," I admit, sniffling.

She leans back and grabs a wad of tissues out of the box on the end table. She hands me some and keeps the rest. "I know you hate all the woo-woo shit Mom and I are into, but I heard something that really resonated with me the other day."

"Yeah, I probably need some woo-woo shit right now." I blow my nose. "Hit me."

"When you go through trauma, there's this little sliver of strength that helps you get through. That strength, that grit, it's waiting, lurking in the shadows, ready to support you whenever you need it. But to truly move on you have to let that piece go. Which is terrifying because you've come to rely on it. But the truth is you don't need it anymore. You've built all these other resources—these strengths and new relationships—and from now those new things will get you through the hard times."

"Are you telling me to quit sports training? Because I can't do that—I'm about to graduate with a degree. It's my job and—"

"I'm not telling you to quit training." She sighs. "I'm telling you that this program isn't the only thing propping you up anymore. It's part of who you are, but not everything. You love it, but I think you love Reese, too, and it's okay to let your guard down. It's also okay if that means you admit you're crazy about a six-foot-four, sexy as hell captain of the hockey team and find a way to have both in your life."

"I admit it." Warmth burns my cheeks. "I am pretty crazy about him."

She smiles. "Then you have to stop running away and figure out how to make this work."

∼

Mom returns after the heart-to-heart is over, probably having been given an "all clear" text by Ruby. Her arms are loaded with bags of groceries and we both get off the couch to go help her in the kitchen.

"If you'll put these up," she says, taking a pan out of the cabinet, "I'll get started on making that Mexican casserole you love."

"Oh!" Ruby's face lights up. "Did you get queso?"

"Yep. With and without jalapenos."

"Thanks, Mama," I say, leaning into her and giving her a squeeze.

"Any time." She rests her temple against mine. I know she has a million questions, and maybe I'll go into all of this with her at some point, but I appreciate her restraint.

I'm putting the groceries in the refrigerator when the doorbell rings.

"I'll get it," Ruby says.

"Make sure it's not a sales guy," Mom calls after her. "Those solar panel people are relentless."

Shutting the refrigerator, I say, "To answer your earlier question, I think I'm going to head back to school in the morning."

Mom's eyebrow raises. "Oh yeah?"

"Yeah, but thanks for letting me come home and figure things out."

She throws her arm around me and squeezes me. "Any time."

"Twy!" Ruby shouts, her voice carrying from the front door.

"Oh my god," I grumble, stepping out of the kitchen, "if you think I'm going to argue with the Jehovah's Witnesses again—"

I stop short. He takes up so much room in the doorway that she doesn't even have to move for me to see him. "It's for you."

My heart lurches and I look from my sister, who looks utterly shocked, to Reese. His eyes are pinned on me, assessing me in that way that makes me sweat. Neither of us say anything and my sister is not one to miss an opportunity to run her mouth.

"Hi," Ruby says, thrusting out her hand. "I'm Ruby. Twyler's sister."

"Nice to meet you, Ruby." He shakes her hand, but never takes his gaze off me. "I'm Reese."

"Yes," she says. "I'm familiar with your work."

He drags his eyes away from me to her. "My work?"

"On the ice," she says quickly. "Big fan. Would you like to come in?"

I snap out of it and blurt, "No!"

Reese's expression falls, and Ruby hisses, "Twy!"

"No," I say again, swallowing. "I'll come outside."

Pushing past my sister, I walk past Reese and out the front door. He follows me and I shoot my sister a look, telling her to shut the door to give us some privacy.

Once it's closed, I turn to him. "What are you doing here?"

Then I look at my watch. "You have practice. And a game tomorrow night!"

"I don't give a shit about either of those things." He reaches for me, and when his hand cups my face, and those gray eyes hold mine, my insides melt. "Just tell me you're okay."

"I'm okay." Better now that he's here. "But you shouldn't be here. The first game—"

"Doesn't matter." His hand skims down my arm and his fingers twine with mine. "Not more than you do. When you didn't show up to practice, I was worried, and then when I found out there was a substitute trainer assigned, well, that's when I panicked. You scared the shit out of me, Twy."

"I'm sorry."

"I was terrified you would do something dangerous—like when you and Ethan broke up. The last thing I wanted was to be another guy that hurt you."

This man. God, how could I walk away from him? "I'm not in that place anymore—partially because of you. I just needed some space to clear my head and I couldn't do that at Wittmore."

"And I should have understood that better," he admits. "You made a decision, and I should have respected that." He grins sheepishly. "I'm not very good at losing." Perseverance is what got him in the position of captain in the first place and high on the list of players for the draft. It's no surprise Reese is the same off the ice. "I never should have asked Nadia to come with me."

"I didn't like seeing you with her, *at all*, although I understand your motivation. She needed a win, and if you'd shown up with anyone else—a puck bunny for god's sake—I probably would have burned down the building."

His lip quirks. "Has anyone told you that you're hot when you're jealous?"

I groan and step closer, pressing my forehead against his

chest. "You're a good guy, Reese Cain. Sweet and loyal. Protective, even when I don't deserve it."

"I'm never going to stop protecting you." His fingers slide under my chin, lifting it until I'm looking at him. "I love you."

"I love you, too."

When his eyes dart to my mouth, all I want is to kiss him. And when he tilts his head and covers my mouth with his, I know for certain that I want everything with Reese—all the time—and I think I may finally realize what I need to do to make that happen.

29

Reese

All my life I've been surrounded by men. After my mom left it was just me and my dad. Outside of that, it was just my teammates, first in high school, then later in college when I moved into the dorm.

Sitting at a table with the three Perkins' women is culture shock.

First of all, the food is fantastic.

"Go ahead," Twyler's mom says, "finish it off."

"Are you sure?" I've already had three helpings of the casserole Alyssa, Twyler's mom, made for dinner.

"Yes," Ruby says from her seat next to mine. "We're awful at leftovers. They'll sit in the back of the refrigerator until they spoil."

"If that's the case," I reach for the spoon, "I'll take it off your hands." I wink at Alyssa. "I'd hate for any of this delicious meal to go to waste."

"Oh my god," Twyler mutters. "You can't turn it off, can you?"

"Thank you, Reese. I'll send the recipe back with you two," Twyler's mom says, rising from the table. "It's easy."

I grin and shovel the food in my mouth. Jesus, it's good, and I didn't realize until now how much I want to spend time with Twyler doing mundane tasks like cooking.

When the pan is scraped clean, Twy and I offer to do the dishes. Ruby and Alyssa vanish, making little effort to pretend they're not giving us space to be alone.

"I like them," I say, taking a plate from her and loading it into the dishwasher. "I wish I'd had a chance to meet your dad."

"He wouldn't have known what to do with you. He wasn't into sports at all. He loved music and art." She smiles at me. "But he would have liked you."

"You think so?"

She shrugs. "He just wanted us to be happy—and you make me happy."

I snake my arm around her waist, pulling her close. These past few days of being apart sucked. "You sure about that?"

"Absolutely."

Coming here was a risk. To my position on the team and as captain. I told Bryant that I had some family business to take care of and I'd be back as soon as possible. He wasn't happy about it, but it's the first practice I've missed in three years, including the time I had the flu. But Twyler is more important than anything—that's what was missing in my relationship with Shanna. We could have gone on and been a hot professional athlete couple that looked good in the tabloids and elevated my profile, but that's not what I want. I want a partner. Someone I love to be by my side. A best friend.

With Twyler, I get all of that and more.

After feeding me, Alyssa graciously invites me to stay the night, putting me up on the sleeper sofa in her office. I hadn't planned anything past showing up at Twyler's house and begging her to take me back. I should be exhausted after the long drive from Wittmore, but as I stare up at the ceiling, I'm too amped up to even think about sleep, knowing my girl is two doors down.

Once the house settles, I get up and cautiously enter the hallway. The dim light casts a shadow and when a figure steps out of the dark, I nearly jump out of my skin.

"Need something, number fifteen?"

"Jesus Christ." I swallow my heart and try to regain my composure. "Ruby. Fucking hell. You trying to kill me?"

Her eyes flick down to my team hoodie. "Just checking to see who was creeping around out here."

"I was just..." my heartbeat pounds in my ears so hard that I can't think of a good lie, so I let my sentence fade off. Her smug grin is enough to tell me she knows exactly what I needed. I narrow my eyes and ask, "Do you even live here?"

"Sometimes." Her nonchalance is followed by a shrug. "My baby sister is really special, you know that, right?"

"I do." Fuck yeah, I really do. Not only is she unique and special. She's *mine*.

"And she's been hurt a lot."

"I know." Twyler's past is a part of her that I've come to understand, a history that makes me all the more determined to shield her from harm. "My intentions are solid."

"If I find out that you do anything to cause her pain," she steps closer. "I will hunt you down and destroy you." Ruby's warning hits like a punch. Her intensity is both intimidating and strangely comforting, a fierce protector of her sister.

"I don't want to hurt her." I say it clearly, wanting her to hear the conviction in my voice. "I love her."

She smiles. "Good. She deserves love. So much of it."

"I agree." My eyes shift back to the room I came out of, a silent indication that I plan on returning. "I'll just head back to bed."

"Eh, go," she says, body shifting from obstacle to understanding. "I may be a hard ass, but I'm not a cockblocker."

I laugh nervously. "You Perkins girls are crazy, you know that?"

"It's the only way we know how to survive." She squeezes my bicep and shakes her head. "Damn, your body is ridiculous. You hiding an older brother somewhere? A cousin?"

I shake my head and with a muttered curse, she enters her room and closes the door behind her. Feeling awkward about getting caught out here, I consider going back to bed, but then say fuck it. It's been too long since I've been in a bed with my girl.

Quietly, I turn the knob to Twyler's room, and step inside. She's curled on her side, her cat curled up next to her.

"Is that cat going to attack me?" I ask, placing my phone on the bedside table.

"With purrs and love," she says, nudging Bertha away. I crawl in next to her and wrap my body around hers.

She sighs, wiggling her ass into my crotch. "That took you longer to get in here than I expected."

"I got ambushed in the hallway." I lift her hair and kiss the back of her neck.

She turns, eyes wide. "My mom?"

"Your sister." I take advantage of her facing me and lick her lips, pushing my tongue into her mouth. My dick tightens, pushing at the cotton of my shorts. I grind it against her thigh. "She's fucking terrifying."

"She's definitely protective." She kisses me back, hips turning to meet mine. The movement makes me harder, and damn, I'm so fucking gone for this girl. "Did you have to sweet talk your way in here?"

"I just agreed to her terms." Pushing my hands under her shirt, I squeeze her tits. "God, I missed you so fucking much." Her nipples tighten into sharp points. "I think your tits missed me as much as I missed them." Impatiently, I yank the shirt over her head and suck a nipple into my mouth. Twyler moans, back arching, and I flatten a palm over her inner thigh, spreading her wide. I rub circles into her flesh, moving higher with each pass, until I brush across her clit.

"Wet for me already, Sunshine?" Tugging her panties aside, I feel the slick, wet heat of her pussy. "Fuck yes, you are."

I push a finger inside.

"I want you in me," she says, hips rising and falling. "Please, Reese."

Her hands grapple with my shorts, and I grab the neck of my hoodie, pulling it over my head and tossing it on the floor. My cock springs between us, already leaking. I want in her so bad that I'm afraid I may come the second I'm in her—but who cares? I've got a lifetime to make love to this woman.

"Condom?" I ask between kisses. "Because I don't have one."

Her hands still on my chest and her nose wrinkles. "Sorry."

"That's okay." I start to kiss down her belly. "More time for me to lick your pussy."

She laughs when I nip her side, squirming from being ticklish. She grabs my face and forces me to look at her. "I'm on the pill."

I raise an eyebrow. "Yeah?" Her hand drops and circles around my cock, giving it a long stroke. My jaw tenses, trying not to rock into her grip. "You're sure?"

"I'm sure." She guides me between her legs, nudging me at

her entrance. I push inside at the same time I smother her mouth, capturing our groans with a kiss. The tight heat of her pussy grips me, and the sensation is amplified by being skin to skin. The friction increases when her legs wrap around my body and her hips tilt upward.

"Jesus, Sunshine." I flex back into her, driving in deep. Palming her breast, I bring my mouth to her nipple and suck. Her nails dig into my back, the pain better than anything I've ever felt before. That is, until the orgasm runs through her, and her whole body clenches around me. It's enough to tip me over, her pussy milking my cock until I come with a final hard thrust.

I hover over her, forearms flat by her head, and look at her. "You're so fucking beautiful."

She twists her head and playfully bites my bicep. "You're pretty fucking hot too."

I kiss her again, just because I can, and take my time rolling off. She makes a motion with her hands. "Give me back my hoodie, Cain."

"You're the one that left it back at Wittmore." I pick the sweatshirt up off the floor. As much as I hate covering her body, I lower it over her head. When her head emerges from the neck hole, I kiss her mouth and say, "You look good in my name and number."

I fall back and drag her into my side. Her hand splays on my stomach, fingers toying with the fine hair on my lower belly.

Looking up at me, she asks, "What were you going to do if I turned you away when you showed up at the front door?"

"I had a plan B."

"Oh yeah?"

"Hand me my phone." I nod to the bedside table.

"You brought a phone, but not a condom?"

"I was trying not to be presumptuous."

She rolls her eyes and I kiss her again. I can't get enough of her.

She presses a hand on my chest, stopping me before I get started again. "Plan B?"

"Oh right." I slide my thumb over the screen and pull up the app. "Plan B was for me to give you these."

She sits up with a screech, then slams her hand over her mouth. We both sit silently, waiting for her mom or sister to appear. When neither do, she whispers, "How? When?" she sputters. "*How?* Where did you get these?"

"Funny thing..." I scratch the back of my neck. "Logan helped me."

"Oh my god. You didn't beat him up and steal his tickets, did you?" She tilts the screen in my direction, showing me the tickets I'd bought two days ago.

"No, but he did help me find them." I run a finger down her neck. "He's a good guy."

"How?" she asks gazing at the screen, then adds, "Doesn't matter. Are you coming with me?"

"I sure as fuck hope so."

Her grin is as bright as the stars, and I know one thing, there is nothing I want more than for her to look at me like this forever.

∿

Twenty-four hours later I'm back in the Wittmore locker room amidst the pre-game fervor along with my teammates. Axel is in charge of the music, playing curated playlists just for games. Reid is rummaging through his belongings, convinced he's forgotten something and then finding it two seconds later.

Pete's here–still unable to play, but planning to sit on the bench for support.

Jeff suits up at the locker next to mine, yanking his hockey pants over his pads. "How pissed was Coach at you when you got back?"

"Mad enough to sentence me to bag skates before practice every day next week." I adjust my jersey. "But not enough to strip me of my captaincy or bench me today."

"That sucks about the suicides, but I'm fucking glad you'll be on the ice with us today." He bumps his fist against my shoulder. "We need you out there."

Just thinking about the hell Coach Bryant's going to put me though makes my stomach churn, but I remind myself of the bigger picture. Getting Twyler back was worth whatever punishment is coming my way. Zero fucking regrets.

Down the row, curiosity gets the best of Reid, who can't stay out of everyone's business. Or at least my business, that's for sure. "So, what's the verdict? You two finally going public?"

"She asked her advisor to go with her to talk to Coach Green. She wants to make sure she talks to him before he finds out from someone else."

"That's fair," he says, pulling up his socks. "Getting ahead of it makes sense."

"But," I add, feeling that warmth spread across my chest that's specific to Twyler, "one way or the other, we've agreed that we're not hiding our relationship anymore."

We finish getting dressed and Axel cuts the music when Coach comes in with a few last-minute words of wisdom about kicking ass and not embarrassing him in front of a home crowd. I'm overly aware that Cameron's here filling in for Twyler. Coach Green gives zero indication of what went down when he spoke with Twyler.

"Reese," Coach Bryant says, nodding at me. Guess I'm up.

"Circle up, men." I gesture for them to join me and the team huddles in a circle. As per tradition, our fists meet in the middle. "This is going to be our season," I tell them. "I can feel it. We're ready and I know that when we hit the ice, we're going to go out there like we're already champions."

There's a chorus of "Hell, yeah's!" "Wittmore!" And one "Fuck'n crush 'em!" from a pumped up Axel. Starting at three, I count us down, and as a team we shout, "Badgers!"

I push everything out of my mind as I go down the tunnel, reminding myself of my goals: winning this game, then the conference, then the whole fucking thing. From there, I'll tackle the NHL. That's my focus as the cold air hits my face and I glide onto the ice, twirling my stick in my hand. Tuning out the crowd, I ignore them and the other team across the ice, and take a hard hitting warmup shot at the goal.

"Dude," Axel groans when the puck gets past him, sliding into the back of the net. "I want to tell you to fuck off, but keep that up during the game. Change nothing."

I skate past him, bumping my gloved fist to his, and retrieve the puck. I pass it to Kirby and hear, "Let's do it, one-five!"

Eyes darting upward, I see her. Twyler's up in the stands, bundled up in a dark coat with a knit Wittmore hat on her head, sitting next to Nadia. Everything else becomes secondary as I skate over.

"Nice shot," she grins, meeting me down at the wall that separates the ice from the stands.

"How did your meeting go?" I ask, resting my stick and hands on the top of the barricade. "Coach Green hasn't let on."

"It went pretty well. I was nervous, but Professor Purvi was amazing, so that helped." She tucks a piece of hair under that adorable hat. "After discussing it, I've decided to switch internships. Basketball is about to start, and Cameron is ready to take over the reins full time."

"What? You're leaving the team?" This wasn't the plan. She was going to go in and explain there are no rules prohibiting an intern and player dating. The goal was to get everything cleared up, not leave the team.

"I'm not willing to go half-in on this," she says, and her fingers tug at the zipper of her jacket as she turns her back to me. Underneath, she reveals a Wittmore jersey, my name and number embroidered on it. "I want everyone to know I'm your biggest supporter."

I swallow. "Sunshine, seeing you in that jersey makes me want to do one thing: slowly peel it off."

A playful smile curves her lips. "Maybe later?"

"Definitely later." I raise an eyebrow. "Are you sure about this? Because I don't want you giving up your dream job for me. If there's any chance of resentment—"

Leaning over the barricade, she silences me with her mouth, effectively shutting me up with a very public, very territorial kiss. Cheers erupt from around us, led by a whoop from Nadia back up in the stands.

"I never wanted to work with the hockey team," she admits once we've broken apart. "Basketball has always been my favorite sport."

"Basketball?" I mutter, incredulous. "Are you serious right now?"

She rolls her eyes. "It's freaking freezing in here, Cain. I'm tired of thawing my hands and feet every time I leave work."

"You're sure about this?" I ask, taking her hand. "Like, absolutely sure."

She nods with determination. The thought of her cheering for me from the stands is pretty damn appealing.

"Cain!" Jeff's shout snaps my attention back. The referees are out on the ice and we've only got a few minutes before the game starts.

"Love you," I tell her, giving her one last kiss.

"Love you too," she says. "Good luck."

We part and I glide back onto the ice, heart racing and a newfound fire in my chest. As the arena roars around me, I know that the fact we worked through this means we can get through just about anything, both on and off the ice.

30

Twyler

MORNING PRACTICE with the basketball team isn't that different from hockey. Tall, muscular guys, ridiculous egos, ruthless competition. The bruises are different, and I haven't seen any broken noses, but the injuries are just as severe. I'm learning a lot from the head trainer about the nuances of the different sports.

The biggest perk is that I'm not a popsicle when it's over. The worst? That I don't get to see Reese while I'm at work. No secret make out sessions in the supply closet or flirty looks over the water bottles. But we've worked it out—grabbing time during the day when we can. Which is why I'm rushing to the coffee shop after morning practice to meet him before classes.

He's easy to spot hanging out in the to-go line, waiting for his order. He's a full head taller than the rest of the patrons. His dark hair hidden under a Badger hockey knitted cap, which only makes his cheekbones more prominent. Damn, my boyfriend is hot.

He's also not alone. Shanna stands across from him, looking gorgeous as always, a dark leather bag hanging over her shoulder that matches her boots. I slow down, unsure if I should interrupt. No, I'm not interrupting, but I'm sure as fuck going to eavesdrop.

"So you and the trainer," she says, hitching her bag over her shoulder. Her nails are pointed and painted a dark red. "I thought for sure it was bullshit just to make me jealous."

"Making you jealous was never the goal, but getting you to understand we weren't getting back together was."

Her eyes brighten and a wicked smirk curls on her upper lip. "So, it is fake. I knew it!"

"*Was*," he admits, "but not anymore. She's the best fucking thing that's ever happened to me." He shrugs. "So, I guess I should thank you for pushing me into that."

"You can't really think this relationship is going to be the best option for you moving forward." She steps closer, placing one of those well-manicured hands on his chest. "I can cut this thing with Brent at any time, and I'll be back in the stands wearing your jersey for the next game."

Circling his fingers around her wrist, he firmly removes it from his body.

"She's all I want, and it's not about what she can do for me. It's what we do for one another." She scoffs at that, and the look he gives her back is one of pity. "That's what you don't get, Shanna. I'm not a business or some kind of enterprise that needs a woman to make me look better. I want a partner that has her own life and her own passions. I want to stand by *her* while she does amazing things."

"Bertha!" The Barista's voice rings out. "George!"

My heart warms, not just from his declaration, but what he does when I'm not around, like handing out our codenames to the barista.

"That's me," he says. "And not that it's any of my business, but I do think you should ditch Reynolds. That guy isn't someone you want to bank on; he's going to be a PR nightmare."

He turns, leaving Shanna watching him walk away as he goes to pick up our coffee.

The expression on her face turns stormy and she turns with a huff. I take that as my cue to step back, hoping to stay out of her path, but no such luck.

"Well," she stops in front of me, "enjoy him. I put in the work getting him to where he is today. If I'd known what he was looking for," her eyes skim critically over me from ponytail to Reese's sweatshirt, down to my tennis shoes, "I wouldn't have wasted all that time."

I close my eyes and will my temper to stay calm, but then I think about Reese and how hard he worked to keep me. I have no doubt he would have done the same for Shanna if she'd been the right person for him. "Reese isn't a ticket to a lifestyle. None of these guys are. They're men who work relentlessly, pushing their bodies and minds to the next level looking for success. That success is never just about them. It's about their team, their family, their future. A man like Reese isn't looking for something pretty to hang on his arm. He's looking for someone ready to go through life with him as a partner. All of it, the ups and the downs, because trust me, there are going to be lot of both." I set my jaw. "Reese needs a woman that loves him. Not someone hitching a ride for their own benefit."

"You really believe that don't you? You really think that he wants to stand next to you—a pathetic little tomboy—when he gets the call?"

"I know it." I step closer. "And he's right about Brent. You're going to regret chasing after guys like that, because he's using you as much as you're using him and one day all of that is going to implode on you both."

Nadia still doesn't want to report what happened to her, but it's going to come out—one day—guys like Brent and CJ don't know when to stop. Shanna's going to find herself in the middle of a huge scandal.

"Are you telling me that because you want me to dump him so your best friend can swoop in?"

"I'm telling you the same thing I told her. You're both worth more than chasing jerseys."

An arm circles around my body, holding out a cup with the name "Bertha" written on the side. Warm lips press against my temple.

Shanna's eyes flick from my face to Reese and she scowls. "Fuck you both."

"Well, we tried," I say after she storms off.

"Yep." He spins me so that I'm facing him and fists the front of my—his—sweatshirt and pulls me to him. "Is it wrong how hard I get every time you show up wearing this? I like everyone knowing that you're mine."

I like it too. Secrets relationships are fun, but exhausting. This is so much better.

"I've got class, but then an hour break." He tilts his head. "You up for some tutoring?"

Room 110. With schedules as busy as ours it's good to have a place to sneak off to in the middle of the day.

"Are you giving or receiving?" I ask, as if I'm considering the idea. "And what exactly are we learning here?"

"Both." He leans over and adds, "I'm giving and you're receiving. Practice makes perfect, even when it comes to eating your pussy."

His grin tells me he's being like this on purpose, just to watch me squirm.

"Your mouth is so filthy."

"You love it."

Fuck yeah, I do.

I love him, too.

~

"That. Was. Epic."

My ears are ringing, and my skin is sticky with sweat from dancing all night. Reese looks down at me and grins, plucking a piece of confetti out of my hair.

"I admit it, they know how to put on a show."

"An amazing show," I gush, spinning around. "Like, the best one so far."

He takes my hand and leads me off the floor with the other fans now that the lights are back on, and the band has left the stage. Yes, we had floor tickets, and Reese humored me as I pushed us as close to the stage as possible. My chest still feels like it's vibrating from the bass and the roar of the crowd. "Just think, one day when you're playing for the NHL you'll have thousands of fans screaming for you like this."

"I only need one fan," he winks, "everything else is noise." We keep pushing forward until we're near the tunnel. His arm is wrapped around my body, protectively, and he looks down and asks, "What makes this one better than all the other concerts you've been to?"

I grab the front of his shirt, a black New Kings T-shirt I bought him at the merch shop. It's a size too small and fits his body like a sexy, fanboy, glove. Stopping him in the middle of the moving crowd, I say, "You being here with me."

"Yeah?" his head tilts, and he grins down at me. My heart

flutters against my ribcage. Being with Reese never gets old. He has this way of always making me feel special and it's important to me that I let him know that he's special to me too.

"Yep." I push up on my toes and kiss him. Ever since we went public, I've become a fan of PDA. Weird.

"Keep moving!" Security shouts, flashing a light in our direction. Reese laughs and holds onto me, making sure we're together as we navigate the crowd.

When we're outside the venue, I say, "You never told me how you ended up getting the tickets."

"I told you, Logan helped me."

"But how? They were completely sold out."

His forehead creases. "Logan showed me a resale forum for serious fans. It's not just first come, first served. You kind of have to plead your case."

I know about this site. I'm actually a member. It's a place for serious fans to keep the scalpers out, making sure tickets or limited merch gets to the right person.

"Let me see," I say.

"Nope." He leads me to the parking lot.

"Come on," I beg.

"Not a chance, babe." He drags my body against his side. "Let's just say I pled my case for being a dumbass and was convincing enough that someone took pity on me."

We make the long drive back to Wittmore and without asking, he heads back to the Manor. The guys are still up and playing video games.

"How was it?" Reid asks, barely looking away from the screen.

"A-mazing," I say, still feeling wired.

"Want some food?" Reese asks, ducking into the kitchen. "Go upstairs, I'll bring it up."

Safely in his room, I sit on the bed and get out my phone,

pulling up the forum. It's not hard to navigate; I've been a member for a long time, but since I've been so busy at school I haven't spent as much time in the community as I used to. Going to the buy/sell/trade section, I open it up and start scrolling. That's when a username catches my eye: OneFive.

I hesitate, looking at the poster of Reese on the wall. His smug, sexy face taunting me.

Nope. I'm totally reading it.

Hey NK Fans,

Confession, I'm new to this group and new to the New Kings fandom. A friend directed me to this forum and suggested I tell my story. I'm stepping into this group with a mix of excitement and vulnerability. Today, I'm here not just to share my story, but to bare a piece of my heart.

*A month ago, I met a girl. No, not **a** girl, **the** girl.*

Our journey began in an unconventional way, a meeting of two souls each seeking something distinct yet vital. I was in desperate need of an exit from a toxic relationship, while she was on a mission to rebuild her self-assurance—something I had in abundance. It was a fusion of contrasts, an unlikely partnership, and yet, it clicked in a way we both never saw coming.

But here's where life played its intricate game. Against every promise to myself, I fell for her. Harder than I could have ever imagined. Yet, in my state of blissed-out self-absorption, I made a grave mistake. I pushed her into a decision she wasn't prepared for, unintentionally scaring her away. That's on me. I admit it, I messed up. In a moment of shortsightedness, I let go of the most amazing girl I've ever known.

Look, I don't know if she'll take me back. I'm pretty fucking sure I don't deserve her. But at the very least I can try to give her the thing she wants most of all.

Let me make this crystal clear: these tickets aren't about me.

They're about her, the exceptional girl who deserves the world. She's a powerhouse of dedication, unwavering in her pursuits; a beacon of kindness that lights up every room she enters. Her passion is infectious, her work ethic unmatched. Even if our paths don't align again in the way I hope (though I'm determined to try), I can still give her this. A chance to witness the magic of New Kings live, to experience a night where the music resonates with her vibrant spirit.

So, fellow fans, this is my plea. Join me in this endeavor, in making a heartfelt gesture that could bridge the gap I foolishly created. Let's come together as a community that celebrates not just the music, but the connections it forges. Let's make sure that the best girl I know receives the gift she truly deserves.

Thank you for hearing me out,
OneFive

I read and re-read the post, then absorb the comments. Several people offered up tickets for Reese's heartfelt confession, including the ones he eventually purchased and gave to me.

A meeting of two souls each seeking something distinct yet vital.

Well, that's one way to describe kissing me in a coffee shop in front of his ex and talking me into a fake relationship.

The door swings open and Reese enters backwards, hands full with bags of chips and a box of cookies. "Axel ate all the pizza," he says, kicking the door shut with his foot. "But I broke into Jeff's stash since he's not home."

"Awesome. I'm starving," I reply, shoving my phone under the pillow. I reach for the cookies and he drops the bags on the bed.

"Don't get crumbs everywhere," he says, sitting next to me. He leans over, going for the chips, but slides his hand under the pillow, snatching my phone.

"Hey!"

"You're up to something," he swipes open my phone. "Texting Logan about the show? Nadia? Posting that video I know you took of me dancing?"

"No!" I grab for the phone but he holds it over his head. "Give it back!"

I jump up, stepping on the bag of chips. It pops under the pressure of my weight and chips explode everywhere.

His eyes widen at the mess. "I literally just said don't get crumbs everywhere."

"This is your fault." I use the distraction to dive for the phone again. "Never take a woman's phone."

He catches me and we fall back, landing in the chair he slept in our first night together. The already broken leg cracks under our weight and we land with a hard thump.

Tangled together, we stare at one another for a long beat, until we both burst into laughter. He sighs and hands me the phone. "Here. Just blur out my face if you post that video. I can't have the other team using it against me on the ice."

I take it from him and confess, "I was reading your post on the New King's page."

"Oh." His cheeks turn pink. "And?"

"It was sweet."

"Yeah?"

I kiss his chin. "No one's ever done anything like that for me."

"Yeah, well no one's ever changed her internship for me."

"But you did this first and I didn't even know it."

"You know what?" he asks, pushing my hair out of my eyes.

"What?"

"That's just the kind of thing people in love do for one another."

"I'm starting to understand that." I rest my hands on his chest. "Thank you."

"For the tickets?" he asks, tilting his head.

For the tickets, for coming to my mom's to get me, for helping Nadia, for teaching me how to let go of my past and embrace my confidence... well, for just being Reese Cain.

I press a kiss to his mouth. "For everything."

EPILOGUE

Six Months Later

"Promise me one thing," Reese says, voice rough with sleep. "Don't ever let me give Axel permission to plan a celebration party ever again."

Over the start of a pounding headache, I grunt, "Deal."

The party had been to celebrate Reese's contract with the Rangers. Axel, looking for any excuse, went all out. There were hundreds of people at the Manor the night before. Kegs, liquor, shots… I feel like I consumed them all.

But it had been fun—so much fun. The weight of waiting for an offer, the meetings with Reese's agent and the negotiations, they'd taken up a lot of time. Time that seems to be running out. It was nice to have a night together that was pure indulgence.

"You deserved it though. Highest signing bonus in the NHL." I'm so proud of him. Proud that he held out for the best deal and is weeks from getting his degree. The first thing he did was call his dad and ask him what color Charger he wanted.

With a speed unimaginable to my hungover body, he flips me on my back and moves over me. "You were too wasted last night to celebrate the way I wanted to—"

"*I* was too wasted? You're the one that sang karaoke with Reid for two hours—only Taylor Swift."

"You have your favorite music. I have mine." He smirks, then dips his head, capturing my mouth with his.

My phone buzzes on the nightstand. When I look over he says, "Don't answer that. Basketball season is over. No one needs you." His lips blaze down my throat. "No one, but me."

As happy as I am that Reese got the offer and everything is settled for him, I can't say the same. I have grad school applications submitted at half-a-dozen universities in the Northeast. I did already get accepted to the physical therapy program at Wittmore, so it's not like I won't go, but staying here is farther away from Reese than I'd like. The other decisions should come in soon—maybe this week—but the wait is fraying my nerves.

What if I don't get accepted to a school near him? His schedule is already going to be impossible, with the intensity of his rookie season and all the travel and away games.

We've already made a million compromises for one another. Can we survive more?

Reese doesn't want to think about it yet—he wants all the information before we even consider a decision. The school, the scholarship offers, the time and distance. Easy for him to say. He just got a million-dollar signing bonus.

My phone buzzes again, breaking me from my spiral. "It could be Nadia."

"Nadia can wait." His kisses move across my shoulder blade and his hand pushes under my T-shirt. What I feel the most is the hard press of his erection digging between my thighs. The thrill of knowing how much he wants me never gets old. "I'm not so sure I can."

Buzz.

"Let me just check. It could be Ruby or my mom."

He sighs, but releases me from his iron grip.

"It's Dr. Parvi," I say, reading the message. "She wants to see me."

"When?" he asks, dipping his fingers under my panties. A shiver runs up my spine, that feel good heat that comes with being with Reese following close behind.

"In an hour." I don't miss the way his eyebrow raises. "And I need carbs to soak up some of this alcohol."

"Sex then carbs." A dark grin curves his mouth. "And I'll give you a ride to Parvi's office."

Reese Cain is hard to say no to, but naked Reese Cain beckoning me with orgasms and carbs?

Absolutely impossible to deny.

~

AFTER BEING KNOCKED out of the Final Four in the semi-finals my work as a trainer intern at Wittmore U was finally complete. I still have a final presentation and a couple of exams, but it's hard to believe I'm so close to graduation.

"Good luck," Reese says, cupping his hand behind my neck and bringing me in for a kiss.

"Thanks. I'm sure it's just a progress check on my final presentation."

Entering the Arts & Sciences building, I head up to the fourth floor to Professor Parvi's office. I knock on the door and her voice calls out, "Come in."

My advisor sits behind her desk, but there's another person in the room. Coach Green.

"Twyler, take a seat," she says, smiling warmly. "Obviously, you know Coach Green."

"Of course," I say, easing into the chair across from her and next to Coach Green. I try not to show it, but I'm totally confused and a little nervous. My internship swap had been approved and signed off by everyone, but what happens if it messed up my requirements? I don't like the sweaty feeling popping up all over my body. "Is something wrong?"

Professor Parvi nods to Coach Green, who clears his throat and says, "We didn't get much of a chance to talk after you swapped internships, but I wanted to let you know that despite my concerns about dating a player, you did an excellent job with the team. You were always professional, punctual, and efficient."

"Thank you," I reply, waiting for the "but."

"When I had a chance to go over the notes you made for Pete," he leans back in his chair, "it was clear you had handled the situation with due diligence. You documented the issue and Pete told me directly that you had been warning him about the possible consequences of wrapping his ankle too tight."

"I should have made a better effort to keep you informed."

He shakes his head. "You did your due-diligence, Twyler. It's my job to follow up on your process and keep track of what you're doing. I'm the certified PT. You're an intern."

"Thank you for that," I say, a little overwhelmed at getting such praise from my former mentor. "I really appreciate it and I'm grateful to hear that Pete's recovering well."

"He should be good and ready for the preseason."

Thank God.

"Working for these teams," he continues, "is a pressure cooker. There's so much on the line. Not just championships, but what they mean. More money. More scholarships. More recruitment leverage. We carry the weight of these young athletes' health on our shoulders. I allowed the pressure I was feeling to color my feelings about you having a personal relationship with Cain, when you did nothing but prove yourself competent and professional." He glances at Professor Parvi and then back at me. "Which is why I recommended you for a work-study program up in Hartford."

I blink.

"Hartford," I repeat. "The Wolf Pack?"

The Wolf Pack is the Ranger's farm team.

"Yep."

"What about basketball?" I ask.

"If your heart is set on basketball, then this may not be the right program for you, but you're a damn good trainer, and I've witnessed firsthand that you have a knack working with the knuckleheads that make up the NHL." His eyebrow arches. "Including your boyfriend."

Reese.

"Did he have something to do with this?" I blurt. "Because if he did—"

"Absolutely not," Parvi interjects. "The farm team has a collaboration with NYU. When they called to follow up on your references, Coach Green and I realized this may be the perfect opportunity for you. You'll go to school part-time and learn on the job training with the team."

"I applied to NYU, but I haven't heard back."

Professor Parvi shuffles a few things around her desk and picks up an envelope. The logo for New York University is stamped on the corner. "We arranged with the program to notify you early and in person."

She stretches her arm across the desk and I take the envelope. "You're serious."

"I know it may not be what you had planned," Coach Green says. "It can take a little longer because you're dividing your time, but it's a good way to get on the job training while also receiving your degree. Bonus, it's in the Northeast."

Where I can be close to Reese. The expression on his face tells me he knows that.

"This is amazing," I say, allowing the information to slowly sink in. "I don't know how to thank you."

"Help those boys get to the Stanley Cup," Coach Green says. "That's how you can express your gratitude."

I'd like to think he's kidding, but I know he's serious. The Stanley Cup is no joke.

When I exit the building, the acceptance letter in my hand, I'm surprised to see Reese's car by the curb. My boyfriend leans against the door, all tall and sexy, waiting for me.

"You didn't have to wait," I say, walking up to him.

"I knew you were nervous." He tilts his head, looking at me in that way that tells me he sees me—all of me. "Everything okay?"

I smile up at him. At my future. At this man I love so much. And tell him unequivocally, "Everything is perfect."

AFTERWORD

Don't miss out on book 2 in the Wittmore U Hockey series, Guarded by the Goalie, releasing 2024 on Amazon.

∽

Y'all know I love my dark romance. I love angst and trauma and atonement and all the things we serve up in a Samgel book. I love true crime, cult documentaries, and endless Dateline episodes on a loop.

But... occasionally I need a palate cleanser. Mostly so I can stay sharp to make sure our degenerates over in Forsyth are given my full attention.

I'm a huge lover of sports romance and fell down the hockey rabbit hole a couple of years ago. I love it. I can't stop reading (and rereading) and there was a point this summer where I was like... I need to work on this (Dark) bonus content, but this other story wouldn't leave me alone. Faking It With The Forward is that "other" story.

I hope you all enjoyed it. As for future books, I am planning on releasing a second standalone in the series, Guarded by the Goalie in 2024. The release date is pushed back pretty far. If you know me, you know there's a lot going on in my life (check out my FB group Monarch's for the details) and I am trying hard not to over commit, but it's my style to release sooner than later.

Thanks for reading!

Angel

Printed in Great Britain
by Amazon